MW01614674

# The Drift of Things

*A Novel*

*The Drift of Things*

©2014 by Ben Schwartz

All rights reserved. No part of this novel may be reproduced without the express permission of the author.

This is a work of fiction. All characters, situations, and places are the creation of the author's imagination, and any resemblance to actual people or places is purely coincidental.

Published by Piscataqua Press
An imprint of RiverRun Bookstore, Inc.
142 Fleet St., Portsmouth NH. 03801

www.riverrunbookstore.com
www.piscataquapress.com

Printed in the United States of America

ISBN: 978-1-939739-33-9

# The Drift of Things

*A Novel*

Ben Schwartz

## To Carolyn

Hey, thank you so much. For everything.

# Chapter One

Her coffin, perched on metal staging, is ringed with rolled out AstroTurf. The glossy wood reflecting our blurred figures has no headstone behind it. I didn't know that you get those later.

"Did you think we kept it in the basement?" Dad said when I asked about it earlier, stepping out of the funeral home's limo.

"No," I'd said, "I just thought—"

"What? That we had one sitting around, just in case?"

"I don't know."

Angling toward the grave, he says, "Have you seen mine around? You never know."

He looks at me and pats his black jacket pockets.

A quiet crowd dutifully follows, cutting through the heat and queuing up behind the two metal folding chairs reserved for Dad and me. I feel forced into this suit, which is Dad's, and my shoulders stretch the seams. There's a good two inches between where the pants end and my shoes begin. I feel like a child.

Really, though, how am I supposed to understand this business about the headstone? With the exception of a series of dead grandparents in elementary school, I've only ever been to one funeral. That was high school, twelve years ago, and I had taken such a variety of substances that I was more concerned with all the grim, accusatory looks and vicious circling birds than the vagaries of the gravestone industry. If there's something to be said for this, my mother's funeral, it is that at least no one suspects me of complicity.

I take my seat next to Dad, twisting to scan the faces. I feel my chair leg digging into the ground, the sun and humidity softening everything. I'd forgotten the summer heat here. When I thought back to home, it was always winter, the town hidden beneath snow. Behind me, women carry their dark jackets and peel hair from their faces. The men wipe at their foreheads and reassume their wide legged stances, hands clasped at their crotches. Dad sits, clutching his skinny thighs, watching as my Uncle Monty asks the pastor if he can say a few words. When the pastor relinquishes his spot, Dad sighs.

"Pat," Uncle Monty says. "Pat and Blake. And Norman, their son, their beloved Norm, were a model for all of us, for all of Garrison City."

He gazes into a distance. "Pat. Oh, Pat."

I'm jealous of his white suit, he must be more comfortable than the rest of us, and his black tie certainly expresses his level of mourning. Uncle Monty gave great birthday presents, until my thirteenth or so. I never heard from him after that, and I can't say it's nice to hear him now. It's certainly comforting to know that Mom and Dad and I were always in his thoughts, always held a special place in his heart. Even as he went through his family troubles, he says, even through that, we were on his mind. It's good of him to bring that up here, in front of his children and ex-wife, glaring somewhere behind me, whom he cheated on with a 17 year old from his store. Family troubles, my ass.

I look through his legs to the coffin. He says my name, pauses. If something is expected of me at this point, I ignore it. Uncle Monty is too busy enthralling the crowd to notice. I mutter to myself, "Christ, shut up."

Dad snorts and snuffles it back. His shoulders shake and hands cover his face. Dammit. I should reach over and pat his back, move closer, something. I could take his hand. Monty seems to be wrapping it up, his voice breaking. I look up after what seems like minutes of silence. He's neatly unfolding a black pocket-handkerchief to dab at his eyes. I roll mine to Dad who's biting his lip, red-faced beneath his beard, hand pressed flat down from his forehead. He's laughing. Cracking up.

I need to look away or I'll lose it. Uncle Monty tosses a handful of dirt vaguely toward the grave and is still holding the death-tainted hand away from his white suit when he approaches for hugs. Dad and I rise. Monty dives at me for a tough guy squeeze, pinning my arms to my sides. I can't reciprocate. He moves over to Dad, still waving that black handkerchief, and places his hands on Dad's shoulders, misinterpreting his red eyes as despair and gratitude.

"Anything I can do, Blake. Anything. You just call me." Monty attacks Dad, pausing only to grab at his pocket to silence his phone, ringing musically. Monty inhales deeply, delivers one final blow to Dad's back and rejoins the mourners, smiling as he checks the phone's small screen.

Dad leans in so close I smell coffee. He says, "Pat always hated him."

"She had good taste."

"No. He's just an asshole."

We stand as final words are said. Dad and I approach the grave, reaching to grab handfuls of stony New Hampshire dirt from a pile dumped on the fake grass. Dad tosses his at the coffin's side, I mimic his throw and the sand slides down smoothly. The larger pebbles drop. Stones clank against the wood and metal, skittering to a rest at the bottom of the backhoed hole.

Nobody moves or speaks or coughs. I feel Dad should be the first to walk away, and I wait for his lead. I see us as the crowd certainly does— two disheveled men in cheap matching suits staring at a coffin. Sweaty hair sticks to the back of my neck. His hair, still holding the same dark color as mine, rises in tufts around that small bald spot. It's ridiculous, it must appear as if we are helping each other, and they're all waiting, watching our reactions to gauge or prepare their own.

We tower before the coffin for maybe another minute until I, wanting to do something, but not speak, reach down and toss another handful of dirt. This clump has larger stones and one gets caught up, coming to rest on the railing surrounding her coffin.

Dad looks up at me, hands still crossed at his waist, "Well. That one should do it."

I shake my head without looking at him. He's hilarious.

"Allow me," he says, holding up a hand, stopping me from doing something I wasn't. He tugs up the thighs of his suit pants and crouches over the edge of the hole to remove the stone. For a moment he doesn't kno what to do with it, and his hand wavers between the ground and the grave. Finally, he tosses the rock at my feet and stretches up for my hand to help raise him. I reach out and pull him up, unsure of when to let go, so I don't. We turn, hands awkwardly holding the other's wrist, and face the crowd. I expect applause; of course, there is nothing.

A collective unease seeps through the August air. On the other side of our folding chairs, they're waiting for us to move, to say something. We're waiting for them to turn toward the row of cars, now blocking the way for the next wave of mourners. So we just watch each other. There are very few faces I recognize looking back at me. It strikes me that everyone here is here for Dad. There is a huge age gap between the little cousins peeling down to t-shirts and the old folks in shawls, with whom Mom had spent her afternoons. If any one I know from high school is still in Garrison City, they have neglected to join today's mourning. There is only one friend in this cemetery, and it's hard to say what his age is. He could be almost thirty, or he could still be an eternal seventeen. I suppose, at this point, that's a matter for larger theological debate.

Uncle Monty is the first to break. He steps forward and takes Dad, who stiffens at the touch, by the shoulder and leads him to the waiting limo, its small purple flags limp in the heat. I remain beside the grave, and when Monty waves me to the open limo door, I make a walking motion with my fingers through the air. He nods and squeezes himself into the back seat next to Dad. The graveyard is close to home and everyone, turning to their air-conditioned cars, seems content to let me walk.

The graveyards in this town match the phone books, more chronological than alphabetical, but the names are all here. The Browns. The Corneliuses. The Stones. The newly enlarged cluster of Means. I'm finally free to remove my jacket. I do, and roll my sleeves, which are actually Dad's sleeves and fall short of my wrists. I look for Fitzy's grave, which turns out to be more difficult than I expected. I saw the FitzGeralds at the funeral. I was too impaired to speak to them or to

5

know if I was welcome, if they also held me responsible. Maybe I spoke to them at graduation, a few months after the funeral. I remember them being there and feeling uncomfortable. They had no one graduating, not now. Fitzy was their only child. I remember wondering then if they thought raising him had been a waste of time. They made love, had a baby, then they had a child, then a gangly kid, then a teenager, then nothing. Then they had nothing, and I wondered what they thought wasn't a waste about that.

There are fresh flowers at Fitzy's grave. HENRY FITZGERALD above the dates and an engraving of the sun behind clouds in the corner. The headstone hadn't been there at the funeral, I know that now, and I disagree with that sunshine in the corner. There should be only an aerial view of the pond with a classic chalk body outline floating in the middle. Maybe just the dignified silhouette of a twelve pack.

It never occurred to me, then, that we were too drunk for anything or too young for everything. We'd been in that spot, in that pond, a thousand-thousand nights and had never lost anything permanently. Until we did.

I wipe my eyes, my face, and offer what I can: a rock placed on the headstone, a memory, a regret. I prop the potted flowers up against his gravestone, as if I brought them. I rearrange them so they lay flat, stems pointing away from the stone. My jacket is on the grass and I lift it, flap it out like a bed sheet, allow it to fall over the gravestone, draping the sleeves down the sides, smooth the lapel over the sunshine.

Stretching out the short walk home, I take side streets and detours past personal landmarks. After my time in the city, Garrison looks so idyllic. These are the neighborhoods considered almost downtown, where the duplexes stand side by side with the family homes, once the distinguished domiciles of the mill owners and bosses. Newer ranches squeeze in on side streets, which cut through the old rolling lawns, now split into driveways and playgrounds. These are different from the devouring brick monoliths of the old mills along the river dominating the downtown proper. They're also different from what you'd find by following the brick sidewalks out to the paved, and past them, out to the roads where nobody walks, out to the woods, trailers, and ponds.

There's the lacrosse practice field, hours a day adding up to months of my life spent there until I found more stimulating things to chase than rubber balls. I can name the families who live, lived, in half these homes. Walking by, I take a count of those where I've had sex, though that game doesn't last long. I open it up to any action, including even blind fumbling over a bra. Names and faces have faded, but not the feeling of those nights. Not the aching for something more, something further, always further, the wordlessness and strained groping until it all reached a point we couldn't pass without speaking, and sometimes we'd work it out and other times we'd subside, reclasp a bra, cinch a belt. The quiet return to a party.

Corny had been one of those girls in the dark, now she's one of those girls who have left and stayed gone. I am back and she's still in San Fran, and doesn't even know. And Fitzy.

Somewhere, right now, Mom is apologizing to him for my teenaged foolishness. They sit, legs dangling from a cloud, overseeing my walk home. She hopes he understands, she really does. I'm not a bad boy. Just thoughtless, or careless, whichever is better, but not heartless, she's saying. I thank her for that, and turn the corner onto our street.

Cars line the curb from the Joneses all the way to our house. The Joneses. We never tried to keep up, at least on the outside, which was Dad's realm. The inside was always neat and organized. All of Mom's little statues aligned on shelves. And picture frames, a curving row of them mirroring the railing up the staircase documenting my growth, school picture after school picture until you reached the landing, where I stare out from under my mortarboard.

Each house looks very similar to the one next to it, and even more like the one next to that. Most of them, not ours, have been built up: a garage with a room above, a new addition to house a new kitchen, something. But not ours. Still the same two bedrooms, mine untouched since high school, down to the Algebra book on my desk, the plaid sheets on my bed. It's been a long time since both bedrooms have been filled and last night the house felt both odd and familiar. There were two adults, but in separate rooms, separate beds. Two different adults.

The lawns are all late summer tan, dead under the sun. They're differentiated, for the most part, by hedges or fences, but not ours. Open to the sidewalk, brown stalks spread over the sidewalk and heartier green weeds poke through, taken over when the grass gave in. Dad always hated yard work and successfully passed the loathing on to me. When the duties became mine, there was a noticeable decline in our already shabby yard. He never seemed to care, even took a little pride in having better things to do than pull dandelions and measure grass blades. Standing between the cars, I remember when Dad, shorts too short, holding a beer can, showed me how to mix oil and gas for a weed whacker before stepping back inside. My junior year, I was allowed one beer after mowing. That was a banner year for the Mean lawn.

I stand between the bulky cars lurking in the driveway, and hold off on entering the house. Just as I decide to take one more walk around our block, the door opens and the Joneses emerge, blinking in their black clothes. Mrs. Jones sees me first and tilts her head, wipes a hankie under her veil. She holds her husband's arm. They never had children. We meet at the top of the driveway; she leans in, and holds me in an idea of a hug, our bodies untouching, for several moments. When we separate, he shoots out a piston handshake.

"Good to see you," Mr. Jones says.

"You, too," I say.

"I only wish the circumstances could be better." He won't release my hand and eyes me from the shoes up like a car he wouldn't recommend buying, not with that wear and tear.

"Mmm. Me too," I say.

Mrs. Jones stifles a sob. "So young..."

"I'll be thirty soon."

He lets my hand go, she holds a purse to her chest.

"We'll leave you to your guests," he says. "Take care of your father for me."

They walk right over the lawn. He points out weeds to his wife and makes scissor motions.

Mom's ladies had landed early this morning. Dad and I erratically orbited each other in pajamas, figuring out how we could both get coffee. They arrived bearing trays of deviled eggs and huge, ornate samovars filled with boiling water. Moments after Dad opened the door every surface was covered with white linen and crackers. A lasagna. Mom would never have stood for that kind of intrusion. Dad and I welcomed it. Food hadn't occurred to us. Now I take a small roll smeared with mayonnaisey thickness.

"I'm so sorry for your loss." A hand on my forearm.

"Thank you, thank you. You, too." I have no idea who that was. They've moved on.

I go to the kitchen, looking for a place to put my sandwich down, and settle on a stack of napkins on the counter. I check in the cabinet above the stove; he still keeps the whiskey there. She couldn't stand to have it in view. Reaching for a rocks glass, I bump into someone.

"Sorry, I was just—hey, Dad." He's put on his old Garrison High baseball hat.

"Hello, Norman."

"How's it going?" I say.

"Great, Norm, just wonderful."

"Yeah, there's a lot of people here," I say, waving my empty glass.

"Your mom was a wonderful woman. She was always...she was always."

"Right. I know. All the time."

Dad motions for me to grab him a glass. I pour us both a few fingers. He refuses to accept the drink until I add another splash. Mourners move among us, nibbling and whispering. We clink glasses.

"Welcome home," he says.

"I'm sorry, Dad. About Mom. I'm sorry."

"Me, too."

We drink. When we're done he hands me his glass and moves as if to reenter the crowd, but turns, hand out, fingers waggling.

"I'd better have one more," he says, more to himself. He bothers his beard a bit and lifts his hat, lowers it. I top us both off.

"Here," I say. "You know, if you want to have a smoke or something, I'm okay with it."

He takes a swallow. "Thanks, Norman, that's helpful."

I shrug. He quit years ago, but I bet there's still a pack hidden around. I could use one. I also quit years ago, a half-hearted attempt to convince Corny to stay in our tiny San Francisco apartment.

"Come on." Dad slips his arm through mine, as if he's an old man. "Let's just get through this."

The weight of his arm feels strange, but it gives me a role as we navigate through our two small rooms packed with morbid, idle guests. I'm his support, whisked in from afar during this crucial time, and that counts for something.

As soon as the last ladies finish washing dishes, and after their husbands and I conclude awkward local sports team talk, the TV goes on. It seems Dad has acquired a taste for crap. He shushes me from his recliner whenever the commercials end and emits barks of derisive laughter at the real life antics of someone's mom in someone's city. This is not the empty evening I would have expected to have after a day filled with Mom's funeral.

I watch him more than the television; his shirt is unbuttoned to the waist. His tie knot rests on the small curve of his new belly. It's hard to remember what he looked like when I was young. It still feels like he's taller than me, but he stops at my chin. We've moved the whiskey bottle between us, on the doily with the strawberry lamp. The vodka is on the floor, just in case. Dad drinks mechanically, purposefully, until his eyes waver. He mumbles something I think is a joke about the show, but I

11

can't understand him. When his head lies back against the crocheted pillow cozy, I take his whiskey and pour the remainder into my glass. The show ends and I find a gangster flick on one of the upper channels. Every time there's a shoot-out, I turn down the volume and check him for any movement. There's none beyond his sudden inhales, held for too long before the next breath.

The house exhales around us, releasing the day's heat and pressures. Lacey curtains wave, ushering in an evaporating coolness. Here we are. I'm back, and essentially alone for the moment. My drink and I take a few inspective laps of the first floor to visit the spaces I haven't entered in years.

The pantry. Dusty snowy day soup cans, classic red and white, linger behind the brighter low-sodium chicken noodles up front. My favorite pop-tarts, raspberry, sit dormant among the cereal boxes. The mudroom: still a pair of cleats in the corner, nestled in a row of leather boots under hibernating heavy jackets. The winter clothes' padded insulation and scratchy high collars appear unbearable, even in the cooling evening. In the bathroom cabinet, old prescription bottles tell their tales of strained backs and wisdom teeth.

The back porch seems tiny under the stars, at the edge of our small field. Two white plastic Adirondack chairs kept separate by a low matching table glow ghostly in the moonlight. The far arm of one is rutted with cigarette burns. The closer chair balances a wine glass on its seat, an inch of particled red is pooled with drowned flies. A small plate on the table is spotted with crumbs and a cookie with one delicate front-toothed bite missing.

No one has been out here yet, since then. The Ladies' Auxiliary

Funeral Corps must have missed it. The wine smells sweet, and the burns have melted the plastic into rough edges. They're old burns, dirty and permanent. I pick up the cookie. Chocolate chip. Stale. The whole thing has the feel of a half-sentence. It's the pause before the bad news.

Dad would have been dreading his last year of teaching, out here that last night, complaining about the school board and another new principal. She would have been listening with the paper in her lap, searching the obituaries and birth announcements. They look across into the small pocket of woods, waiting to count the tenth or thirtieth deer of the season. They don't discuss her diagnosis. She jokes about the yard; he hopes she's joking. Talk turns to their possible retirement, which turns to their familial past, which turns to me, a nation away. Mom sighs and folds the paper. Dad looks over and takes her hand on the table. She's surprised, but returns his look. On their way upstairs, she drops the paper in the new recycling bin, leaving behind her last sip of wine.

I almost bite the cookie, but instead, rub the bit off teeth marks, where her mouth was, against my lips. I place a light kiss against the cookie, hear the smack in the dark, before going inside to put my Dad to bed.

# Chapter Two

Dad has dodged every phone call. I've received none. There's a knock on our door every few days, then we look at each other, usually over drinks from our seats in the living room.

"You expecting anyone?" he asks every time, and by now it's taken on a hint of insult. We both know the answer.

He pushes himself up with one hand, the other reserved for whiskey, and goes to the door in sockless moccasins and hardly buttoned button-down.

"Blake. Oh, how are you two holding up?" It's always a woman's voice. They're a diligent corps of death watchers.

"We're holding in there. Staying tight."

"I brought a casserole. Now, I put the heating instructions on top of the foil, all you have to do is—"

"I'm sure we'll be able to handle it. Thank you." Dad doesn't let her get through the simple instructions.

"Oh, I just know you will, the thing to watch out for is when to take the foil off." I hear the metallic wrinkling of foil.

"Thank you," he says, closing the door and yelling to me. "Guess."

"Another green bean with crispy onions?"

"You want some?"

I usually do. We heat it up, careful to take the foil off for the last ten minutes, and eat in front of the television. A few days later there is another knock, and we return the casserole dish, empty, breaking one of Mom's cardinal rules. Booze bottles have migrated from the cabinet to the counter top. The wine glass on the porch remains untouched.

The moments when Mom seems to be around, we do not speak. And when we feel alone, our conversation centers on TV channels or cocktail choices. I've yet to go farther than the new grocer, haven't even taken the long way through town. Once, through misattention to my route, I drove past Fitzy's house. Slowing at their driveway, I saw several people on the porch, laughing and swinging on the same porch bench I used to sleep on if I couldn't make the three-block walk home. They seemed happy and nicely unaccusatory. The rest of town, though, each corner and alley holds some memory. At the gas station by the grocery store, I expect to see myself, too skinny and laughing, kicking the door open, brandishing a case of underage beer to cheers from a waiting car, Fitzy sitting on the hood.

Dad hasn't asked, yet, what I plan on doing. Or better, why I'm still around. I don't know what I'd say, and I think he knows that. His summer vacation is drawing to its end. I've been using that as a vague endpoint. A time for decisions.

I couldn't produce my education degree when Dad asked for it, seeing as, he said, it has the highest expensive-to-useless ratio of any thing he's ever bought. He begins asking about my old job in San Fran, prior to the pizza place, running an after school program for screwed up neighborhood kids. Finally, this morning, he got to the point.

"They've been trying to fill the position all summer. No takers," he says over coffee and Pop-Tarts. "Special Education. All the kids I kick out. You would love them."

"That does sound tempting."

"I talked to the boss yesterday. You could interview tomorrow." Dad sips a few times before looking up. I'm not sure if this is an order.

"I don't know if I'm up for that. I decided not to be a teacher after all, you know?" I say.

"Hmmm. Good decision." He looks back down at the paper.

"It's my old school."

"It's mine, too."

"And you work there."

"I do. For another year."

"Nah. Can you pass me the classifieds? I'll find something more suited to my natural lack of abilities."

He flips a page. He does not hand me the classifieds.

"What time tomorrow?" I say.

"9:00. Clean yourself up. You look like shit."


He's right, I think, looking in the mirror before bed, in the light of a tilted desk lamp. I need a haircut, or maybe a hairstyle, if there's a difference. I want my beard back. From the eyes down I look just like the last photograph on the stairs, but my eyes have sunk. The skin is building around them as if someone is digging a hole, the dark dirt piling around the edges. My eyes have always been blue, bright enough for strangers to comment. They've probably kept me in jobs and relationships for longer than anything I've actually done. I put on an interview smile; it moves aside some of the darkness—for a moment. I push some hair down right above my eyebrows, then hold it back, slick

17

against my head. Not bad, but my forehead is nearly as pale as my eye whites. I blame the yellow light of the desk lamp, not the booze, for my appearance. Tomorrow I'm going to need to borrow Dad's nicest clothes. If I want to make this work.

Dad is elsewhere this morning, but there's coffee in the pot and toast, not pop-tarts, rising from the toaster. I eat at an angle, keeping the crumbs off Dad's shirt and tie, the same ones I wore to the funeral. He's left the car keys in the middle of the table, next to a comb. He's still hilarious.

The interview is with Deidre, Garrison High's head of Special Ed. She's a square woman in a round dress and the whole thing consists mainly of agreeing that Dad is a great guy and how tragic Mom's death is and how bad things happen to good people and do I want the job? There is really no way out at this point. I take her tour of the Special Education rooms, dubbed "The Learning Center", as if the rest of the school isn't, and like that, the number of Mr. Means at Garrison High doubles.

He's on the porch when I get home, in the chair with the burns, two cigars long as my forearm and a sweating bottle of champagne on the table. He doesn't turn. I take hold of Mom's seat, carefully, so as not to knock over the wine glass. The grass stretching out into our patch of woods is brown; trees have sucked the moisture up into their drying leaves. He has a small white towel on his lap, a yellow bottle of lighter fluid, and his venerable silver Zippo. Bony legs stretch from the towel to brown loafers. The Zippo lights with a click, scratch, and fwoom. Again. Again. His fingers move deftly, finding the old muscle patterns as he spins it around, flipping the top and bringing the flame with a snap of his fingers. He gives it a small toss so it lands, lit, clutched in his fingertips.

"Champagne?" I wipe a line of condensation from the green bottle.

Without stopping the lighter show, he says, "I thought it might be in order."

"Did they call you?"

"No."

"Well, I didn't get it. They wanted someone with more experience. Any experience. I guess they were looking for someone who wanted the job."

"Pop the cork, Norm."

"Really. I flipped out when they turned me down. Demanded the job. You'll be lucky if you still have a job. I called the lady a fat bitch."

"You would have been correct. But now she's your boss. Pop the damn cork."

I do, and it doesn't arc gracefully through the yard. The cork, actually made of plastic, shoots into my palm and some unexciting foam runs down the bottle.

"What do I do with it now?"

"Pass me that glass."

"Mom's?"

The wine glass is sun-hot, any liquid has now evaporated, leaving incomplete circles of burgundy stained sediment. Dad lifts it to his nose and inhales, starts to say something, then spits into the center. He wipes around the inside with the towel from his lap, staining it red. Holding the glass to the sun, he seems satisfied, and raises it to me.

When it isn't filled immediately, he turns, and I see his face. His old trimmed beard is back, smooth lines separate hair from skin, red from heat. He's had his hair cut into neat deviations, separated by a ruler-straight part. He's an old photograph taped back together. His eyes, light in the sun, jump between mine and the champagne bottle.

"How about it, Mr. Mean? Let's celebrate," he says.

"Please, Mr. Mean is my father. Call me Norm." I say, and pour.

"Those kids are going to walk all over you."

"That's what I tried to tell them today."

He drinks down the foam. Now that the wine glass has been removed, the other chair is available, and I sit, matching Dad's sun-glared stare over the burnt yard. The bottle still holds some of its refrigerated coolness. I stick it between my legs, let it soak through the fabric until my thighs feel white and frozen.

"You didn't bring out another glass?" I say.

"The bottle is glass." He sets aside his Zippo cleaning project and unwraps the cigars.

When I tip the bottle back, foam fills my mouth, and I shoot forward, coughing champagne through the porch rails. It's all over the interview shirt and tie. I strip down to a soaked t-shirt, which is refreshing. I make a pile of bubbly-soaked clothes, topped with borrowed shiny shoes and flimsy, damp dress socks. The second sip goes better, but not as well as the third, and when I lean back Dad is handing me a cigar, already lit.

My immediate coughing sends smoke out my nostrils, burning furiously, but briefly. I try to cool it with a swig from the bottle, but it's too quick, and champagne joins the smoke in the air.

"Can I grab you a sippy cup?" Dad says.

"Fine. I'm fine."

"Good, because that's the finest champagne Store 24 had to offer. It'd be a shame to spit it all out."

"I got it, I'm good," I say.

"Let's hope that's true."

"We can always hope, can't we?"

"That's all we can do, Norman."

The sun slides smoothly over the day, stretching the roof's shadow across the dry field. Eventually it covers a small bike, abandoned by a neighbor's child in the heat. Dad's talkative, telling horror stories about high school special education. I listen to his accounts of the screaming, chair throwing 15-year-olds who can't subtract and will soon be my charges. Kids raised by wolves in mom's clothing. When I was in school (just thinking this puts me solidly into adulthood, a first step toward becoming that didactic teacher the kids dread) such kids existed, I'm sure, but they fell victim to the cruel Darwinism of childhood. Either they were shamed enough to leave everyone alone, or just to leave. There was a dropout age for a reason—so they could drop out. There was no responsibility to coddle, nurture, or educate them. They could always get a job with an uncle a few towns over. I certainly drank at my share of 'just dropped out' parties in the woods, at the pond, or in some dilapidated trailer they shared with vague cousins.

Every story leads Dad to another, the angry underprivileged subject of each related by blood or address to the next. The champagne leads to gin, a new bottle, bought this morning. He's been busy, and I feel good. It's nice to be employed and still not have to work for another few days. It's good to sit out here and drink and smoke cigars, though it seems dangerously closer to cigarettes. These are the old times we never had, as if Mom should be inside, maybe baking something.

We're past talk, through the smoke, and I think I just poured the last of the tonic. We never had limes. I have that satiated stretched skin feeling of long sun and plentiful drinks. Dad's quieted, examining his cigar stub for another drag.

He's unsuccessful, and looks at me until I look back. He says, "Where's that waitress with our burgers?"

"No shit. I'm starving."

He stands. "Let's go. You're driving."

"I've been drinking all day."

"Fine. I'm driving."

We ramble inside to bump around, pee, and check our reflections for sunburns. The house still holds the day's heat. Mom's porcelain kitties and photographs of ourselves judge us from the shelves. If she were here, she'd run to the store for us, clicking her tongue. Ensure that we listened for a buzzer to go off. She's not here, and I watch Dad fumble through the dish for his keys, smooth his hair in the small mirror by the door. I stand aside, allowing him to finish his routine. He checks pockets, pats his butt for his wallet, breathes into his hand. He smiles up at me. "What? I'm the one driving."

"I'm not saying anything."

We pull onto the old street in Dad's newish car, the one Mom wanted. It still smells flowery and laundry crisp thanks to the candle shaped air freshener hanging from the rear view. Our street winds through double sentry rows of trees and setback homes. It's been here long enough to allow the landscape some passage. I can pick out the neighborhood newcomers by their family-style trucks parked on the street, garages too overflowing with equipment and grills.

Garrison City creeps outward, starfishing from its five-street downtown, which once encapsulated an entire world. The old mills hold the center of town in place, everything else revolving around them. Anything on the outskirts is there because a block-long mill building takes up any potential space downtown. When I had the run of the place, downtown was clearly differentiated from the rest of the world by its brick sidewalks. Once you hit the concrete, you were outside town, even if crossing the street got you to an old mill-worker bar, you were not downtown unless you had brick. Our house is in one of the first neighborhoods built for those workers, and by the time I was in high school nearly everyone I knew came from farther away. I gained some credibility as the kind of guy who knew downtown.

Dad hums while he drives. Tuneless songs he couldn't name if pressed, except maybe that it was a big hit by that guy who wore a hat. Before you were born. I fidget with the radio, scanning rapidly and perusing the few CDs Mom bought after discovering the car had no tape deck. I almost put one in for a laugh, but return it to its case, afraid of what we might hear. Talk radio seems safe in lieu of talk. Dad seems to have a destination in mind, so I remain quiet as he coasts through stop signs and takes the corners wide.

"Pizza or burgers?" he says.

"Burritos."

"Burgers it is."

Downtown is busy tonight, people out walking in this finally cool evening. They hold hands and drink through straws. They window shop in all the little stores, new since I left. The old brick is still everywhere, but cleaner. Scrubbed. Window frames have been painted, refreshed in subtle shades to match the signs hanging over each doorway. I feel like all my memories have turned sepia, a monotone compared to this pastel street. I want a huge old photograph to cover it all. An overlay that will replace everything as it should be; eventually I can poke holes in it, allow the changes to arrive one at a time.

We're stopped at a light. There's the fountain, spraying its lily-shaped shower. The benches surrounding it were the spot where we'd meet. I'm glad to see that kids are still lining the benches, lying over each other. One plays guitar. We never did. They think they are subtle when they couldn't be more obvious. A girl sits on a boy's lap while another boy stares, desperate to touch that short summer skirt—maybe feel a little skin against his own. We did the same, but we did it with a far greater sense of ownership and disdain. In cooler clothes.

The light changes, and Dad keeps up his determined driving. We've passed a dozen restaurants that by the law of averages must have a burger or two. We thread Dad's drunken needle between gas stations and their identical counterparts across the street. I worry over his driving skills and whether he even remembers our mission this evening. Food. And possibly more drinks. Maybe he's just driving, too embarrassed to let on that he doesn't remember why we are on the road. Oh, Dad. Another restaurant's welcoming lights fade beyond the rear window, and I can't hold back.

"Where the hell are we going?"

"Tuesday," he says.

Oh shit, he's farther gone than I thought. Is it even Tuesday? I don't know, but I can guess that's not where we're going.

"Tuesday?"

"Two for one burgers on Tuesdays, Norman. One," he points at me, then himself. "Two."

I play with the radio again, finding a great song, and I sit back. He's on top of things. Two for Tuesdays it is, though I swear we're closer to home now than when we left. After this afternoon, here without our bottles, we've sprung back to silence. Everything is a test. This has the feel of Dad dropping me at practice, or at a friend's house, Mom assigning him as driver—so we could talk. Maybe have THE talk. Which he eventually did, on the way to a friend's house, where a good laugh was had about it. By that time, on that car ride, I had hopeful condoms stuffed in my backpack under a warm six-pack. He seemed relieved as I was when he finished his speech. If he had said 'penis' or 'love' one more time in the same sentence, I would've leaped from the car.

I'm on the verge of jumping out now, just to eat. Thankfully, he slows to a coast and pulls into a red chain restaurant.

"This work for you?" He clunks into park.

"At this point, sure."

We're seated in a booth and I'm done with the menu before our waitress, Brittany, hands it to me.

"We'll have two burgers and a couple beers. Thanks," I say.

"Do you want Rancheros or Bigelows?" she says.

Nobody says anything. Brittany seems unsure of what to do. Finally, Dad says, artfully, I feel, "Medium rare, please, and Budweiser."

"Yep," she says, looking away as she accepts our menus.

We rearrange the abundance of tabletop advertisements and gaze at the locally themed decorations hanging haphazardly from the walls until he speaks. "So. How is Julia doing?"

"Corny? I imagine Julia Cornelius is doing just fine without me," I say.

"And you?"

"I'm doing just fine without me, also."

He doesn't respond.

"Christ, Dad, we've been together every minute for almost two weeks now, you tell me, how am I doing?"

"Just fine. I imagine."

"How are you doing?"

"Well. I suppose I'm doing just fine, as well."

"Well, that's fine," I say.

Our beers arrive, ridiculously tall and delicious. We both take long sips, making the same satisfied sound when we put them down. Nothing caps off a day of liquor like cold draught beer. We raise our eyebrows at each other, in agreement. He points at something over my shoulder.

"I know that guy," he says.

I look over both shoulders until I find what he's pointing at. There's a framed photograph of a very clean-cut looking kid in a robe, accepting a diploma from someone who looks like the monopoly man.

"He died in Vietnam. I think," he says.

"He looks so happy."

Dad looks at me as if I've said something stupid. "I think he probably was."

"I guess. But Vietnam, that's rough."

"He didn't know that. Then. He didn't know what was going to happen."

I shrug, really looking around this place. These decorations, this theme—it's demeaning. There's Garrison memorabilia everywhere, like Garrison no longer exists. It's as if an invading army came through and built this memorial to those they destroyed. There are photos of last year's graduating class, the year spelled out in the green robes the boys wear. The girls surrounding them in white robes. Smiling kids in pretend police uniforms smugly hold plaques beside the town's one lonely symbolic police horse. Sports teams kneel on their helmets, coaches on the end of the line up in their green and white polo shirts. Stoic sepia women pose in their dour dresses, their names hand drawn over the image. Where do they get all this stuff? In every town this restaurant drops on, there must be teams of scavengers scouring the countryside, digging up décor.

"Hello? You going to eat that?"

"Just thinking," I say, and set to preparing my burger.

He's already three bites in, ketchup on his cheek. "Not bad, huh? Two for one Tuesdays."

"One." I point at him. "Two."

"Maybe you did learn something in my class."

The burger fills me perfectly, leaving exactly 20 oz. free for the next beers Brittany brings to our table. We sip at them, feeling growing pressure from the hostess table to move on. Sated, worn from the sun and the gin and the beer, oh, and the champagne, we sit until Brittany bounces back with our check. Dad gets up to pee, leaving me alone and hoping he doesn't expect me to pay. I don't even have a credit card or a wallet in my borrowed pants. I still wear the t-shirt I spilled champagne on earlier.

I look over the faces in the row of graduation pictures, young and unsure in their tilted caps, futures unwritten, I'm sure at least one of those nervous kids had a hand in our burgers tonight. Others are dead.

"So, you got this?" Dad says on his return.

"Ooh, I don't seem to..." I make a little show of patting imaginary pockets on my chest.

"For the pleasure of your company," he says, and tosses a few bills on the table.

At the door, Dad pauses and says he should piss again, old men, you know? I wait outside, in the present, free of the museum inside. It's the purple dark of late summer. People have built up in a line by the door, mirrored by the line of SUVs turning in. Dad reappears, walking strangely, his hands at his crotch.

"You're driving."

I have to take the keys from where they hang below his belt, because he won't raise his arms. I curve the car past the traffic and pull out, away from town.

Dad's quiet, probably disapproving of my choice of route. We pass row after row of stores: Videos, coffee, and cell phones. I see trees silhouetted beyond the buildings' roofs, a star. He shifts around in his seat, changes the radio station, then shuts it off.

"Turn down there," he says.

"I was going to go down Sixth and over to Central."

I turn where he indicates, a completely unfamiliar street. There are street signs where there were never streets. Ornate signs tantalizingly advertise developments, listing vague prices, "Starting in the low 300s!"

Dad snorts. "Nothing low about 300. Turn here."

"There? It's a dead end. Cul-de-sac."

"Norman."

I turn, the lit sign sliding by the window: "Barbados Pond Estates: An Elliot Development."

"Shit. Dad. Fuck. No." I hit the brakes hard, right in the road, and put it in park, a hand on the shifter, ready to reverse.

"We're fine, just go on. You gotta see this. What they've done."

"I don't care what they've done. Let's go home."

He looks at me under the yellow dome light, points ahead.

"Just take a spin around the circle."

He puts a hand on my leg; I breathe in and put us into drive. Swathes of flat, bright green glow on either side, broken by smooth black paths. We creep through like stalkers, casing the joint. The houses are massively set back from the road, huge rectangles stretching into smaller wings. Everything is silence.

Each lawn simultaneously sprouts a small sprinkler fountain, and the curbs reflect our lights like a runway, leading us forward. I need to use the wipers because the sprinklers are splattering the windshield. They keep time with my heart. We continue to the end, where the road takes a graceful twist around a circle of grass centered with a granite monolith.

I roll us to a stop at the curve's apex and smell water on pavement. This house we're parked beside is enormous. Its lawn is less austere than the others, strewn with stuff, just stuff. Blue tarps, corners held down by bricks, mar the grass. A ride-on mower rests idle, sprinkler water raining down. The grass flows a gentle slope behind the house, where I can just make out a circle-shaped absence of trees. Every light is on. No noise, though. Not a sound spills from the closed windows.

"It's back there," he says. "The pond. Behind that."

"That," I say.

"Behind it."

I rev the engine in neutral. "Why are we here?"

"I thought you might want to see. To know."

"I see."

"Things move on, Norm. Houses are built. Families swim."

"I see," I say and drop into drive.

"That's all."

I need the high beams through the back roads home. It's starting to get dark earlier; school will be starting soon. We drive without the radio, the engine nearly as silent. The clicking blinker is the only noise as we turn into our driveway. Dad reaches over my head and presses the garage door open, but I shut the engine where we sit and stare at the glow of the dashboard.

Dad stretches out strangely. He straightens his legs, lifts his shirt, and reaches an arm down the top of his shorts. He produces a narrow black rectangle, a picture frame, and hands it to me. His door opens. The interior illuminates. He leaves slowly, following his long legs into the driveway.

In my hands, smiling up at me and clutching lacrosse helmets, are Fitzy and me. An enlarged newspaper photo broken into pointillist dots. Our arms around each others' shoulder pads, our heads touching, we're holding our fingers up, number one. Number one. When I wipe the glass dry, looking through the open car door, the stars have fully revealed themselves.

# Chapter Three

## Blake

Blake slows the car to a stop at the school doors. This feels so familiar, dropping off his son. Everything he thinks has gone for good always returns. Norm doesn't open the car door. He looks as if he may ask Blake to pull out, drive around one more time, as in second grade, before he can leave the car's familiarity. Blake thinks that if Norm asked, he would do it. Then keep driving.

"Good luck on your first day," Blake says.

"That's not funny. That's exactly how it feels," Norm says, fidgeting the door handle.

He looks at his son and sees all the hurts over the years, all the could-have-beens. He's a good-looking boy, a man to other eyes, still not completely formed in Blake's. Norm wears another borrowed shirt and is freshly shaved. His hair is longer than Blake likes it, but his mother would have approved. Norm has her unruly hair, and she always wanted it long enough to pet. Blake says, "They're all good people. Mostly, anyway. No one is going to hurt you in there."

"That's what you said the first time you dropped me off here."

"Don't be so dramatic. You're on the other side of the desk now."

"Where are you going? Don't you have to be here, too? Or do you already know everything?"

"I'm going to grab some breakfast before this thing starts for real."

"I thought they had food here," Norm says, one leg on the pavement.

"They call it food. You're fine. You look good. Suck it up."

Blake curves through the bus drop-off lane past the parking lot toward the main road. He looks back from the stop sign and sees Norm checking his reflection in the half-opened door before pushing through, and he smiles. He's glad they'll be working together. It will give them a topic to rally around, to discuss over dinner and breakfast and during commercials. Forever, it seems, he hasn't had to think about conversation topics. With Pat, their natural routine talk covered the same dozen topics, agreeing over coffee, and disagreeing over drinks. Through the years since Norm left, they'd had the same rotating discussions, each one picking up where another had stopped. Everything was decided upon.

For ten years or so, Blake has been thinking that he was sick of it, that he had fallen into an inescapable rhythm in a tired marriage. They'd ask questions to which the answer was already known. What do you think of the new principal? Where was it we had that great pie? Decades ago they'd forgiven each other their differences of opinions. Which one of them hated the new buildings downtown? At the moment, he can't remember what had been there before they were built and can't think of a reason to hate the innocuous structures. Yet, now he recalls thinking less of his wife, for a moment, when she mentioned, from behind a newspaper, that she was excited about all these changes. Then there'd been the doctors and their diagnoses. They gave every word a stopwatch's weight.

Where did he get his coffee before the franchised drive-through, which they insist on spelling 'thru', opened up outside town? He conjures the image of a silver cylinder with a screw off cap, which doubled as a cup. It seems so ancient now.

Blake orders into a machine tucked inside a giant menu. The staticky voice sounds familiar, and he drives the ten feet forward to a window. He recognizes the girl's face. 'Melody' it says on her nametag, and immediately he pictures her in his classroom, twirling her hair and biting a pencil. He thinks 'C-' and gives her a genuine greeting, asks if she is ready for school. She rolls her eyes and says that at least she doesn't have to take math this year. He laughs and says he wishes the same. She says 'yeah' without smiling and Blake takes the bag of doughnuts and Styrofoam coffee. He places them on the passenger seat and turns back to the window, smiling too broadly.

Blake says, "My son is teaching at Garrison this year."

"My brother has you for class," Melody says.

"Does he chew on his pencil?"

"Huh?" Melody pokes her visored head out the window and looks down at the cars lining up behind Blake.

"I'll go easy on him."

Blake sits at the window two more moments before offering a one-sided goodbye and pulling out, against the incoming traffic.

He feared the growing redundancy of conversations where he and Pat would talk about how they used to talk. These meta-conversations had risen large in his mind, and he had feared them. Pat had had her activities, her groups and her few leftover accounting clients, old widowed women who knew nothing of taxes, and there had been no need to retire from them. What would those women do now? It occurs to Blake that he should call them before tax season. But they already knew. He'd eaten their casseroles.

He rests his hand on the bag of doughnuts, the engine silent. His usual parking spot was left empty for him, though the Garrison High parking lot is overflowing this morning. Retirement now seems superfluous, and he feels guilty for that. Pat is gone. Norm is an adult, or working on it, anyway. There had been two things: Pat and teaching math. One of these has left him, and the freedom that provides seems enough. Blake won't ever say it out loud, he barely says it in his head, but it is definitely a profound freedom that he feels. It's intimidating.

The house is hard, yes, with its radiating collection of memories and the fact that he no longer has a side of the bed. Certainly, Blake feels like a bit of an asshole for these feelings of relief. It's novelty, perhaps. All the immature decadences in which he can indulge—he can almost make himself believe that they'd really been taken from him over the years, that it was Pat who took them. This is not what he expected whenever he had dared to imagine her death and his solitude.

He closes the car door behind him and pictures the school cafeteria. He knows precisely who will be sitting where and with whom, knows just where he will sit and what will be said, and for once, in thirty years, he is looking forward to it.

# Chapter Four

Watery coffee and hard bagels. No creamers or cream cheese, only Styrofoam plates and some powder that is clearly not dairy. The packaging offers no further explanation. My first official day on the job—stick on nametag and everything. I had thought, years ago, that high school was intended only to humiliate the students. A quick glance around and one sip from my institutional coffee-type beverage proves that wrong. I add the powder to my coffee, proving the label accurate. Nothing dairy would ever turn that shade of gray.

Dad's an old pro at Welcome Back Breakfast. He's just walking in with a Dunkin' Donuts bag and an enormous coffee. He sits with the gym teachers, sharing his doughnuts and laughing. Teachers approach him in tight clusters to offer their condolences. Each exchange ends with the entire group following Dad's finger to watch me cringe into my coffee. I offer weak waves in return. Hardly anyone has actually approached me. Only two other new teachers with whom I had to sit through painful small group pep talks at yesterday's Get-to-Know-Each-Other-Fun-Fest actually seem glad to see me.

These two had chattered excitedly about the kids and the importance of hands-on projects and solid lesson plans and how nervous they were and how exciting, how exciting. The big guy cried. Just thinking of all the good he could do, he shed quiet tears. The other guy, wispy-haired at 23, patted him on the back, saying he was going to be just great. I hadn't said much, and continue that approach today.

Garrison High's two newest, peppiest teachers move from group to group introducing themselves. I can't imagine summoning that much energy in here. I ate four years of lunches in this room, carefully unsupervised by some of the same washed-out paunchy professionals here today. I feel just as unsure now as my first day freshman year. At least then I had Fitzy to sneak around with. I'm curious about the kids and working with them tomorrow; nothing has been made clear about my actual role. It's been a long time since I've been around high school kids. I can't imagine they're much different than we were. I've been trying to recall one cool teacher, one that had it right, to model myself after, but I can't. Being in this room certainly brings no one to mind.

A few teachers approach, and I survive a couple of clipped conversations.

"Norman Mean. Well, if there was ever a face I never expected to see again."

"You stepping into your old dad's shoes?"

"I was very sorry to hear about your mom."

"What the hell are you doing here?"

I smile, shrug, or make ponderous nods to each inquiry. Dad has filled me in on who is still here and who has left and under what circumstances. I don't feel ready to speak to these remaining stragglers as an equal. At any moment I expect to be ridiculed or sent out, back to the car to wait for my father to finish his workday and take me home.

Not much has changed in the cafeteria. Not the barely multi-colored tiles or the inspirational banners: "Responsibility + Respect = Success at

GHS!!" "Every 'A' begins with 'U'!" A mezzanine looks down over the caf from the second floor, providing distraction for every student walking by and creating the perfect spot for projectiles. They've added a high metal railing around the whole ledge. There must have been some terrible accident.

All around, these people burble about their summer vacation escapades. The beach. Books poolside. France, finally, France. Nothing at all, it was wonderful. Wonderful. I realize this has all been an awful mistake. I don't belong here now any more than I did then. The moment those front glass doors swung open, I was hit with the same old angst, nonsensical but visceral. One day on the job, and I'm already an embittered old bastard. If I left now it would save everyone so much embarrassment. There's no way I'm going to honestly convince pissed off teenagers that they shouldn't feel the way they do. They're right. And I was wrong. Wrong to ever get talked into this job or to leave the constant summer vacation of making overpriced pizza in San Francisco. Or to ever leave here in the first place.

The assistant principal, Sullivan, gives a double-fingered whistle from the mezzanine. In his Madras shorts and boat shoes, he's got the look of an old coach moved up through the ranks thanks to back slaps rather than competence. Everyone cranes around to look up at him. He claps his hands and holds them together at his chest for a moment, letting the last of the conversation piddle away.

"All right, folks! Let's move into the auditorium and start another great year!"

His voice falls flat on the assembled crowd, with the exception of my two new fervent colleagues. They're halfway up the stairs, clutching notebooks. Conversation resumes in their absence.

"Let's go, staff! Summer's over and the kids will be here tomorrow, just as excited as we are."

"Shut it, Sullivan!"

That's the ancient gym teacher next to Dad. He draws a united laugh from the cafeteria crowd.

"You, too, Flynn!" Sullivan shouts down. That draws a bigger laugh.

In the shuffle I end up beside Flynn. He smells like the locker room he's ruled for decades as a lackluster dictator. Mismatched windbreaker ensemble, wrinkled. I didn't know that windbreakers could get wrinkled. Word is he quit drinking, though he's keeping true to his past by maintaining the look, attitude, and smell of a constant hangover. I wish I was hungover. It would give me something to think about through the upcoming inspirational speeches.

Flynn pushes through the crowd with admirable disregard. Younger teachers get nudged aside, the heels of their hip sneakers stepped on.

"You really want to put up with this bullshit?" Flynn says.

"No. Not really."

"A penny's worth of advice?"

"Sure."

"Don't."

He slips into a student bathroom. I'm left in the crowd, balancing a tiny white coffee cup in my hand. The coffee is still gray. We're marched past the row of front doors, the sunlight blinding, showing tempting white rectangles on the opposite wall.

This auditorium has been the site of innumerable boredoms: Previews of school plays, class election assemblies, emergency school-wide meetings to discuss the seriousness of smoking in the bathrooms or something else for which Fitzy and I were directly responsible. So many inane adolescent gatherings. Today is no different.

The new principal manages to be both perky and dowdy in a flowery overmatched ensemble. She tries to build a new collegiality by urging everyone to sit in the front, up here, where she can see all our pretty faces. No one moves and she orders people to move. One minute into her reign, and she's already broken under the weight of decades of Garrison's educational bitterness. We all follow orders and grumble our way to new seats. Only Flynn remains in his original back row, feet up with a newspaper spread over his legs.

I end up a couple rows in front of Dad, with all the other newbies. I hear him invite me to sit next to him, and I choose to ignore him to avoid climbing over more seats.

"Come on back, Son. Keep your old Dad company." He's doing this on purpose. People down both sides of my row turn to look. I kind of shake my head, like, oh, isn't he a card. In front of me those two new teachers turn in unison, wondering how I could possibly disobey such direct orders from an honored professional. With each new entreaty, they drop a shade paler. Big guy mouths, "Just go." Wispy nods, increasingly concerned. There's no fucking way I'm going anywhere now, and I spread out wider in my undersized theater seat.

The principal begins her introductory speech. Wispy and Big Guy flip open notebooks and click their pens, entranced. When she gets to the part where she introduces this year's new teachers, I listen for my name and stand, and remain standing, as per her request, until all names are called. There's a surprising number of us, and I feel like I'm standing

39

forever, facing the long green curtains on the empty stage.

Then I feel a light tap on my back. I don't turn. Another one, higher this time, on my neck. This is now actually worse than high school. He's shooting spitballs at me. I can hear his row giggling, and I throw him a pleading look. Stop.

After all the new teachers are standing, there is the obligatory applause, and I hear a loud "Nooooormaaaaan!" over everybody's clapping.

The remainder of our morning meeting is uneventful. There is a half-hearted award ceremony for teachers who have been here astonishing lengths of time. Decades. Dad receives a plaque, winking at me during his photo shoot. He seems to have gotten whatever it was out of his system and, when dismissed, we wander off separately to meet with our departments and set up our classrooms.

Our Special Ed room, The Learning Center, is actually a small maze of semi-connected rooms on the second floor. Two windowless classrooms are attached to the hall, one with a third carved out of it through thin walls and a doorless doorway. The other larger classroom has been halved to hold two small offices, one for the department secretary and one for the big boss, Deidre. She's decked it out with lacy curtains and wallpaper borders to create a forced air of country kitchen homeyness.

A group of middle-aged (and then some) ladies enter and find seats among the mismatched tables and orange chairs. They're hauling an impressive array of canvas bags and milk crates overflowing with books. Chatting amongst themselves, they give me sidelong glances without eye contact or introductions. With no real surface to gather around, I remain standing. While they don't seem warm or welcoming, at least no one is shooting spitballs at me.

The largest one, in a bright red dress and sequined shoes, addresses the room. "Should we set up some tables, do you think?"

"I don't know. No one told me what we're doing," the dowdiest one says.

"Should I have my list of students?" the oldest one asks. I can't say exactly what it is she's wearing.

"I said no one told me what we're doing. So, I didn't know what to bring."

"I think we should set up some tables, don't you?"

Now they all finally look at me.

"Okay," I say. I don't move. They remain nameless and haphazardly seated.

I figure out then, that as the one male, all responsibility for moving moderately heavy items falls on my shoulders. I put my stolen pen and scrap of paper on the nearest table and slide it to the middle of the room. I take a quick count and gather enough chairs. I sit in the middle, they collect their bags and, huffing a bit, seat themselves around the table.

"What about Jean? Do we have a seat for her?"

"Hmm, Jean."

"And Sally."

"Yes. And Sally."

Putting all their passive clues together, I figure that I should get two more chairs. I squeeze them in, and the ladies continue speaking.

"I think that's all of us."

"Is Andrea here today?"

"There's enough for her. Do I need my list?"

"No one told me what we're doing today."

"Should we put two tables together, do you think?"

I'm not moving. Of all people here, do they honestly think I would know if we have enough chairs? It looks like Big Boss is here, anyway. Her rank is clear by the crushing number of bags she totes in. All that baggage hangs beside and behind a bold polka dot number. She drops into the seat across from me. I smile at her. She giggles and exhales with a squeak.

"Hello, everyone. Does anyone know what we're supposed to be doing today?" Deidre says, and her hair remains lacquered in place, musk ox curls at her chin, as she swivels her head between us.

"No one told me anything. I don't know," one of the ladies says.

The ladies begin the meeting around me. Mostly someone just says a name, presumably a student's, and everyone cracks up, reminiscing. I smile and hide my sheet of doodles. After forty or so minutes, Deidre stops speaking and stares at me.

"Oh goodness! Norman!"

"Hello," I say.

"Ladies, I'm sorry, this is Norman. Our new case manager. One of us now."

They all greet me then. Smiles and waves like I just walked in the room.

"He's Blake Mean's boy," Deidre says.

"Oh, my, no!"

"Poor Blake. His wife. Such a loss."

"Terrible. I almost went to the funeral, you know."

"Tragedy."

"Oh, my, that was your mother!"

"No!"

There's a sliding of overburdened chairs, and I'm suddenly inundated, covered by perfume and polyester. They're bumping each other to get to me, still in my chair. Huge breasts and rough hair rub against my face. One of them is crying, pulling tissues from her sleeve to dab at her mascara. Deidre resettles herself in the plastic chair and rests her paws on the table.

"Well, goodness, I hope we all feel a little better now."

I certainly don't. "Yes. Thank you," I say.

We pull through our shared sadness for the next hour and manage to divide the few hundred Special Ed kids between us. Deidre reads a name from her multi-page scrawled-over list, and someone says, "Oh, I'll take her." Or "I might as well, the rest of the school already hates me." The oldest one even says, "Sure. Why the fuck not?" She's my new favorite. When there is silence after a name, it stays silent until I volunteer. When I do, they all tell me how much I'll love working with so-and-so and how he really just needs a male case manager and he'll be fine; last year they got off to a bad start together, but they're sure that with me that won't happen. I agree that we'll probably get along swimmingly and that some of these kids just need someone they can talk to, you know? They nod sympathetically, and we move on to the next name on Deidre's list.

The principal's crackling voice announces lunch over the loudspeaker, and all the ladies begin gathering their bags, cutting Deidre off mid-sentence. Moments later, they're gone. Deidre continues talking

43

to me as if there had been no interruption. I end up with the last five kids at the end of the alphabet and uncomfortable stares from Deidre. We're across from each other for many seconds before she sighs and says, simply, "Lunch." She collects her baggage and walks out.

The Learning Center looks anything but. It's still recovering from a deep summer cleansing, with nothing in place. All the tables are covered by inspirational kitty posters: "Hang in there!" and colorful charts comically portraying the four mathematical functions waiting to be put back up on the soft, thumbtack walls. Worn maps of different world regions rest unexamined on shelves. Glancing at them on my way out, I notice at least three countries that no longer exist.

The sound of more awkward conversation rises, spilling up over the mezzanine and down the hall. I fold my scrap of paper bearing the scrawled list of assigned names, each one a tangled history of abuse and neglect, into my pocket. I know I should probably put this paper in an important folder somewhere, but I have no desk, no file cabinet, and certainly no idea of what I'm going to do with these kids. I also know I should probably go mingle with my new co-workers, but I don't.

The side hallway to the parking lot is empty. I duck my face away from the surveillance camera, hoping whoever watches is busy bitching about the year ahead over cold cuts and sweaty cheese. Thankfully, Dad still keeps a spare key in the gas tank cover. I start the car and lean my head against the steering wheel. The familiar voices of wacky local radio, still crazy after all these years, calm me as I pull out onto the main road. I think there may be some casserole left, and I head home.

# Chapter Five

Sometime during the first week of classes, both bushy-tailed newbie teachers appear in my doorway as one entity. They have lost their shine and look a little hazy around the edges.

"We wanted to see how you were doing," Big Guy says.

I can't quite seem to separate their actual names from the ones I've assigned them, and do not call them by any name, for fear of speaking their nicknames out loud. "I'm good," I say.

They allow their shoulders to fall and exhale as one. "Oh, that's good."

"Yeah," I offer.

"So good," Wispy says.

We smile at each other, relaxed in our good-ness.

"How are you guys doing?" It finally occurs to me to ask.

And there go those shoulders, tensed back up to their ears. They look at each other and at their own hands, dancing before their chests. "Oh, you know."

"Sure," I say, and I mean it.

"It's harder than I thought," Big Guy says.

Wispy nods. "Go on. Tell him."

Big Guy takes a practiced, calming breath. "Yesterday." Another breath. "One of the boys told me to shut the fuck up."

"It's true." Wispy says.

"Oh, wow. Yeah. I mean, that's tough," I say, thinking that that's how half my kids introduced themselves over the past couple days. And, mostly, I respected their wishes.

Now we all frown at each other in our shared frustration. Big Guy takes a step forward, and for a second I think he's coming in for a hug. I involuntary retreat backwards, and sit at my desk. Big Guy steps back into position.

"That is probably harder than you thought," I say.

They agree, and continue standing. I find myself nodding in time with them.

I have nothing more to say to them now, after this confession, than when they first materialized at my door. I don't have the skills for professional adult talk. Or maybe I just don't care about them or their swearing students. Both, probably.

It's a relief when Dad knocks on the doorframe, holding his battered briefcase and dangling a key ring from his finger.

"Contract says it's time to go," he announces. When nobody moves or responds, he raises the briefcase and slaps the side twice, his keys jangling. "Chop, chop."

They both startle easy and turn to leave in opposite directions, bumping each other. "Right! Goodbye Mr. Mean, and uh, Mr. Mean."

"Good night, boys. It only gets worse," Dad says, grinning hugely.

"Nice, Dad," I say when they've left.

"Oh, you'll all be crotchety old men in a few years, too."

"Comforting."

"Let's go. We're late," he says, looking at his bare wrist.

46

"For what?"

"Leaving," he says, and executes a military turn into the hall.

Dad has withheld any actual expressions of pride. He laughs at my stories and tells me he's sure I'll figure it all out. Or not. It's not going to change the students any. It's just accepted that we now teach together, that this is our life; he seems happier than before school started. The routine seems to have done us both some good. It gives us cause to get up early and sets a standard time to begin drinking. I can think about tomorrow instead of yesterday, or the last thirty years. We talk solely about school until we talk about where to order dinner until we talk about what's on TV. Mom would be proud, if it weren't for the whiskey bottle on the counter.

I don't know why we avoid talking about Mom; we're still trying to get to know each other. Having barely returned for more than a quick required holiday visit or a guilt-driven long weekend, I think coming back reset some sort of internal clock. Whatever sort of adult I had become in California stayed there. Being in Garrison erased all the years I've been gone. When I left, I remember thinking it was the only option. Julia carried me away with her, and I mistook that for maturity, for dealing with the past by starting the future. Now, it seems like it may have been an unhealthy cocktail of teenage lust and utter fear of ever bumping into Fitzy's parents at the coffee shop.

We don't talk about that either. Fitzy. We don't talk about him. Or our trip to the pond. The photograph of me and Fitzy rests untouched on my desk under stacks of legal paperwork from the school district— both nearly incomprehensible.

This afternoon, Dad and I will take the roundabout route home, stopping at the liquor store outside town, to avoid 'the goddam school board', and we may pick up a pizza or some burgers. If we get burgers we'll sit on the back porch and eat them until the quiet becomes too much and he'll make a poor joke as he leaves to turn on the television. I'll weigh the benefits of staying on the porch or watching TV. I'll find new justification for not leaving the house, refill my glass and listen to Dad's commentary, pretending this is maturity.

# Chapter Six

"Hey, why don't you break out some work, try to get caught up in math?" I asked one of them this morning, a 14-year-old boy draped across my desk, completely worn out from the stress of actively doing nothing. Three weeks into school, and he is done. Spent.

"I already did. I have, like, an A, or something now."

"That's great. Did you get anything new today you could work on?"

"That asshole wouldn't give me anything new," he said with a look of complete disdain, like I'm an even bigger asshole for not knowing that.

What a bunch of losers. I have a hard time reconciling my memories of teenage pride with the crude immature arrogance of these kids. It's still 90 degrees outside, and the kids have bitched about everything, contradicting themselves with every complaint. I'm still not sure what I'm doing here.

"Why wouldn't he give you new stuff to work on?" I say.

"I don't know, I guess I have to give him all the old stuff."

"I thought you did."

"Fuck that! That guy's such a dick. He hates me or something."

This is before eight in the morning. They must go to bed bitter and marinate all night. And it's not even just the students the adults in the room are barely better. There is a clear hierarchy, I've come to discover, in the world of Special Education.

It's our own unique realm, almost a separate institution from the rest of the school. No one truly wants to associate with us, and even we're all only here by default. Either we weren't certified in what we wanted to teach, or there were simply no other jobs. There are only a few women who voluntarily entered "sped," and they're so damned heartfelt. Here because their own child had some sort of problem, and they so badly want to help others with the same issue overcome the obstacles this cruel world places before them. They're as obnoxious as the kids.

There's Deidre, of course, she's my direct boss in the building. Above her is the district sped director. I only ever hear from her in solid blocks of page-long e-mails, giving directives about paperwork, so she doesn't really count. An assortment of specialists come and go, working with the really banged-up kids on things like walking or holding a pencil. I sign off on their forms without knowing their names or what they've done to the children. Then there are the case managers; that's me and all the ladies I met on my first day. Our job is essentially to ensure that the kids on our case load, who have been diagnosed with some sort of disability, get everything they need to succeed handed to them on a silver platter and fed to them with airplane noises. We're hidden in The Learning Center, waiting for the Regular Ed teachers, somewhere above me on the chain, to become so infuriated or frustrated that they send down our kids.

The lowest caste consists of the paraprofessionals. They're assigned to work with specific kids in the classrooms. Their sour-faced countenances beside furious, swearing children complete the picture of Special Education at Garrison High. As a group we make up the largest department in the school, a ragtag bunch, a motley crew—a street gang without the swagger, coolness, confidence, or competence.

This morning I crept in with my plastic bag lunch, always an embarrassment, like a hobo with his bindle stick, and hid behind my desk. Desks, actually. I rescued two old beat-up wooden relics from the loading dock just as the garbage truck was pulling up. Dad likes to get here early to prepare lesson plans and grade homework, and even though I have none of that in my vaguely educational position, he's my ride. And in the morning, no matter how early I arrive, Phil the paraprofessional is here before me.

Every early morn, Phil squats and performs his calisthenics across the green tiled room. He grunts a number with each leg extension. His polyester pants strain to contain his buttocks. The small buttons on his short sleeve button-downs can't hold out much longer.

He's the kind of bald that shines, which is fine, except I'm pretty sure he waxes it. His head is luminescent. His horseshoe hairline is shaved around the top edge, only he doesn't do the required upkeep and stubble creeps up toward the crown. He's like Friar Tuck, minus the sense of fun. He's a devotee of oddly homoerotic Russian strength training journals, which I didn't know existed until a couple weeks ago. Phil's been on a half-day schedule for years, well before I got here (which puts even him somewhat higher than me on the hierarchal tree), due to a flooring project he has going on at his trailer. He's putting linoleum down in his living room, which begs several questions: How long can such a project possibly take? And who puts linoleum down in their living room? It's not his exercising here every morning that bothers me, it's just that after all these years of dedication, you'd think he'd look better.

He's not to be confused with another para, Big Buff Phil, who's training to be a professional wrestler in a neighbor's garage and is on such a strictly regimented caloric intake that he only sleeps in two hour bursts in order to eat cans of straight tuna. These two men work with children.

Today is our second day of standardized testing, and there are many things wrong with this. The first being the excruciating boredom it elicits from our kids, the second being the name: New England Common Recordable Objective Standard, or NECROS. The administrators keep throwing the acronym around like they don't get it or maybe there's been some directive not to acknowledge the clear reference to sex with dead people. Either way, three hours of NECROS isn't appetizing.

The room is beginning to fill, and I hide behind my computer. The few kids here at this hour are going crazy. Despite all medical research to the contrary, high school kids seem to have plenty of energy this early in the morning. They yell, play grab-ass, and chase each other in autistic circles. Someone grabs a pencil from someone else, and it's not like the kid is going to actually use that pencil, but, shit, he wants it when someone takes it. There are repeated cries of, "She's not my girlfriend!" from a small kid with glasses who clearly wishes the opposite was true. They're loud, but each sip of coffee decreases their volume a notch. The other paraprofessionals sit around the classroom tables, watching Phil work out, drinking coffee, or perusing the want ads. They bitch about the kids who are bitching about them at the next table.

It's been strange, this past little bit, figuring out what my job is.

When I first heard 'Special Ed teacher' I imagined myself at the bottom of a pig pile of oversized, happily drooling teenagers with children's haircuts, but it's nothing like that. It turns out that I'm just extra help for kids who've been fucked up by a wide array of things: the full range of abuse, drugs, parents, and/or bad birth. Others just need a place to go when class becomes too much. Some are just genuinely unlikable.

Destiny, one of my freshmen, is here moments after the first period bell rings. I'm surprised to see her here, only because this is where she's supposed to be, due to the NECROS.

"I'm not fucking going." She drops her enormous purse, a formidable handbag really, and all its attached pins and key chains with witty sayings rattle and clank across my desktop. She stares at me, snapping her gum with one leg crossed tightly over the other, the dangling foot at the end swinging crazily in heels she can't handle.

"Oh yeah?" I say.

"Yeah. She's a cunt. I'm not going."

"Okay. Stay here then."

"What?" Her foot stops twitching.

"Stay here this period."

"Why?"

"So you don't have to deal with that bitch."

"She's a cunt."

"Either way. We have testing today."

"I'm not taking that fucking test." She gathers up her bag, sweatshirt and cell phone, which she's not even supposed to have in school, and starts flipping the phone open and closed.

"Come on, it'll get you out of class for the next few hours." I stand

53

and go through the attendance list for the NECROS. Lots of kids scheduled for sex with dead people today.

"I'm not taking that fucking test," Destiny says.

"It's not a fucking test."

"Bet you wish it was." She stops fidgeting with her phone and looks up at me. Her gum snaps. "Whatever. I'm not doing it."

I really don't want this conversation to be overheard by anyone. I don't even want to hear it myself anymore. "You know what, Destiny? You have to take the test, half the school does, so why don't you just kick back for a while and fill in some circles?"

She stands, clutching her possessions, and pauses to scream, "Fuck you!" before storming into the hallway. I can hear her hitting lockers down the hall.

The table of paraprofessionals stares at me, their styrofoam coffee cups frozen to their lips.

"I guess I can cross her off the list, huh?" I say.

They rotate back as one and continue their conversation. Shouldn't they be in a class somewhere?

I look down the hall. Destiny has disappeared. She's someone else's problem now, though I'm sure she'll be returned shortly. They always come back. The paraprofessional table rises and clears with no goodbyes. Phil has left to share his Russian strength training secrets with the next generation. At the ringing of the late bell, the students also leave, absently ignoring my goodbyes and questions about their lateness. I've turned into the teacher who asks such things.

Soon the tables are full, and I compare the faces to the names on my list. Ollie's missing. So far, Ollie is my favorite. He's a freshman at sixteen who could pass for twelve. The baggy gangster clothes that other kids wear so smoothly look like child's pajamas on Ollie.

While not actually preparing for the exam, he eventually arrives stocked with a bag of crap candy, which he says is for energy. This breaks the 'no food' rule, but I let it slide. He smells like Swedish Fish. He says hi through a mouth already showing bright red stains from the candy and walks right past me to stand on the back of an older girl's wheel chair. From anyone else this could come off as offensive. It's not only because he's dumb that he can pull this off; it's that he has no idea he's dumb. He barrages her with questions about horsepower and burnouts and wheelies, and it makes her laugh.

"All right, kids, let's get this over with," I say.

Ollie stands next to the seat he had yesterday, only today there is a large girl leaning across the table, knees on his seat and huge ass up in the air. Her turquoise thong a flag for the class to salute.

"Get the fuck out of my seat," Ollie says.

"It's not your seat. We don't have assigned seats. Right, Mr. Mean? You said? Yesterday?"

"Can you just move for today? What's the big deal? Come sit at my desk."

The girl rolls herself off the chair and roughly tugs her shirt down to the top of her stretched jeans. "Uh! Whatever!"

"There, Ollie. It's all yours."

"Sick!" He sits and begins digging through the candy bag.

I hand out the tests and pencils. For minutes, the room is quiet. Destiny seems to have found someplace to hide. Ollie is contentedly filling out random answers, working his way through the bag, when he bursts out with an impressive swearing explosion.

"Shit! Shit! Motherfucker shit ass shit!"

I walk over and kneel beside him, try to calm him, quiet him, so the others don't get sucked in, start a chain reaction. "Ollie, what the hell are you doing?" I say quietly.

"My fucking mom!"

"What about her?"

"Her butts!"

"Your mom's butt?"

"No! Shit fuck! She bought me all this candy after work last night!"

"So, what's the problem?"

"Her fucking butts! In the bag!" Ollie rummages around the Nerds, Swedish fish, and Jolly Ranchers to produce an unopened pack of Marlboros, bright red and clearly out of place in this room. Other kids are laughing and pointing, asking for smokes. Ollie throws his head down, hiding tears with teenage aplomb.

"Just bring them to her after school. No big deal." I awkwardly pat his back, he's so small.

"She'll be so fucking pissed I got suspended again." His face is bright red, and he rubs angrily at it, disappointed in himself, at how hard he has to try to keep it cool. I have to stifle a smile.

"But you're not suspended. At all. Everything's fine, hey, let's go talk in the office."

Ollie throws his test on the floor, something for the crowd, and flings the rest of the candy in an arc across the room. "Fucking take it!" Adults nervously watching from their corners begin to converge on us now that he has clearly done something they can punish him for, their hands extended and childish reprimands ready. I hold them back with a couple of calming gestures, fingers out, slowly waving them down. I got it, I got it.

Every paraprofessional in this room has had it out with Ollie, and I'm sure I'll hear about every incident later today, with them telling me that today was the final straw, this can't happen anymore. I'll tell them I understand, and they'll say that they're sure I handled it, they're sure, it's just that, well, you know. I know.

Ollie is in his corner in the office, crying and holding the Marlboros. He wants to squeeze them so badly, his hands are clenched white around them, but his mom, while she may be mad about another suspension, would be fucking furious about crushing a pack of her butts.

"You're not in trouble, you know." I hand him the box of tissues.

"I brought fucking butts to school, and you're telling me I'm not in trouble!"

His pinpoint logic is supposed to floor me. He knows how these things work.

"Just put them away and bring them to her after school."

"I'll get fucking suspended again if I have butts at school."

There's an opportunity here. "Your mom works at Dunkins, right?"

Sniffle, snot. "Yeah."

"I'll bring them to her after the test. Tell her what happened. C'mon, it'll be fine."

"You know my mom?"

Christ, I've spoken to her in this room in front of him a half dozen times since school began. "Yeah. I think I'd recognize her."

57

"She won't be pissed?"

"No." I'm not sure about that. "She'll be happy to have a smoke after work."

"Yeah, she will."

"See, it's fine." I stand. "Let's go back out there and finish up."

"Can you hold these?" He hands the sweaty Marlboro pack to me.

"Sure, Ollie. No problem."

The room turns to watch us reenter. Ollie offers only one challenging, "What the fuck you looking at?" to the room. Someone was kind enough to gather his test. I get him going with a few heavily hinted answers and return to my desk to plan my excursion to the Dunkin' Donuts.

I imagine walking in, catching Ollie's mom's eyes from the back of the line. I'll smile to show her that Ollie's fine and wait my turn. When I get to the counter she'll smile, and I'll hold up the pack of smokes. "Oh God," she'll say and ask the manager for her break. We'll sit out back, on the curb by the dumpsters, and share a laugh without much conversation. She'll smack the pack on the palm of her hand and tear off the cellophane in one smooth motion. With a flick, she'll produce two cigarettes and smell them before handing me one. We'll smoke in silence, then look at our watches, shrug, smile, and have one more, wishing our days were truly done.

# Chapter Seven

## Nikki

The quiet, clustered bar conversations remind Nikki of her time at the hospital. The hushed tones and immediate importance of shared secrets fill the space between her and her customers. This is group therapy. Nikki plays Doctor, nodding approvingly at each revelation and filling prescriptions. The tall rectangle windows, orange with October's late afternoon sun, look out over a parking lot; same view as the hospital. The dust motes dance their last round before evening hides them. This time will be the best part of her night, slicing lemons and limes in the twilight, listening to the talk of men in between their work and their women. They like her, mostly because, and she knows this, she is not their boss or their wife.

These are the men who drink the same drink every time. She can have it resting at their usual spot before they order. And they like that. Nikki can determine how their day went or how they're getting along with their wives within moments. It's a nuanced intimacy. When they see a drink waiting for them, and say to Nikki, "Maybe I want something different tonight." That's a bad day. And depending on which guy said it, and whose boss is a woman, she can tell whether the problem lies in the office or the bedroom. These noticings seem simple, but the doctors in the hospital knew nothing more than this, not more than Nikki. They made huge assumptions, extrapolating a life from a gesture.

She learned a lot at the hospital. About other people. And how they think, how the seeds of their psychoses sprout and fester, spreading like blight into their bones, choking out everything else, blocking their sight. How easily people decide to see only what they choose, even if it doesn't exist. The Doctors, her family, they all wanted Nikki to be cured. They wanted her to stop telling them she had visions, so when she did, they knew it was true. Nikki knows more now than before, and for that, she is glad.

What she does not know, cannot get at, is Norman Mean's role, and how it relates to her own. At this juncture, that isn't clear. Nikki trusts in her odd prescience, her knowledge of the future that had come in blurry flashes, more frequently at some times than others, but is becoming clearer. There were no faces for as long as she's had her visions. Just colors, shouting. Disconnected scenes and water. Lots of water. Then one day, there's Norm's face, his hands, sticking out clearly from a blur of motion yet to occur.

It's not until the sun is gone from the windows that these men leave. The bar is empty. Their replacements, coming soon, won't appreciate Nikki in the same way. They won't get the same drink twice; all their orders will be colorful and syrupy. She'll have to take off her sweatshirt, allow her tits to help her collect tips, but that's fine. You can't expect to work at a place that hires its bartenders by breast size without having them come in handy once in a while. The cleavage doesn't bother her as much as the uniform, the blue police shirts and accompanying badges which complete the theme of The Lock Up. It doesn't really matter, though, as long they keep coming in, and eventually he'll come in. Or she'll figure out where to look.

The hospital gave her names for what she experiences and even if none of them fit perfectly, they all added up to something she can live with. Even if she, herself, had to properly name it. It isn't a hallucination, she can distinguish it from the reality of the present. It isn't a dream or delusion. She prefers "vision." "Vision" makes sense to her. It sounds promising and heroic, not insane.

If when she went to the hospital she, and everyone around her, thought she was crazy, and when she left she knew she was sane, then it makes sense that the hospital fixed her. It would appear that they stopped something from happening, removed some malfunctioning extraneous bits of Nikki that took away from the flowering effectiveness of her whole.

But, Nikki knows, that's not at all what happened. She told her family that's what happened, and her doctors. But that's not what happened.

Nikki grasps the power of a small, well-twisted manipulation or the perfectly casual lie. These men at the bar don't need to know the extent to which her mind travels forward. They just want their drinks and camaraderie. Not her predictions. But they aren't predictions as much as sureties. Visions. Of water and the beginning of something, or the end of something. Or everything. But it's hers unlike anything else in the world, more than her apartment, job, or clothes. It comprises Nikki more than her thoughts or body, either of which she's more than willing to share. But her vision is solely her own. For now.

The limes are all sliced. The lemons are done; she cleans the knife and cutting board. Absently sliding open all the cooler covers, she checks on how well stocked she is for the night ahead. Looks good. It's always shocking to think of the long process, the hundreds of people it took to make all these beers arrive at this bar and then to know she'll be dumping all the empties in the dumpster in just hours. All for the delight of the roving droves of frat boys who will appear as one at the bar, drink in unison, and leave in a blurry rush. It makes much less sense to her than does her vision.

Lately, the colors have been more vibrant and her reaction to them more visceral, but still manageable. The water used to sneak up on her slowly, her feet sweaty and legs becoming numb, the feeling moving up until the spot behind her ears buzzed. Then her mind filled from the bottom, like a bathtub draining in reverse with the treetops in the scene scraping against the sunny roof of her head, eventually leaving her hair wet and mind empty. She would come to, unsure of what had happened, exhausted and infuriated, aware of the time lost.

Everything she had done to keep them away seemed only to encourage them. The drinking was useless and drugs carried their own problems. But they did give excuses. Nikki could be drug crazy, not plain crazy. People seemed more comfortable with that, and no one got together to have visions the same way they got together to do drugs. It is much more sociable to be an addict than a prophet.

Her family could blame the drugs for the hospitalization, if that was easier for them, but it wasn't Nikki's attempt to beat the drugs, because those she could understand and handle. She wanted to take her head back from something that was yet to happen. At the hospital she'd seen the crazies. The damaged girls and boys, their bodies used and minds wasted. It comforted her to know she wasn't that. There had been those who spoke ceaselessly of things unseen by other eyes. And she wasn't one of them, but she wondered if maybe those crazies just weren't cut out for whatever she has been chosen for. If perhaps they were like her, only weaker.

"Chosen" isn't a word that came easily to Nikki's mind, to her worldview. "Chosen" implies more than she had been willing to accept. First, that there is something beyond herself that fills her mind, and second, that she has to do something with these visions besides make them go away, which had always been her instinct.

Nikki's been good since she's made genuine attempts to understand, rather than eradicate, her visions. For the last couple of months, she's been able to make out some new small detail every time: a word, the trees, the height of water. That makes her think things are drawing to a conclusion. But with Norm Mean appearing in her head—she can't quite get that. It was almost more frustrating when his face became clear. What the hell was he doing there? It even took her a while to place him. She knew that face somewhere, but you'd think if he was part of some master plan of which she had celestial knowledge, then they would have more of a connection than a few shared drinks or hits. They'd gone to high school together. She even remembers, after some deep looking back, some conversations they'd shared, just as she'd begun her drug-addled attempt to rid herself of visions. But Norm Mean? What the fuck?

When she'd heard that his mom died, she immediately felt responsible. Ridiculously removed responsibility, she knew, but still, somehow at fault. As if her visions had conspired with the universe to bring him back to town.

To her.

It is this strange connection, between herself and Norm, that occupies her mind as she wipes the counter clean, wiping at the overlapping half-completed circles the drinkers have left behind, proof of their presence clear as tracks in the snow.

Nikki digs around under the register to find her smokes. If she doesn't have one now, she may not get one. She figures they can't be killing her that quickly if her life hasn't caught up with her visions; she's got some time left. In the rush of water and people and Norm Mean, she cannot see her own face, and so doesn't really have much of a timeline as to when all this will happen. Norm looks reasonably young in the flash where she can make out his face, though it's hard to tell, so Nikki thinks things should be happening soon, start moving along any day now.

She'll wait, of course. Nikki would have left town a long time ago if she didn't have this pesky destiny. Despite her fondness for the late afternoon regulars, she's not here at the bar out of an inherent love of the service industry or a shrewd career move. The bar is in town. And now Norm Mean is in town. When the two meet, Nikki will be at the crux, as curious as a tourist, waiting to see how one thing flows to another.

# Chapter Eight

"Norm," he says again, pointing at the commercial on the screen. "What movie was that guy in? With the hair? And maybe the car?"

"I don't know, Dad."

"You've seen it. It's got that other guy, also, who married the blonde one." Dad waves his rocks glass in thoughtful circles.

"I don't know, Dad. Just toast him anyway."

"You're right, Norm, that's the attitude!" He pushes himself to a half-stand off the recliner. "Here's to you, sir, and to that movie you were in! Cheers!"

"Dad."

"Cheers!" He turns to me and drains his glass, eyeing me over the rim. "And to you, Norm! No one better to share this next drink with!"

Dad downs the whiskey until the ice cubes fall around his mouth. He clacks the glass down and sits back, looks at me and touches his finger to his nose. "Not it."

He's grinning, mashing his big old nose around with his fingertip, and nudging his empty glass toward me, across the small table separating our recliners. "Thatta boy, help out your old dad."

I take both our empty glasses to the kitchen counter, which Dad's been referring to as the bar. After topping his off, I put mine in the sink with the dirty silverware we used on our take-out dinner.

"Here you go, Father."

"Nothing for you?" He raises his glass immediately.

"Nah, you know what? I kind of feel like going out tonight. You know, I haven't really been downtown since I've been back, so…"

"So, you're leaving me? Heading out on your own? Sick of sitting around nursing drinks with an old man?"

"Dad, no, I just feel like going out for a while. You know."

He takes another sip and turns back to the TV. "Well, it's about time."

Tonight he pours his own whiskey and watches TV alone. No conversations about students past and present, their parents he taught and principals long dead. I'm walking downtown in the present. Finally, this Friday night, something outside of the house seems to have allure.

It's cold enough when I open the door that I almost grab one of my old jackets; stiff, thick canvas, worn at the wrists from whatever it was I used to do, then I remember that I'm in Garrison now. This is warm. It's not cold cold, not like it will be soon, but the chill is enough to make me think I've been here too long. I'm not back for a visit, though Mom certainly would have appreciated one. I'm past the funeral. I have a job. I even have my own clothes now; no more picking through Dad's plaid and khaki showroom. There's no good reason not to go downtown. None besides whatever private prohibition has been keeping me at home. Dad won't notice I'm gone until his drink is. That's fine. We both needed something to smooth my way back into the house.

The streetlights buzz on as I walk, and I look up at each lighting, wondering if I did that. They light very little but themselves. It's not quite dark here on our street. Cars at the intersection don't yet have their headlights on as they wait their turn, stopping to let me cross to the brick sidewalk part of town. These are all apartments now, with porches and yards. Another street to cross before the buildings turn to brick and the apartments rise taller, above sandwich and repair shops. The streetlights here seem brighter. Maybe it's just gotten darker.

Crossing over Fourth St. brings me into the heart of downtown, where the narrow one-way streets lead Boston summer tourists into a torrent of horns. I used to sit on the benches by the fountain, across from me now, laughing and cursing the visitors with the traditional "Masshole!" war cry. The braver tourists would occasionally stop at our bench and ask directions to some restaurant or museum. They would invariably receive directions to the 'health club' across the river. The one that everyone around here knew was really a whorehouse.

That's probably gone now, or maybe it's just cleaned up and charges more. Downtown is crowded. The parents leaving restaurants balance sleeping children and hold the door for the next wave of customers, the drinkers. Girls shivering in small shirts lean on each other, laughing past me. It's hard not to turn, watch them pass. Their guys walk three steps behind, comparing their girlfriend's asses. Talking sports. All headed somewhere. I check out their clothes.

My recently-purchased clothes still hold a new chemical smell. I traded nearly a whole paycheck, the biggest of my life, to the chain stores on the miracle mile in exchange for a whole new me. I think the last time I went clothes shopping, with the intent to leave with more than a new pair of jeans or a shirt for a job interview, was back-to-school shopping with Mom. It's been maybe fifteen years. Essentially, this was also back-to-school shopping. Though with Dad waiting, drinking in a bar in a restaurant in the middle of a parking lot, it had a different feel.

I had the students in mind as I picked out clothes. Did I want some air of authority? As if a crisper white, a stiffer collar, would make them listen. Or did I want something a little hipper? See kids, I'm cool. You should listen to me. If we had a fabric in common, maybe they could make it five minutes without a burst of swearing. I took a weak middle route, jeans, Chuck Taylors, a few nice shirts, nothing any self-respecting high school jackass would admit to relating to. Nor would I, but weeks of pleading with ragged teenaged zombies have left me with little self-respect. They can't help it, even if they don't make it easy. The one thing they do well is help me remember. I was like that, probably worse. If they knew half the things that happened in those halls when I was there, well, I hope they'd be impressed.

I remember the sense of ownership I felt walking this street. This was my town. I held a map of its narrow streets and alleys etched in my mind. I was Icarus proud. This town was our own. Cocksure, high-noon swaggers carried us to the spots we were sure only we knew; the same spots where our older brothers, sisters, or fathers had also hid. I wasn't even old enough to go into the bars, half of them now gone, replaced with classier versions of themselves. Still a neighborhood bar, but now the sign has to inform us of that fact, as if swilling belly up at the bar beside your neighbor isn't fact enough.

Tonight on this street, my first cigarette in forever seems only natural, not forbidden. Required even. A part of being here, like the leaves skittering and blowing up from the asphalt. Unlike my first life here, I feel Dad would be jealous, rather than derisive, of my smoke. I almost feel he should be here. The cigarette helps me push through the crowd; people fade aside at the tall smoking guy's approach, pull their children away from the possible contagion. All these people out for a night on the town, afraid of people out for a night on the town.

On the corner of what is optimistically referred to as the "upper square", a new bar sign reading "The Lock Up" drips a blue glow. I get it. This is the old police station. Beneath the sign, blue-skinned drinkers in Red Sox shirts line up. They all share matching hats, worn jaunty and cocked. I walk along the crowd's perimeter, peer over their loyal sporty heads, and follow the building's face into the alley separating it from a notorious apartment building, The Orchard Street Hotel and Apartments. By all appearances, it is still earning its notoriety. Music, arguments, the smell of macaroni and cheese, and crushed beer cans are all tossed carelessly from the windows into the alley.

In high school, if you knew someone, as I did, who lived in one of those squalid rooms, then, man, you were raised above the level of apprentice teenage drunk. If you were welcomed into one of those rooms and offered a can of beer like it was nothing, maybe even the half-smoked joint from the ashtray, you were established. And the drunks who lived there had gone to school with one of your teachers, and you would learn what a pussy that teacher was and how he was hated by high school kids, even when he was one. The squalor was romantic, and the layer of filth nothing but a cool patina. Who needed school or a future when everything you wanted could be had right here in the Orchard Hotel and Apartments?

Despite the crowd lining up at the front door, IDs at the ready, most of the bar staff seems to be back here in the alley, smoking. The front of the house waiters, bartenders, and bouncers are distinguishable from the kitchen crew by their dark blue shirts, tight and cleanly adorned with badges. That's cute. The kitchen crew smoke faster and more earnestly, with more dedication to what is certainly going to be a lifetime habit, rather than something a waitress can shake her head about in ten years, "I can't believe I used to do that! Oh, college was crazy!" The cook's snap-up white shirts are filthy and stiff at the waist from food spills that spread south to their jean fronts. Their hair is either long, tucked down the back of their shirts, or shaved to the skin, the scalp demarcated from their face with thick beards or tattoos. The waiters have clean white towels tucked into their belts like loincloths and little gelled-up patches of hair spiking over their foreheads. The waitresses and bartenders tie shoes and adjust cleavage in the red light of the exit sign.

All but one. I bump into her coming around the side of the building as I'm looking up at the apartments, getting ready to light another cigarette. She seems to be scanning the crowd out front. I say sorry. She gives her head a little twitch to look past me, her dark hair pulled back into a thick unruly ponytail hanging behind her with its own agenda. Without looking at me, she waves her unlit cigarette. "No problem," she says.

"You want a light?" I say.

"No, I'm good—" In the middle of looking to either side of me, she catches my eyes, "Oh. You're here. Yes, I'd like one. Please."

I hold out the Zippo and snap it open for her, trying to remember the last time I lit a girl's cigarette. I can't remember when I spoke to a woman who didn't work in The Learning Center, and was therefore actually pleasant. The only girls in my life recently are fourteen and pissed, just completely furious.

The flame burns the tip of her cigarette, but she isn't paying it the necessary attention, doesn't inhale, so the flame doesn't really light the cigarette, only burns it down.

"Hey," I say because she's just watching me through the flame. Her eyes are large and heavily lined above a small nose. The kind you could draw with one small curved line, far above her lips. Her body would require many more curving strokes.

"Oh, got it," she says and inhales, removing the butt with a practiced hand. She exhales sideways. The stream of smoke floats back between us. She flaps her hand through the air and dabs at a spot behind her ear, like putting on perfume, "Sorry."

I quickly light my own smoke, to show her I don't mind, also blowing my smoke sideways until we're again enveloped. She seems a little older than the other waitresses and bartenders, experienced. Maybe it's just the casual, wild hair. A black sweatshirt almost zips high enough to cover her cleavage. Her jeans are worn to her shape. I wouldn't question being shut off by her. Despite this, she seems strangely nervous —stares at me, then looks away to smoke. I have no idea what to say. Thank god for cigarettes filling in the conversational blanks.

"Is it tonight? Are you coming in tonight?" she finally asks.

"Here? I don't know. Isn't this place new?"

"So? "

"I don't know. I grew up here," I say.

"Maybe I'll see you inside."

"Yeah, inside. That line, though, I don't know."

"Are you asking me to get you in?" She smiles and smokes.

"No, no. Why? Could you? I think I'm just walking around tonight, you know?"

"Okay."

"Yeah, I drink at home," I say.

"Figures." She laughs and stamps out her cigarette. I take a look at mine. Still a few drags left. "Thanks for the light. I'll be inside until close."

"Okay. Thanks. You're welcome."

She turns away down the alley to the side door, then stops. She looks back at me.

"I knew, you know," she says.

"Yeah?"

"That you aren't new. I know that."

"That's cool. Okay."

She walks the rest of the way down the alley and says something to the assembled workers, who scuff the ground and smoke, putting off going in, knowing that there's no assured break once they do. They laugh with her and follow her into the bar, the last guy looks back out at me. I wave and he slams the door.

'I drink at home?' What the hell was that supposed to mean? I really need to get better at this, I'm too old. I never even asked her name.

My cigarette is done. I drop it and stamp it out like a regular smoker: These habits, the motions that come with them, don't go away. The line is moving, everyone letting everyone else know by cell phone. They're rowdy amateur drinkers. Excited, they discuss what they'll order and how many they'll have. Walking past them, on to something quieter and darker, I keep my head down, realizing that downtown isn't where I meant to go tonight. Leaving the busy streets behind, I follow the brick sidewalks to their end. I use the white line on the side of the road as a guide. I'm going to the pond.

# Chapter Nine

The pond looks impossibly small. A crescent of pavement, sprinkled with colorful children's toys, curves the miniature shoreline until meeting the dam. The low dam wall flattens out the far side, separating the pond from the stream. It can't be the same spot where the ultimate midnight challenge was the cross-pond swim. We'd swim from the shore to the dam, scrambling up the low wall and looking back at the distance we'd crossed before sliding back in. The Dawn Cross-Pond Challenge. Across and back, ending in the perfect teenage excuse to remove clothes and sit shivering by a campfire, draining beer from shaky cans. That was the penultimate challenge, I suppose. There was one more to be made by firelight. Sparks rose to the stars where our futures lurked, soaring in bright clusters.

I barely remember what I wished for then. To be back here checking off recent changes like a bitter old man? I do remember all that talk, if not the words, the naming of our future addresses and the collective assuredness. It was always me who claimed I had all I needed right here. Right in this spot, man. And then it was me who left. Of course, that was after Fitzy. There was no staying after that.

A dog barks close by, revealing how far from wild these woods have become.

I walk straight into the water from behind someone's house, headed for the pavement across. My quiet splashes mingle with the low gurgle of the stream, running through a small pipe in the dam before coming to rest in this basin, hand dug generations ago by a harder working man than me.

It's cold in the night air and water squishes around the little holes on the sides of my shoes. My jean cuffs float toward my knees; in the middle of the pond my shirt skirts up around me. I dip my hands in and break the surface; sticks and leaves rub my legs. With my head sunk back the houses slip from view, and the stars fill in perfectly the empty spaces among the treetops. My feet float up until my shoulders dip below the surface. I allow the invisible tension of the water's surface to carry my weight.

The pond still holds the memory of that night. The water fills my ears and I hear one voice plucked from the chaos, "Norm, help. Something's wrong." All the other voices I hear come from my head, from that next day and the years after, "It's not your fault. You did what you could."

I let the pond cradle me. I allow the trees to draw my sight up to the stars, which become sparks and fall around my body. The sizzle of them hitting the water stirs something in the murk beneath; my back arches up to keep me afloat. I paddle my hands a bit, rotating my body. The trees appear to spin around the stars. The water leaves odd pinging echoes in my ears. My clothes spread in the water. I straighten my spine against Fitzy's dead fingers, a tremble across my back. They hold me steady, raise me above the water line. Higher, my clothes hang limp. He's speaking now, I hear his voice, but his words are muffled by the water in my ears. Tilting my head into my chest, I can almost make them out. It's still unclear, I try to focus, but become distracted by the floating and the stars and find myself back, standing in the water, alone and soaked.

That dog barks again and a door slides open. The treetops gain a glow. A voice from outside the pond floats in beneath the stars. Dog tags clink and claws scrape against wood.

"Lacey! Lacey!" A man's voice calls out from the light. Behind the glare, I make out the back of a house, lined by a large deck. He is on that deck.

I sink my feet back down into the muck and stand straight, the water seeps in just over my belt buckle. My vision adjusts until I can see the oversized house with a deck backed by glass. A golden retriever sprints down the elaborate levels of stairs into the yard. It comes barking to the edge of the pond, only feet from me.

"Shit," I say.

"LACEY!" The man is silhouetted against the light in a baseball hat and what looks like pajama bottoms. He is clearly not expecting an interloper on his pond this evening. Hands cupped around his mouth, he calls out again.

"Lacey! Get back here! Jesus F'ing Christ."

I'm still, trying not to disturb the water, shivering in the air.

The man twists momentarily back, and the night sky is sucked into light. The yard's clutter is shown in garish relief. That dog makes a sudden break back to the house before turning on its hind legs, back to the water's edge, and doubles its barking.

I whisper reassuring words to it. "It's all right, go on, go away. Good girl. Nothing to see here. Go on, girl."

The man's tone drops. "Who's there? Lacey! Who's there?"

Another voice, a woman, calls from inside. "What's going on? Steve! Is someone out there? Steve!"

"I got it!" Then quieter, "I fuckin' got it. Christ."

The man steps out of shadow and morphs to recognizable. It's that Steve. Steve Stone. It's him. Here again, somehow. I'm split between turning, paddling back into the dark, to home, or running forward through the yard.

If I left the house tonight, I suppose I can leave the pond. I take a few sloshing steps to the edge, my shoes crunching the pebbles on the pavement. "Hey, Steve."

"Who the hell's there?" He jumps back, and the dog is going mad.

"What the hell is going on out there? Listen to me, Steven!" the woman's voice says.

"I don't know, Sherry. Hold the fuck on!"

I step through the edge of the light, from the pond to the yard and look up to the deck, squinting against the flood light. "Steve? It's me. Norm. Mean. Steve Stone? I'm back."

Steve leans over the railing and shields his eyes on the sides of his hat brim, as if looking down a hole, then he stands straight, hands on his hips. "Norm?"

"Hey."

"What the fuck?" Steve says.

"Steve. What are you doing here?"

"What am I doing here?" He leans both hands on the railing, then crosses them. Recrosses them. Mutters something I don't catch.

The dog stops barking and wags at my feet, now that I have Steve's tepid approval. She's looking for a rub and sniffing the pond on me. The woman shrieks again from inside.

"STEVE! What, exactly, is fucking going on here?"

He turns his head. "I got it Sherry! I got it!"

"What the hell, who's in my goddam yard?"

"Is that Sherry Elliot?" That screech, that particular tone, even after years, is immediately recognizable.

Steve looks down at me, then back inside. Speaking just loudly enough for me to hear him, he says, "Yeah, that's her. Sherry Stone now, man."

"Isn't that a clam?"

"She's Sherry Stone because we're married. You're thinking of a cherry stone."

I nod. "Right. Cherry. I didn't know you guys got married."

"Nine years now."

"Wow. I haven't done anything for nine years."

"You've been gone."

"Yeah, I've been gone longer than that."

"Well, there you go."

I laugh. "There I go." I nudge the tip of a red kayak about the size of the pond. I'm shivering, shaking from the water, my clothes clinging. Steve is still mostly shadow; the floodlights outline his round shape on the deck above me. The deck is raised on many pillars, looking down on everything. With our hands on our foreheads to block the light, we appear to be saluting each other. He's a captain, on the prow of his ship, coming across a castaway, considering the situation.

"Mind if I come in?" I say.

"STEVEN! Will somebody please tell me what the hell is going on out here?" And there is Sherry, a shadow materializing in the porch light. She looms enormous behind Steve, twice as wide. Damn, she got huge. Then she kind of pulls herself in at the sides, wraps wings into herself, and I see that she is wearing a flimsy kind of robe, now tugged tight. There. Now she looks like I remember, wiry body and hair, small shoulders with a head that always seemed a little too large. Prettyish. Always ready to outdrink you. She doesn't appear to have been domesticated, except for that robe. Like a raccoon with a bar of soap. Her narrow silhouette appears beside Steve's looming circle.

"Sherry, Christ, come on, it's Norm. Norman Mean, from high school? Remember him—"

"Whoever is in MY yard better get their ass off my property right about fucking now!"

"Hey, Sherry," I say.

"How the hell do I know you?"

Steve touches her and simultaneously steps away. He says, "Sher, it's Norm. I don't know what he's doing here, but it's okay. It's okay?"

"Hey, Sherry," I say.

She leans on the railing, her robe falling loose, and snorts a breath down at me. "Norman the fucking Mean. Good Christ. How are you doing, killer?"

"Good. How're you doing?"

"I heard you were dead. Or sick. Or something."

"My mom died."

"That's it. I knew it was something." She nods.

"Jesus F'ing Christ, Sherry," Steve says. He claps his hands once and whistles through his pinkies. Lacey leaves my side in a sprint and takes the levels of the deck in just a few strides.

Sherry turns to him, and says in mock quiet, pretending I can't hear, "What? I can't say that? Steve? I heard that, I can't say it?"

"Nice to see you, Sherry," I call up from the yard.

She blows a shot of air from her nose and turns on Steve. "You coming to bed?"

"In a few, Sher."

She wrenches open the door so hard it slams into the frame. She walks through before it shoots back and closes itself with a click. She's clearly done that before. The yard goes dark. She's good.

Steve and I face each other from different altitudes in the dark. The air is tense, everything inhales—further—and holds it...

"LACEY!" Sherry screams from inside.

The dog immediately leaps from Steve's side and scratches at the glass, whining and turning to Steve, to the door, to Steve. He leans over and flicks the slider open enough for the dog to disappear. The air molecules shake themselves loose from behind other air molecules. Everything exhales.

I'm still on the edge of dark, in the yard. "Sherry seems good."

"Shut up. What are you doing here, Norm?"

"I don't know. Bored, I guess. Wanted to see it, you know?"

"Yeah."

"How can you look at it everyday? You were there."

"That was a long time ago. We were kids. Shit fucking happens. Shit happened."

"You think?"

"Yeah. No. What do you think?"

"I just wanted to see it. It's freezing out here."

"Yeah."

"Can I come in?"

The ridiculousness of that idea sends Steve's head back for a moment. He eyes me sideways like a lizard, looking for the catch. There's a noise from the house, and lights go out around us. Steve and I stand separate in the sudden dark.

"Shit. You know what, Norman? I don't see any reason in the world why you can't come in."

I try to remember what was where as I work my way through the dark yard and its detritus. I find the stairs and take all the corners to where Steve is standing by an open door. The house through the glass door is blackness. I'm so cold that as I begin to walk through the door, I bump into his outstretched arm, and for a moment I think he's blocking me from entering. I look up at him, ready to throw some swears around myself, but he's only trying to shake my hand. I take it.

"I was very sorry to hear about your mom."

"Yeah. Yeah, me too."

"How's your dad doing with it?"

"I don't think he's noticed yet," I say and immediately regret the joke. "He's all right. He's doing okay."

"And you?" He's still holding my hand, shaking it a bit, squeezing hard, and I almost say something stupid, but it crosses my mind that this is genuine and I forget to answer.

"You doing okay?" Steve asks again.

"I think so. I'm cold, man."

Steve reaches his hand inside and flips a switch, the kitchen lights up. "Nice," I say.

"Thanks. Sherry's Dad built all these. That's how we got the water view."

"The water view?"

"The pond." Steve nods and gives me a quick once over, surmising my condition, clearly not pleased with it. My shirt clings unattractively, and everything is speckled with pond muck. My sneakers are pooling out their own ponds on his deck. Sherry wouldn't have let me in, that's for sure. I almost say something. Something like, "Never mind, I'll stop by at some better time," or "Hey, do you have any dry clothes?" but I feel that Steve needs to be put on the spot a bit, let him make the call.

He squinches his lips up and gives me another up-and-down before sliding the door open all the way. I wipe my feet on the mat, a nod to his good decision making, and enter. I take one step to the side and let Steve in to find more light switches. A row of three lights flick alive, spotlighting a slick kitchen island, three stools arranged neatly on the closest side.

"Nice place," I say, hoping he doesn't go into the typical home owner bullshit about fixing up the spare bedroom, and the basement's not done, but it's getting there, and it's always something and you know how it is, but I don't. I don't care how it is.

Steve walks around the kitchen island and produces a couple good beers from the double-doored fridge. He pops them with his teeth, hands me one. "It's nice. But it's weird, you know? Being here."

"Because of the pond?"

"No, Norm, not because of the pond. Because it's weird," Steve says.

83

"Looks that way."

"Does it?"

"Playing house."

"You don't know half of it."

"Thank god," I say.

"It's not that bad. Being grown up." Steve tilts his head, listens for any noises. "Here, let me grab something."

I sit alone at a stool, dripping, thinking how strange it is to be in a different home. Steve returns with a large bottle wrapped in a velvety bag.

"You must be grown up. We never drank that by the pond."

"Sherry's brother gave us this when we moved in. He owns that new bar downtown."

"In the old cop shop?"

"Yeah, The Lock Up. Been there yet? It sucks, but it's all right."

"Sounds great. Yeah, I walked by. It was too busy."

He pours a couple glasses, about three fingers deep, and grabs two more beers, placing them unopened on the island. He's hunkering down. Something occurs to me. "Hey do you know anybody who works down there?"

"Where? The Lock-up? I work the door sometimes, but I try to stay out of it. That's Sherry's family shit, you know?"

"I guess." I let it drop.

"Cheers, man. Welcome back."

"Cheers. Thanks, I'm not sure if it's good to be back yet, though."

"Either way," he says and takes a drink, then gives a quick grimace. "That's good."

I make sure to drag my swallowing out a second longer than his, hide my grimace, and agree.

It's quiet for a few beats as we smile at each other and sip our expensive scotch. Searching for something to talk about, we play the name game for a while, taking long sips to fill any quiet. Steve fills me in on who's still around and doing fine, who's still around and currently incarcerated or just getting over it. Who works for the city and crashed the snow plow drunk into the police chief's car, stuff like that, and before I know it we're laughing our way into another silence. Now with a much lighter bottle of scotch and a collection of empties decorating the counter. I can't immediately think of anybody else to ask about. The night now seems to call for something else.

"So, you like it here?" I say.

"Where? Sure. Garrison City? Why not, right? It's home."

"Garrison, yeah, but I mean here. The circle. The pond."

"Barbados Estates? Sure," he says.

"Sure?"

"Yeah, man, I fucking love it. Fucking love it. Is that what you want to hear?"

"If it's true," I say.

"You always were kind of an asshole."

"Me? Naw. You're thinking of someone else."

Steve laughs and leans back on his stool, stretching his arms like he's getting ready to say he's turning in and it's late and he has to work, and, you know.   "No, Norm, I'm pretty sure that's you."

"How about Sherry?"

"Do I think she's an asshole, too?" He leans forward, hands on the counter.

"No, the other thing," I say. "Does she like it here?"

"Or, 'Do I like her?' Is that what you mean?"

"Either way." I shrug, lean back, casual. Take a sip.

"We're good. It's good. Sherry's great, man."

"Oh yeah. She seems great."

Steve points at me, his finger sticking out from around his glass, over our empties, and he's about to say something with his eyebrows creased, but then his goatee mustache opens and he starts laughing. Hard. He's drunk. I am, too, and I need to spit a mouthful of scotch back into my glass, but miss most of it. Steve's shaking his head. He's worked his laughter down to a smile.

I'm smiling back. "I'm sorry. That's your problem."

"No shit, huh? No, it's fine. It is what it is."

"Isn't everything? Everything is what it is, that's not an answer, or anything."

"No, but it is what it is."

I nod and drain what's left of the scotch, hold the glass upside down and peer through it, to the ceiling, out the windows, at Steve.

Steve takes a long swallow and repeats himself. "It is what it is."

I drink my beer, thinking back. "Sherry graduated with us, right? A year ahead?"

"She left our junior year."

"She dropped out?"

Steve puts down his glass. "You don't remember?"

"I remember her being around a bunch, the pond and stuff, but then not graduation night or anything."

"She had a kid, man."

"What?" This seems new to me, but it starts to reemerge from the high school portion of my brain.

"You never paid attention to anyone. It was a big deal. Her dad made her go live with her uncle and shit. It sucked for her."

"She had a kid with her uncle?"

"Shut up. Her Dad just made her split town for a while. He was fucking pissed."

"Really? I kind of remember now, it was that guy. Shit, with the cars..."

"Travis," Steve says.

"Travis! You got it. What a loser that kid was."

"You don't even know half of it."

I want to laugh some more about it, small town shit, but then remember we're talking about a real person. One who is, in fact, upstairs smoldering in anger. "No. No, I guess I don't."

Quiet.

It occurs to me to ask, "Who's got the kid?"

"She should be home by now."

"What? She's alive? Here?" I say, looking behind me.

"Jesus F'ing Christ, Norm, what the fuck is that supposed to mean?"

"Nothing. Nothing, I just forgot about all that, you know? Of course the kid's around."

"Destiny."

"I guess, yeah, that's how things happen," I say.

"No. Destiny. That's her name. Destiny. And it's past her curfew, not that it seems to matter."

"So, she lives here, with you guys?"

"You want her to travel with that fucking carnival? With her dad?" Steve says.

"I don't know."

"No. You don't."

Quiet.

"She's a freshman. Yeah, she should be here any minute. Christ, maybe you know her? Right? You work at the high school now."

"Maybe."

I know her. I know exactly which Destiny she is—Destiny Elliot. I just never put the last name together. I'm pretty sure it has to be that Destiny. She's a bitch. Takes after her Mom, I guess. I make a note to be nicer to her on Monday. Or not. We'll see.

Steve bursts out, "Things change. It's not the same like when we were kids."

"I know that."

"Good. Because you're here now. You work here now. You're among us—get used to it."

"Among us? What are you? Aliens? Natives? I am 'us.' I guess I know all that."

"Good."

"Good?"

Steve takes off his hat and runs his hands over his hair, down his face. Stretches his arms again. I feel I should go, but don't. I drink some more.

He takes a deep breath and a drink. "Look, I'm sorry about your mom, I really am—"

"What does that have to do with anything? What does my mom have to do with whatever?"

"I'm just saying, Norm, you've been gone and you can't just come back like you never left. That's all. I've been here this whole time."

"You never left the pond. Leave now if that's what you want, what are we talking about here?"

"Nothing. Norm, we're talking about—"

A door slams, a car horn sounds loudly and a second too long. Lacey barks upstairs. I hear her claws clack, racing down stairs, then she blurs by the kitchen. She knows where she's going.

"Goddammit," Steve says.

He stands, surveys the countertop and begins picking up bottles in threes and putting them in a bin beneath the sink. He takes the glass from my hand and puts it in the sink.

"What?" I say.

"She's home. Finally." He stands straighter and clears his throat, ready to speak up.

"What's going on?"

"Shh. Wait."

Another door shuts and footsteps on stairs. Destiny enters. All jangling keys and purse and backpack, phone to her ear, swearing and laughing, walks to the fridge without a word or glance at either of us. It's my Destiny. She flicks her hair, blonder than her mom's, but just as wild, and rummages through the fridge, scattering her shit all over the counter, leaving a trail of shoes and hair clips in her wake. Lacey wags and pants, staying a constant foot from Destiny's right leg.

"Do you know what time it is, Destiny?" Steve says in a deeper voice than I've heard all night.

I watch. Destiny's face follows her hair out of the fridge; she has pizza slammed in her mouth, phone still at her ear. She snorts through the pizza into her phone, "I know, right?"

"Destiny," Steve says.

Her head pops back out with a giant can of something. To the phone she says, "I gotta go. Yeah. Yeah. He's a total dick. Yeah right. See you."

The fridge closes and Destiny stands there, phone in her jeans pocket, holding pizza. "What?"

"Do you have any idea what time it is?"

She takes a bite. "Naw. You?"

I swallow my laugh. Steve throws me a glance, then focuses back on Destiny.

"It's late. That's what it is. Late."

"Oh."

"Your mom was worried sick. She's upstairs."

"Yeah, right." She takes a huge bite of pizza, turns to me. "Hello, Mr. Mean."

"Hi, Destiny. How are you?"

"I'm fantastic." She swallows. "You?"

"Good," I say.

"I bet."

"Destiny," Steve says. "You're done. You're late. Get to bed."

"Whoa. Calm down."

"Go!"

She pulls out her phone, presses a few buttons with her thumb, and without looking up says, "I was going to bed anyway. It's been a crazy night."

She turns and walks away from us. She calls to Lacey, at her heels already. Then she's gone. I look at Steve who is still watching the open doorway. I watch with him.

From around the doorframe Destiny's head pops out, about knee height. "Good night, Mr. Mean. See you on Monday."

Her head disappears, and Lacey's replaces it for a moment before we hear them both moving up the stairs. Steve is silent.

I hear a door open and close. Water running. Then Sherry's voice comes down the stairs, and it's hers, but not like earlier, smoother.

"Des? Honey? Come sleep with me tonight. I'm lonely in here."

"Right there, Mom. I gotta clean up first."

"Thanks, baby. Bring Lacey to keep us warm."

Steve picks his glass of scotch from the sink just to have something to slam against the counter. "Jesus F'ing Christ." He wipes at his face and the hair under his hat again, and I know I shouldn't say, "There room in that bed for all of you?" But I do.

"Oh shut up, Norm."

"Just asking."

"You know? It was good to see you, man." He's stretching again.

"Yeah? Hey, go easy on her tomorrow." I stand, my shirt's finally dry, except where it sticks to my jeans. A murky pool spreads out from under my stool.

"What are you talking about?"

"Destiny. In the morning, just remember what we were like. She can't be that bad."

Steve starts around the island, making his way to the deck door, to open it for me. Apparently, I am to leave the way I came in. "Stay out of it. You don't know what it's like around here."

"No, but I know what you were like, and it was way worse than that. That's all I'm saying. It kind of sucks being a high school kid." I rise and stand at the door, almost gone.

"Christ, you got kids?"

"No and neither do you. She's Sherry's."

Steve slides open the deck door. "It doesn't work that way. Good night."

"You out of beer?"

"No. Just good night. I'll see you around town now, I'm sure."

"Yeah, and now that I know where you live…" I take a step into the kitchen, away from the exit, for no real reason.

"Go home, Norm. It's late and I already have a world of shit to deal with tomorrow."

"Who doesn't?"

"What the fuck are you talking about? Why do you care so fucking much?"

"I don't, it's not that—" My shoes slip on the smooth wet floor and I go down. Hard. The side of my face lands on that metal track rail thing that glides the sliding door back and forth. I know it's bleeding bad. "Ow. Shit."

Steve bends down immediately to help me up. He holds my forearm and shoulder and eases me up. I stand and lift the bottom of my shirt to cover the cuts. It's immediately soaked through, the blood spreading shockingly across the white fabric, soaking thread after thread.

"Christ, you okay?"

"I guess. Yeah."

"You good to get home?"

"Yeah. Yeah, listen…that night…"

"I know." Steve says and slaps me a bit on the shoulder, but I guess I'm a little light headed and I go down again. Steve, again, bends right over, but this time I stay down a moment to clear my head.

"What the fuck is going on here, Steven? Can you tell me what the fuck is going on?" There's Sherry.

"Sherry, it's fine—"

"Fine? This looks awful far from fine, Steve. Awful fucking far."

From where I'm lying, I can see Sherry's feet and the hem of her robe. They both look worn.

"I was just leaving, don't worry, Sher," I say from the floor.

"I wasn't friggin' worried. But you should be. Don't fuck with my husband, Norm. Don't fuck with my house!"

Steve says, "Sherry, no, it's not like that. It's fine."

"Go home to your dead mom!"

"Jesus, Sherry, let him get up."

I get up to my knees, one hand still on the floor. I think I can make it out the door. "Wow. Sherry."

She flies over to me and grabs my bloody shirt from the back and tries to slide, tries to push me out the door, swearing uncontrollably. When I move to stand she pushes me forward, the floor is so slippery. I finally straighten myself, and she's slapping my chest, repeating, "Get the fuck out." Each time she says it she changes which word she emphasizes. Behind her, Steve stands, his arms half extended, shaking his head, possibly talking, maybe screaming, but he's useless against this onslaught. Behind Steve, Destiny stands in the doorway holding her phone and clutching a teddy bear to her. She's wearing a tank top and that's about it. A few strings run above her thighs. It's hard to see past Sherry. She is cracking the fuck up. She loves this, has probably already called everyone she knows.

I'm on the deck now, and Sherry seems unwilling to cross the threshold. She stays in the kitchen, pointing and shrieking. Steve and I make a quick eye contact. He shakes his head and throws his hands in the air, turning away. Destiny is out of sight.

Sherry slides the door shut and closes all the lights. It's cold and dark, the change disconcerting. I don't move, but after a moment it feels awkward to listen to Steve and Sherry argue in their kitchen, so I move on.

I stumble down the stairs, every step squishing, and the light goes out behind me. I'm standing alone in the dark yard, the only sound is the pond's low gurgle. Blood runs down my wrist when I touch my cheek. It's pretty bad, but I barely feel it. The blood itself bothers me more than the pain. It makes my hands clammy, and I flap my fingertips against my palm a couple times just to feel them stick. The pond looks more intimidating than it did earlier, and I stick to the edges, unwilling to trudge through and feeling unable to float. I've traded my buoyancy for drunkenness, taken in so much liquid that it's messed with my displacement. I can't trust that water to hold me.

I step on a rake. A few plastic pails get crushed beneath my clompy footfalls until I make it around to the dam and opt for the direct route down a driveway, out in the open. The moment I step on the driveway two rows of lights blaze to life. I walk right through them to the circle at

94

the end of the cul-de-sac. There's no sound behind me, and I continue down the curving road past the shutters that don't shut and the decorative wells that don't draw water. The houses line the road, arches around a coliseum.

I let my curiosity sneak around their hedges and bedroom windows, and I can feel their secrecy and sense of security pushing back. I let my shirt and my blood dry in the moonlight, reflecting off mica in the pavement. Each house is perfectly locked up and square, holding everything in, oblivious to this passing disturbance.

# Chapter Ten

I've stopped bleeding by the time I reach The Lock Up. Still shivering. The windows are darkened, the sidewalk empty, and with my nose to the cold glass, hands cupped around my face, I can see the few people left inside, downing shift drinks or collecting empties. She's there, hefting huge trash bags from behind the bar.

I walk around the side, to the alleyway by the Orchard Street rooming house, and lurk by the dumpster, try to light a crumpled damp cigarette. Even the infamous rooming house is quiet, the day's disputes momentarily settled. There is no good reason to be here. I feel like a creep waiting for a bartender who probably gets hit on a thousand times a night, our only relationship being that I almost bumped into her. Then I lit her cigarette. Put that way, it doesn't seem to count for much. But I'm here. The night can't get much worse. I've already been beat up by the mother of one of my students while she watched. I've been swimming in the pond where my friend died. There's not much else a bartender could do to top that.

A cook and his companion open the side door; when they see me they take the quick corner behind the building. I assume they're avoiding me, filthy and bloody in the moonlight. A moment after they disappear, I smell drifting weed smoke. Alright, maybe their quick disappearance is not due to me or my appearance. It could be that bleeding drunk guys are an everyday sight back here. I don't know, I've forgotten how these nights go. For a moment, I consider going to join them, taking a couple friendly hits, floating home, and maybe not making a fool of myself in front of this strange girl. A crashing in the dumpster brings me back to the alley.

"Well, I can get you in, but I don't know," she says, very close to me. "It couldn't be as much fun as where you were already."

"No. No I guess it couldn't."

We look each other over. She takes out a pack of smokes, looks at the crumpled white twig in my hand and shakes out two cigarettes.

"Thanks."

"You're welcome, Norm."

I still don't know her name.

"Can I use your light…?" I say.

"Nikki. Nice to meet you."

"Nikki. Can I use your light, Nikki?"

"If you promise to let me take you home. It doesn't look like you can take much more of this night." She looks at the sky. "Morning."

"I'm fine, really, just fell, you know? Looks worse than…yeah. Thanks." I light her cigarette with her lighter. I've forgotten the comfort a smoke can be.

"Sure," Nikki says.

"Fine. I'm fine."

Nikki shakes her head in a way that makes me stand up straighter.

She says, "I didn't think you'd come back."

"Well, I was having so much fun…"

She snorts.

I say, "Yeah."

"I'm glad you did, Norman Mean. Welcome back."

"Thank you. It's wonderful to be here."

"I'm sorry about your mom."

"Thank you. Me, too." I feel a lot has gone by me, as if this is already something I'm piecing together a day after it's happened.

"Come on in, you look like you could use a drink."

"It's the light back here. It's unflattering."

"That must be it," she says.

She turns and walks back down the alley. Without looking back, she props the door with a stool and disappears inside, cigarette smoke rising from the cold ground, veiling the doorway.

I walk through the second door opened to me in invitation tonight. The few workers left inside look up. The weed-smoking cook and his friend are huddled over a golf video game, almost the only light in the place. Only pretend golf and neon beer signs. The last waitress and waiter are mating at the bar, her long legs lying across his lap while he rubs her feet. The jukebox is still at full bar level. I don't recognize the song.

I sit many stools down from the foot rubbing couple and crouch over to hide the blood on my shirt. Nikki puts a big beer and wet bar towel down in front of me.

"Thanks." I lift the beer and begin to move the rag around the bar top, thinking I'm helping her close down.

She laughs. "For your face, Rocky. Just throw it in when you've had enough."

My beer and Nikki finish up at the same time. We're the last two left.

She is leaning against the counter opposite me, amongst the taps. Her head is tilted inside her sweatshirt hood.

"I don't fucking get it," she says.

"What?"

"Everything."

"No. Me neither," I say.

She nods at my empty glass. "Another?"

"I think I'm good."

"Does anybody else?"

"What?"

"Let's get you home."

"And out of these wet clothes?"

"If that's what it takes, Norm, I'll do it." She hops off the counter, landing lightly. "I've been waiting long enough."

I don't know what she means by anything, nor am I sure I want whatever she seems to be offering. I follow her out the back door and wait while she double checks doors and taps numbers on the alarm keypad.

"I swear I'm the only one who uses this thing." She quietly swears at the blinking light. "But who gets bitched at when Sherry finds out it was off?"

I take a guess. "You?"

"Damn straight, Norm. Me." She tries another series of numbers. "There. Let Sherry bitch about that. We need to go before this thing goes off."

"Sherry?"

"She's a bitch. Her brothers own this place," Nikki says.

"Sherry Stone?"

"Yeah. The Clam. You'd know her as Sherry Elliott, probably."

"I know her."

Nikki slams the back door behind her. "Christ, Norman, you remember her?"

"She leaves an impression."

"And me?"

"You're still impressing."

"Smooth, very impressive." She takes my face in her hand, turning it to look at the cuts. I cringe at the touch, not the pain, but turn back quickly, hoping she didn't notice.

"Wow. You don't get out much do you?" She hands me another cigarette and holds her lighter out, we both lean in and light up together.

"No, not recently. No," I say.

We stand. Nikki smokes and scopes me out. I let her, too tired to think of anything witty. Finally, she shakes her head. "I don't get it."

She nods down the alley. "I'm over there."

"If you want, I can just walk."

"I offered, Norm."

"I know, it's just—"

"It's just what? Christ, what do I have to do?"

"What do you mean?"

She inhales deeply, looks into the night, and says to no one, "What the fuck?"

I watch the sky with her for a moment. No answer appears.

"You live at home?" she says.

"Doesn't everybody?"

She stamps out her smoke. "I'm leaving. You coming?"

I stand at the car door looking at the piles of CDs and trash on the seat before she shoves it all on the floor. "Sorry. I'm a mess."

"Me, too."

Another feeling I've forgotten is the strangeness of being in somebody else's car. My feet push around empty coffee cups, papers, and just stuff. It seems so personal and strange to be here, driving down the familiar route to Dad's house. My house.

She sings along with the radio on the quick drive home, having one more cigarette without offering one, which is fine. As her little car approaches home I realize I never gave her directions. When the headlights shine on Dad's bumper, Nikki slides it roughly into park, and we sit, the engine still running. The lights still shining. She takes a deep breath and turns to me, looking very young in the dashboard light.

"Listen, Norm, it's like this—"

"Do you want to come in?" I don't want to know what it's like.

She pulls back, looks out her window, looks at me. "Yes. I do."

"Good," I say. I stand in the driveway, resting my hands on the cold metal of the roof, listening for the engine to stop. I feel a slight power shift in the energy between us, a little lift on my side.

The engine dies and here we are. I can't believe this. I haven't even tried to get laid in the longest time. I wish I wasn't bloody and drunk.

She rummages around the driver's seat, pops out with her purse, and slams the door. "This is as far as I know where to go. Lead the way."

"It's around here." I meet her at the back bumper and guide her like a butler, touching the small of her back. Then remove my hand. To cover the moment, I tell her how we're going to go in the side door and then up the stairs, but we have to be quiet, and if she has to use the bathroom, or anything, she should probably do it downstairs so we don't wake up Dad.

I'm still talking loudly about being quiet when we're standing in the living room. She looks so out of place. I'm suddenly protective of the house, the furniture, and aware of the eyes in all the photographs, and I stop talking. She's hugging herself; Dad drops the heat to nothing at night, which makes his regular naked hallway appearances even more shocking. Oh God, don't let him come out naked tonight. This will never work, and I turn to tell Nikki that when she kisses me, and somewhere between realizing what she's doing and kissing her back, I decide this is going to work very well.

# Chapter Eleven

## Blake

Blake sleeps naked again since Pat died. He's chalked it up to comfort, as he has many things he feels are deserved these days. Be it cold sheets against his skin or warm whiskey on his tongue. He'd only really stopped smoking at her insistence that it stunk up their house.

Moments ago, dreaming he had been in a field with a faceless woman, maybe Pat, maybe not, on a picnic, he hadn't been able to produce the right silverware because of the mice. It had been frustrating but not revolting. Blake had just wanted to pull out a fork so she could start eating, but every time he reached in the mice would bite and swarm. He is glad when Norm's noises downstairs wake him. The side door shuts. He hears Norm's voice and realizes there must be another. Blake's first thought is: I should call the FitzGeralds, let them know Henry is here and safe. But as he wakes fully he knows, of course; that isn't the truth. A woman's voice, then a long silence, some kitchen noises, Norm's voice. Then nothing.

Blake clears his throat, preparing for a hallway greeting in the green glow from the clock. 3:23. It's been almost twelve hours since he has spoken out loud, since Norm had restlessly left their house late this afternoon. Death is a strange thing for those left behind. For the holes it creates. Lately it has become clear who did the talking in the family, and her silenced voice seems to hush them all.

There had been so many times Pat had passed the long-distance phone to Blake, telling him Norm wanted to speak to him. It was never true. She had called Norm every time. Unless Norm needed something, she had called. So many forced banalities over the years at her insistence, the whole time Blake feeling apologetic for participating, knowing that Norm wanted to forget about everything. Now he feels he may have been wrong. Hearing a voice from far away would be a great comfort.

Each time Norm came home over the years, he would pace the house. The clocks couldn't move fast enough, dinner couldn't be done sooner. His flights always arrived late, left early. The half dozen or so times he'd dropped in always concluded with a pre-dawn drive to the airport, the two of them listening to the radio, not speaking—which had been Pat's hope when she insisted Blake drive him to Boston without her.

Blake takes comfort in Norm's surreptitious entrance downstairs. He tries to imagine who could be with him and smiles at the ceiling, at what Norm must be feeling. Each noise which floats up the stairs, under the door, brings precise images. He can see the nearly empty uncovered plates in the fridge. He knows exactly what Norm is reaching around to get a certain beer, the one Blake knows he's grabbing. He sees foam rimming the can as it whooshes open. Blake knows all this as surely as if he is standing beside Norm. And his guest.

Pat had never slept naked before they were married. It had been such a delight to watch her become accustomed to it. At first, shutting the light and allowing her clothes to fall only as Blake raised the sheet. Then the almost strutting nudity, a confidence reserved for him, the feel of clean sheets against smooth skin. The sudden warmth of another's body. There was a first time for that, and a first time he said he'd stay downstairs to finish a movie, and she had gone on to bed alone. Blake remembers her final night; they had gone to bed together and she died naked. But for so many years previous, from fleecy nightgowns to the thin cotton shorts of summer, their skin had again become only their own.

Water rushes through the old pipes. A toilet flushes, and Blake knows the exact pressure it took on the handle to make that happen. He clears his throat a few more times, says a few practice lines softly in the dark. Two sets of footsteps come heavy up the stairs. The railing creaks under the weight. Blake rises from bed and looks down at himself; every time it's not what he expects to see. In his head he is somewhere around 27, in another body. The doorknob is in his hand, ready to turn when Norm reaches the landing.

The strange footsteps move quickly past his door and down the hall. There, now Norm's steps stop before the bedroom door. Blake pulls it open.

Norm is paused at the door, half-crouched, listening. His eyes go directly to Blake's nakedness. His shirt is bloody and muddy, gashes runs across his cheek in three parallel lines of dried blood. Blake says nothing.

"Hey, Dad."

"You're home."

"Yep."

"Goodnight."

"Goodnight, Dad. Hey, there's somebody —"

"That's fine."

Blake watches his son, balancing two beers, make his way down the hall to his childhood room. Norm gets to his bedroom door and turns, raises a few fingers from a can in a low wave and disappears. When the door closes it steals a slant of light. Blake stands a moment in the dark, then returns to his bed, still warm, and thinks of his son. He hopes there was a time when Norm lay naked, his hand on a lamp beside the bed, and for the first time watched a bare breasted girl slide everything off, walk around the bed, and slip into sheets he had raised for her. He hoped Norm smiled as nervously as she did before shutting the light and seeking her skin.

# Chapter Twelve

Thank God Nikki made it in without walking into naked Dad. I nudge the door with my foot, balancing the beers. When the door clicks shut I look up. Nikki stands, bare feet poking through the end of her jeans, her back to me, in her blue bar shirt.

"Here you are," I say, holding out a beer.

She turns, a hand out for the beer. "Here I am."

"Cheers."

We sip. It's terrible beer, nothing I need after tonight, but it's something to do with our hands. Something to focus on. Having her here, having someone else in here for the first time in years, forces me to see everything anew, with her eyes. And it all looks ridiculous. I live in the room of a seventeen-year-old. There's a model airplane on a bookshelf, beside a lacrosse trophy from middle school. This is not impressive.

Nikki takes a long sip as she looks around.

"Nice place," she says.

"Sorry. I haven't been home in a long time. I guess they kind of just left it alone the whole time."

"She must have missed you very much. While you were gone."

That had never occurred to me. It seems strange now to think of it. I guess it had just seemed like such a good idea to leave.

"I guess so," I say.

"You didn't miss it here?"

"No. God no. I couldn't wait. We left right after graduation."

"We?" she says.

"Me and Corny. We left like two days after graduation."

"Julia Cornelius? Really?"

I nod.

"Julia, huh?" Nikki raises her eyebrows, impressed or disgusted, I can't tell.

"She's still out there."

"For good?"

"I have no idea what Corny's plans are. We haven't spoken for a very long time."

Nikki stops riffling through papers on my desk and walks to me. When she arrives, standing so close I can feel our bodies almost touching, she says, "You look like shit. Does it hurt?"

Nikki raises her beer, drinks, and I need to pull my face back so the can doesn't hit me. When she swallows, she holds the cold can against the cuts on my face. It does hurt, a bit, but I don't move because her face is so close to mine. Her hair smells like a bar, but flowery underneath, nice. We stand like that for too long, I keep my arms at my sides, holding my can by the top, concentrating on the weight in my hand, so I won't notice her heat or breasts. I feel myself pushing out, the flies on our jeans touching. I'm sure she can feel my heart in her chest.

I say, "If you want, you can —"

"What? What do I want?"

My face is numb from the beer can and she kisses me, her lips dry against mine, resting there until I push back, and she slides the can behind my head, holding me to her until our lips are wet. I drop my beer on the floor, ignore it, and rest my hands on her ribs, sharp lines beneath her shirt. She pulls me closer, both her arms behind my head, her mouth wide. Our teeth touch, linger, and scrape again. Then beer runs down the back of my neck, freezing, spine-tightening, and I pull back. She laughs.

"Sorry. That was an accident," she says.

"I hope so," I say. I wipe at the back of my neck, looking over my shoulder, and I feel her hands on my stomach, under my shirt, right above my hips, and I draw back at the feeling, almost ticklish, but deeper. She puts her hands flat against my sides, against my skin.

"It's okay," she says and slides my shirt off, exposing me. On her way down to kneel and kiss my stomach, she puts her beer on the floor next to my dropped one. And yes, it is okay. I reach back and shut the light. Her hair is the same color as the darkness. Her face ghostly in the cold, blue reflected moon. The air is chilled against the skin on my legs. She lifts her arms, and I reach down, pulling her shirt over her hands at my chest, then they're lower. I hold her shirt against my face, feeling the cotton and inhaling, before I drop it, rest my hands on her head and feel just how thick Nikki's hair is.

When she stands, our naked skin slides and rubs, catches, our mouths everywhere but our mouths. I kiss the spot behind her ear she's been touching. She pushes me away, at arm length, holding out my hands, far apart. I feel completely exposed, but I let her look. No one has looked at me like she is, taking stock of everything, recording. She lets go of me and falls on the bed. Nikki arranges herself under the blankets, not really making room for me, just getting comfortable among the mess of plaid flannel sheets and light blankets. I slide in beside her after she lays her head on the pillow.

"You don't remember me, do you, Norm?"

"How could I have forgotten? I haven't even passed out yet," I say and push down the pillow so I can see her face. The way she isn't smiling makes me uncomfortable. "No, I guess I don't. Should I?"

"No, not really, I suppose. We were never friends, it's just that..."

"Just that, what?"

"I remember you, that's all. We had a few classes together senior year."

I try to take the years off her face and put her in an old desk. Nothing.

"You sat in back," Nikki said.

"You were always up front?"

"Yes. Usually."

I pull the sheet off her, letting me see all her skin, so pale in this light, her dark nipples and black triangle hair stand out like an advertisement. I slide my hand from the back of her knees, over the curving split and up the sharp bumps of her spine, until I hit the back of her neck.

Nikki rolls over, away from me, slides up the bed a bit so the middle of her back is in my face. I kiss her spine, tracing vertebrae with my tongue, and she takes my hand from her neck and puts my three middle fingers into her mouth. It is so nice, I enjoy it so long that I don't notice when she falls asleep. I use her hip to pull her body closer, rest my lips against her back and match our breathing until morning.

It's been a long time since I woke up with someone. We speak in quiet clips, asking how the other slept. Warm enough? Yes. You? Yes. My hand feels forbidden resting on her side, late night intimacy gone with the moon. There's a terrible taste in my mouth. I breathe shallow and turn my head away when I speak.

Nikki sits in bed, pressing a sheet against her chest, and looking around my old bedroom. I lie flat, my head at her hip, a sheet up to my waist.

"Do you remember me, yet?" she says.

"I remember everything."

"Good. Everything was nice." She reaches down, one hand still covering herself, holding the sheet.

"So," I say, trying to keep everything nice. "We had a class together?"

"We did, Norm. You may have been too busy to notice."

"What was I busy doing in class?"

"I don't know. Trying to figure out how to get beer to bring out to the pond, probably," she says.

"The pond? Did you go out to the pond?"

"A few times." She pokes me hard in the chest and allows the sheet to fall, exposing herself but covering my hand. I stare at her skin, knowing exactly how it will feel when I touch her, and wanting to, but I put it off just for the wait. "You're staring."

I feel her thigh through the sheet, move my hand up until it's warm. She makes a sound. I imagine the feel of her nipples hard against the center of my palms, but I just keep looking at her.

"What?" she says.

"Nothing."

"Something. You're staring at me."

"Yeah?"

"Yeah." She raises her arms straight above her head, her hands flared out and tilts her head, the sheets fall lower, but her expression doesn't change. She looks away, out the window. The sun is also revealed, glinting off the old trophies and Nikki's small earrings. "I remember when it happened, you know."

"What," I begin, then realize what she's talking about. "Oh. That."

"Fitzy. The accident."

"The accident. Was he in the class we were in?"

"Right next to you. Against the wall."

I take my hand back.

She says, "I remember feeling terrible for you. I think everyone did."

"Everyone felt something for me. Anger. Suspicion, maybe. Not terrible. Not everyone."

"We were kids." Nikki runs her hand over my chest, pushing the sheet down, lifting it and looking down. She smiles. "It was awful. But it wasn't your fault."

"Maybe. That's not how it felt. Feels. That's not how it feels."

She moves herself around, lays her head on my chest, and reaches further down beneath the sheet. "Sometimes I think that certain things, well..."

"Certain things what?" I move up the bed enough so her hand is even further down the sheet. Her fingers close on me.

"It's just that some things are meant to happen. And I know how it is when everyone thinks something that isn't."

"Isn't what?" I say.

"Isn't true. Or different than the truth they think is true. Do you understand?"

"No." I say, rolling quickly so I'm over her, her hand still holding me, flat on her back. Before I kiss her, I say, "No, I don't understand."

She places me against her with one hand, the other against my face. She's so warm, I need to hold my breath in or I'll be everywhere. I push just enough against her, she raises herself, slightly, but enough.

"Me neither. I don't know if anyone does." She moves her hips away from mine, moves them back. Then I can't hear a thing.

Waking up for the second time is just as strange as the first. Nikki isn't in the bed, and for a few half-sleep moments I think she's left, then I see her sitting, wearing only one of my t-shirts, with a few of my old shoe boxes open in front of her at my desk.

"Morning. Again," I say.

"Morning. Still. You got a pen in here?"

"There should be one in that middle drawer."

"Next to the crumpled diploma or your old bowl?"

"Are you my mom?"

"Norm, if I was your mom," she pauses to write something on a photograph, "I'd be dead."

She stands up, completely exposed from the hips down and hands me the photograph. I keep watching her as she bends all the way over to pick through our clothes, balancing on one leg to slide her panties on and arching her back when she buttons her jeans.

She stands by the door. "I'm going to get some breakfast." Then she's on the other side of the door, and I still sit in bed.

After a minute, the door still hasn't reopened. I look down at the photograph in my hand. It's an old high school picture, the edges blurry with motion, but with a row of grinning faces across the center. A group of kids, clearly of a certain era with their haircuts and clothes, arms around each other, in every hand a beer can. I am there, in the middle, and Nikki has circled the face two down from my own. On the top, over the blurry white green of trees and sunlight, she's written: "That's me."

I assume, as I get dressed, that Nikki has left, that she has walked quickly down the stairs and out the side door, as we had come in last night. That Dad has no idea she was even here, or that, at least, we were quiet enough for him to credibly pretend otherwise.

I hear his laughter as I start down the steps. It echoes, fading just as another peal spreads against the walls. I sit on the landing and listen to the murmur of Nikki and Dad talking. His low even tones and her lighter voice roll around the house. I think pictures might fall, vases smash. A woman's voice.

"Norman!" Dad greets me when I enter the kitchen. "I didn't know you knew Nicole."

"Me, neither." I give a look past my dad at Nikki. She just smiles and hides her face behind an old white coffee cup. Her hair is a mess, her blue shirt, with the badge and 'The Lock Up' on it, is wrinkled.

"Nicole was the star of my honors Calculus class a few years back."

Nikki smiles over her coffee and says, "Oh, Mr. Mean, it was more than a few years ago."

"Well, I remember it like it was yesterday. B+." He looks at her, beaming, then at me. He punches my thigh. "Norm never took Calculus.

116

Said he'd never need it."

"Norm!" she says, scolding. Then to my dad, "He probably just couldn't do it."

"His mother and I always suspected as much." Dad is leaning towards her and she's laughing. Not even looking at me.

I start to pour orange juice into an empty coffee mug, and Dad actually slaps my hand and tells me to get a glass.

I take my mug to the coffee maker, and Dad signals over his head to bring it to the table, top off their cups. I stand next to them like a waiter as they raise their mugs to me, still talking. Nikki rubs her toes against my shin as I pour the coffee.

"You know, Nicole, young Norm here works at the old school, now."

"So I hear."

"Hard to believe, isn't it?" He looks at me with maybe pride.

"Mr. Mean, I never would have suspected. That's the truth." Nikki reaches over and touches the back of my Dad's hand over his cereal spoon. He turns to me.

"Oh she's delightful, Norman. It's good to have a little laughter around here." He bends toward Nikki. "He's been moping around for months."

I turn my hands palms up. My Mom died. Your wife's dead, I want to say.

Nikki mirrors his inward lean and says something I can't hear, but it rocks my Dad's head back with laughter. He's still chuckling as he gathers dishes from the table, a Mean house first. My dishes, though unused, are collected as well. Nikki and I watch each other over the empty table. Dad pats my shoulder on his way out, almost conspiratorial, and says, "Nicole Follansbee and Norman Mean."

Alone, Nikki looks fairly smug across the flowered oil-cloth covering the table.

"Proud of yourself?" I say.

"What?"

"You've made yourself at home."

"I felt welcome," she says.

I can't look at her without remembering last night and imagining more. "You are welcome."

I drink from my mug, listen to Dad humming up the stairs, watch Nikki look around.

"Thank you," I say.

"It was my pleasure. Really." She smiles beneath eyes angled slyly, then looks shy, which appears to be a foreign emotion for her. Uncomfortable.

"I guess you never can tell what's going to happen," I say, and it seems like a fairly innocent thing to say, a little square maybe, but she laughs harder than she should.

"I don't know about that," she says and puts down her coffee to rub her neck.

I walk Nikki to her car and toe pebbles around while we say our goodbyes with her jotting down her schedule at the bar and me promising to come by. I look up at my bedroom window, closed and far above us. She is at the end of the driveway, and I'm standing, waving, when she stops, lowers the driver's window. I run over.

"Hey, Norm."

"Yeah?"

"Cheer up. It's okay."

I slap the door and stand straight. Nikki leans low, her head twisted to fit out the window. I hear the same song we heard on the way home last night.

"I know," I say.

Her car disappears around the corner, and I don't want to go inside. Saturdays are long, with a tendency to drag toward a dismal happy hour. I don't think Dad's new found good humor will help. I decide to walk down our street, follow the trail Nikki's car left in the air. It's sunny, a few clouds motionless with the chill, but the kind of chill that promises to be forgotten. I think of camping, of mornings watching the sun rise, shivering. And younger, counting stars with Dad in our backyard, tracing the beam of his flashlight, pointing out constellations. Eating the cookies my mom brought to us, her robe wrapped tightly around her. "Stay out with us!" Dad would cajole her. She would decline, claiming this was boy's stuff, and I was never clear what she was referring to, the stars, the night air, or just the fact that she wasn't there. Rough stones would poke my palm as I leaned back. The flannel of Dad's old jacket brushed my cheek as he reached across to point out the tip of Orion's sword, the cold air and the warmth of the cookies.

I begin to jog down the street, just for the feel of my legs. It's awkward in jeans and t-shirt. To the few people around who watch me pass, it must look like I'm being chased. I have no idea of when I last ran.

By the time I reach the brick sidewalk, I'm leaning hands on my knees, boozy sweat dripping down my neck. I can smell it and decide that's probably enough for my body this morning. There should still be a few twenties in my pocket, and the coffee downtown must be better than the coffee at home.

Downtown is busy. Old men morning regulars on benches fold newspapers into readable squares and scald their loose mouths with black coffees. Local crazies lurk among the cafe tables smoking butt-end cigarettes. One moves a broom, not really sweeping, just tapping the bristles into piles of dirt. I'm not sure whether a kind coffee shop employee gave him the broom, maybe to make a show of working for a coffee, or if he arrived with it this morning. Maybe he brings it every morning, ready for a day of work. But the brick sidewalk is a tough clean, and he doesn't really seem up to the task.

No women, it's only the men who chain-smoke through town. These are the same crazies who were wandering the streets when I was in high school.

The big guy by the bench trying to sell a young couple some old spoons. No? Maybe a Bad Company 8-track? That guy used to buy us beer, though we only used him as a last resort. He would charge extra and want to come hang out with us after the transaction was made, lingering and asking where we were going to party. He always said that: "party," and every time it seemed outdated, like your guidance counselor calling you "man" and asking if you liked to smoke "the reefer." It would come down to me to deal with and deny him, probably because I lived closest to town, and was therefore most citified and worldly. Granted, it was an assumption I had carefully fostered, but still, I wished one of the kids from the woods would have just told him to fuck off.

I cross the street, my arms straight down my sides, deep into my pockets. I take quick steps through the crosswalk, only my lower half moving. I can't see Garrison as it is now; everything I remember has been camouflaged. Recognizable remnants lurk beneath fresh paint. The corner store which sold Hustlers from a low shelf, covers in clear sight, now has a wine list in its many-paned window. What had been the movie theater, then the camera shop, now hawks pastries with names unheard in this state ten years ago.

Maybe it's not the new stores, Garrison's fresh image, that bothers me. Fine. Redecorate. Touch things up. I can accept the facelift, even the new demographic which demands it. If everyone who lived here had been moved out, trucked further upriver to another dilapidating mill town, leaving Garrison to rot under cappuccino nutmeg dustings and SUV fumes, then this quiet little town would be just that. But it's not. All the old animosity remains. Ask Nikki how many Garrison High Green Wave football players settle the same old scores every Friday night? How many of their fucked up children do I cajole into bitter silences? Everyone has learned to order new foods, pay higher prices, even enjoy it, but they all remember. They know.

Every corner screams responsibility. Each back alley calls out dark memories of secret beers and secretions spilled on the asphalt. All the old apartments, gentrified into condos above cutesy stores, hold tales, full of empties and empty of innocence. They all tell me I never should have left, and I respond that I never should have returned. It was foolish to believe that time removes anything but pages from a calendar, pages piled and marked with red Xs, each scoring an anniversary of a crime to which I can't confess.

The cafe in front of me always sold coffee, but it came in chipped mugs with two eggs and toast. Now you have to order from one part of a counter and wait at another. I prepare an order in my head, large coffee. Bagel. Cream cheese.

When the lady in front of me opens the café door, to allow her small dog out, I see a familiar profile shadowed by the drink cooler. Destiny. I take a sudden left away from the entrance and duck quickly behind a little tourist information booth they've set up in the square. I pretend to peruse the flyers and ads which have been pasted up with hand cut tearable phone number tags. Lawn mowing, dog walking, and bands looking for bassists. I take sudden interest in all these things.

Destiny stands inside the café door, surrounded by her gaggle of catty friends, all snapping gum and cell phones. A couple boys stand awkwardly around them, clearly not sure of their role, but feeling that they are with girls, and that counts for something. Goddam, this is a downside of working at the school. The girls are gathered at the counter, the boys linger behind, praying their baggy pants off that the girls will finish ordering and start undressing.

I glance from the information booth to the door; it opens and closes, busy day. Every time it opens, the girls are closer to completing their complicated, sugary order, taking sample sips and handing the small cups back to the black-haired tattooed girl behind the counter, throwing rehearsed attitude in the angle of their heads and the purses swinging from their arms.

I'm running out of things to look at, and my hangover is making me feel awkward just standing here. I think about leaving, but decide that would be cowardly and ridiculous. I'm the adult. The girls now come toward the door, and I angle myself to leave the tourist booth between us. Just let them pass by, stroll in through their wake, and take my coffee to go. Drink it by the river. I feign sustained interest in the posted flyers, waiting. Oh look, open auditions for barbershop quartets. I go so far as to rip off a number, just to keep the idea going that I am only standing here out of deep interest. Working my way around the booth's octagon, I come around to the other side, by the arranged cafe tables, and quickly duck back around.

Vice-principal Sullivan is there. Sitting with his wife, whom I think was my 6th grade teacher. I didn't realize. There are a thousand Sullivans in town. Shit. I don't want the effort of sustained conversation, nor do I want Destiny to approach me while I'm talking to the vice-principal. Now I'm obviously trying to hide, peeking around the far side of the booth.

"Hey, Mr. Mean." Damn it. She came up on me from behind.

Giggle, giggle, whisper, snort, slurp, giggle. I hate these girls at this moment. Loathe everything about teenage girls and the poison they spread through our culture. Look at them, smirking and slurping the chocolate syrup off the sides off their goddamn oversized plastic cups.

There are roughly five of them around me. It's hard to keep an accurate count, they move as a herd and wear similar colors. They blend with each other and keep an ever shifting balance of distance and contact between them, each movement dependent on unseen emotional contingents. The two boys keep their distance; they're talking, pointing, and laughing to themselves, aware of the girls focusing their attention elsewhere, and deciding to act the part of playing it cool. I keep one eye on the Sullivan table; they seem not to see me. Maybe they're avoiding me as completely as I'm avoiding them.

"Hello, Destiny. Nice day, huh?" I say. I touch the cuts on my cheek, thinking to cover them.

Her eyes are on me, her hands hold the drink, her lips suck on the straw, her purse swings in opposite rhythm to her hips. "I guess."

"You guess?"

"Yeah, I fucking guess. Whatever."

"Well, it is," I finally say and turn away, avoiding their eyes, afraid to catch a glimpse of too much of that newly displayed cleavage and then be stuck there.

They giggle. En masse. Destiny is clearly in charge here. Her shortened giggle stops the others. Silences them.

It is her turn to talk. I'm not sure whether my role as teacher extends to downtown. Should I scold her for swearing? Walk away? Passing the breeze with these girls, doing the nice thing, is that what people do? They seem to be looking for something. She's the one who approached me.

I say, "It is, but there's no need to swear about it."

"Whatever," Destiny says. A little echoing chorus of, "yeah," "whatever," floats behind her voice. I get it. They're bad girls today.

"Whatever is right," I say, feeling how lame it is the moment I say it.

"My mom hates you." Destiny swirls ice around her drink. "Steve might, too."

"Oh yeah? That's nice, Des."

The girls look at her, giggles at the ready.

"It's true. They were talking about you this morning. I said you were nice, and Mom got wicked pissed."

"Oh."

"Wicked pissed."

"You mentioned that."

"What? I tried to defend you." She angles her head at her bony neck. "See? I'm nice."

"I never said you weren't."

She just stands there in the pants they're all wearing, belts way below their waist, disappearing their hips. The boys join them, growing impatient with the lack of attention. All but Destiny turn to jump on them, beg them for sips of their drinks and refuse to give them back, an excuse to play keep away, get their hands on each other, share germs. It's only me and Destiny. She looks at me, giving me a quick up and down, but it has a practiced air, like she's seen it in a movie. Her favorite actress playing powerful, seducing the leading man. I look away, but don't move.

"Yeah, I gotta go, Mr. Mean." Thank God. The Sullivans are rising, clearing their table. We're right by the trash, and they're headed our way.

"Me too, see you Monday." I'm already turning away.

"Yeah. Right." She turns and skips a few childish steps to join the others, reclaim her fragile monarchy.

I hurry across the street. The whole exchange leaves me feeling a little too hollow for coffee. The cracks between all these bricks, the sidewalks, the buildings, the doorways, they all absorb the sun, leaving me shadowed, holding a strip of paper with a stranger's phone number who's looking for a baritone to complete his quartet. That's not me, I'd never be able to keep the time right. Watching Nikki cross and uncross her legs at my desk in only a t-shirt seems like a long time ago—she and Dad laughing at the table.

I fall out of the slipstream. Time's current lifts. It has carried me and this town and Nikki and the sunshine all the way to this morning, but we've hit a split. And I got dropped behind. I watch from the banks as the old men continue to fold their papers, and the crazy men sweep and smoke. The kids find excuses to paw each other, and they should, they all should think about pawing each other and smoking and reading. It's a day for all of it. Coffee is definitely out of the question. I need something of more substance, outside of our quaint little square with its maintained brick garden boxes and clean flags.

Leaving my spot on the sidewalk, stepping into the street, feels like stepping onto an escalator, or subway car, where you have to do the instant physics required to match the new speed. I ignore the imagined stares of the crazies, which is probably good because they are probably imagined, and I don't want to make a scene. It looks like rain, I tell myself, focusing on the one fluffy blemish marring the blue sky. I head for someplace darker and private; there is no burden on me to enjoy the weather. I can leave that to everyone else.

There is only one place to go this time of day, this close to downtown, but out of its eye. That place is Jimmy's.

# Chapter Thirteen

## Blake

The house is quiet once again. Breakfast dishes rest in the sink and coffee cools, television seems obscene after this morning's cheer. Blake tries it anyway and finds he was correct. Its canned laughter and false cheer squeeze out the last echoes of this morning's high mood. He isn't jealous of his son's evening romp; he remembers the needing of closeness, of another's body, the newness and fulfillment and fading of initial desire. But he isn't jealous. Not exactly.

The clock claims it is too early to switch from coffee, and Blake wishes he still smoked, just to add that cutting edge to the caffeine. A cigarette could keep the cap on the bottle. Maybe. He walks through the house, and the word 'totter' keeps popping into his head. Blake doesn't want to believe that he is a widower who totters around on Saturday mornings. He purposely avoids weekend yard work. Even besides his hatred for all things lawn-oriented, he does not want to appear to need to keep busy. The magazine articles, the co-worker's advice, they all suggest gardening or exercise, finding interests. He presumes they mean beyond drinking.

The old men sailing their radio control sailboats at the duck pond. Discussing ohms and wind direction, he won't do that. There are no papers to grade, he's been easy on his students lately. Looming retirement has softened his resolve. He's had the same lesson plans for a decade or more. They work, and this close to retirement, he isn't changing, no matter what the eager young presenters at the teacher's workshops tell him about progress. Blake has seen enough progress to spot the cycles, and he knows where he is on his circle—right on the top, about to close it.

A younger version of himself lived life in a straight line, a true 180 degrees. Blake had envisioned the lives of others as lines, as well. Some lines parallel, never to touch his, but going on into their own infinities. Others formed rays, hitting his and running with it for a while, before sprouting off.

Norm is a ray, conjured from some human mathematical magic where 1 + 1 formed 3. His and Pat's lifelines were skewed, crossing once and running close, but never really touching again. Now, Blake sees the graph paper of his life filled with circles, curves crossing haphazardly through neat, light blue squares. Circles like galactic charts with gravitational pull invisibly drawing some things closer while pushing others away, all very much beyond his control.

He touches tabletops, doilies protecting surfaces from lamp bottoms and picture frames encapsulating years of life. Norm as a baby, Norm starting kindergarten, unsure as ever, the same half smile as his graduation picture. These are the moments where circles cross, points that bind trajectories. Blake runs his fingers, with their grey hairs and foreign folds, over shelves of knick knacks: pale white vases and figurines. It seems Pat placed all these here yesterday, without his knowledge, and then died, leaving him to ensure everything stayed in place. Dust accumulates. Its small circles of imperfection build a slow amnesia.

Blake found that having a third person at the table this morning brought out an old sense of camaraderie. Something between his table seat and hers teaming up on Norm's. Was it always like that? He had settled into an old role, kept an old circle round, picked on his son, kept him out of the circle. Nikki's moans early this morning, floating down the hall, and her laughter at breakfast were cleansing. Blake makes a point to talk with Norm tonight; he tries to think of things they had done when they were both younger. Maybe they could check on the constellations, share a drink. A drink.

Blake had, for the first month or so, still kept his bottle in the cabinet, where Pat liked it, out of sight. Now it usually sits on the counter, a sort of to-do list, a reminder to stop at the liquor store after work.

The contents of his house become oppressive, he feels their weight. The silenced piano slowly pressures the beams, the windows' rectangular forces bend their frames. Blake feels this.

Norm made the clay bowl by the side door at a summer camp, presenting it with pride when he and Pat had come to pick him up, after two weeks, his longest time away from them since birth. "Now you won't lose your keys!" Norm said.

Now Blake empties it of his watch, keys, and wallet, briefly opening the last to check for the green flash of bills. It is time to leave the house.

# Chapter Fourteen

The opened doors cough out the trapped smoke and beery breath of customers now decades dead. Signs advertise beers no longer brewed, the cigarette machine bears the name of a brand I don't think has been smoked in my lifetime. If these major changes in the commercial world go unrecognized by Jimmy's Bar, then I suppose it's not surprising that nothing else has changed.

If you didn't already know Jimmy's was here, then you'd never know. There's no sign. It's nestled inside a dingy neighborhood, behind a small row of stores still awaiting the effect of Garrison's renaissance. It looks like a two-story house, which it is. Just that the second floor is filled with pool tables, and the first is, for some reason, set about three feet underground, made to look like a basement. The only natural light comes from a series of small head-height rectangle windows.

Entering, I see Roger. I swear right where I'd last seen him. It's nice to see him still alive. I had given him only hours to live last I saw him, and that was over a decade ago. We are alone in the bar. Strange half walls break the sprawling open space into drinking corrals. They're strangely similar to the classroom dividers in the learning center. Three tightly packed pool tables abut the old Centipede video game. It had been such a point of pride to beat a regular back when that's all I really wanted to be, sneaking in here underage, ordering Cokes until midnight or so, when laws seemed to disappear. Randomly placed card tables are pushed together and surrounded by scattered chairs, still lingering from last night's conversations. On my left runs the Formica bar dotted with stained and cluttered ashtrays—one for each stool. At the end, beside a tray of wizened lime wedges, is Roger.

"Morning, Roger." I take a stool, a polite three down from his.

"Aaeyah," Roger mumbles, not unkindly, and begins descending from his stool, a painful maneuver requiring multiple grips on the bar and stool while his Velcro sneakers seek the sticky, ashy floor.

I fight the urge to offer help. Roger has become increasingly orangutangish with his short bowed legs and slumped shoulders. His hair has grown gray and wispy as cigarette smoke over his ears. A limp handlebar mustache dangles beside his mouth. I stand almost twice his height, and picture resting him on my hip while he reaches for bottles, suckling messily before smashing them and screeching.

Roger ambles his way behind the bar to face me. I can't believe he is still allowed to tend, especially while a pint glass of ice and whiskey awaits his return. He goggles his eyes up at me.

"Pabst, please."

He leans, looking me over. "What?"

I clear my throat, put on a smile.

"Just a PBR. Tall boy, please. Thanks, Roger."

He flicks himself into motion, sliding open several metal coolers before locating the Pabst and handing me one unopened. My change is roughly correct and after deliberating over the quarters, I leave a dollar. Roger works his way back around to his drink, the straw in his mouth before he's fully reached the stool top.

I feel an inch higher off the ground as the beer whooshes open. This morning's exploits seem safely contained outside these walls. This is a much better choice than coffee. It's only Roger here, and he can't remember me, all those years and beers ago.

The Pabst is freezing in my hand. It's delicious, and the first sip quickly becomes the second, and the third. After the first half, I can sit back and see that there has been some change.

Crammed above the bar, beside shelves balancing repetitive bottles of cheap booze, there are two flat screen TVs. The one down the bar, farther from me and Roger, is silently showing a brightly colored cooking show. A flamboyant man is preparing a highly stacked dessert. This is all going on above a worn, hand-scrawled sign reading MENU: Pop-tarts $1.00, Slim-Jims $1.25.

Roger has a remote in his small hand, which drops and rise from behind the tray of old bar fruit, changing channels on our screen. He's flicking between The Karate Kid washing classic American cars and Burt Reynolds in a cowboy hat talking into a CB. There doesn't seem to any timing to his switches, just back and forth: Burt Reynolds, Ralph Macchio, Burt Reynolds.

The beer goes down quickly, and I try to start some conversation with Roger so I can slip in my request for another without sounding demanding.

"So, how's things, Roger?"

No response.

"How's business today, Roger?"

Ralph Macchio turns into Burt Reynolds turns into a commercial turns into news turns into another movie. The channels are flying by.

"Roger?"

"Roger?"

I have to stand on the bottom rungs of my stool to lean over and get a good look at him. He's face down on the bar, the remote clutched in one hand and his drink in the other.

"Roger!"

The channels continue to switch.

I look around for someone I know is not there. It's only him and me. Maybe only me. I'm behind him, looking and repeating his name as a mantra. There's still nothing. My hands reach out. I can't quite bring myself touch him, but he's still not moving. I shake his shoulders a bit; he feels loose enough.

"Shit."

Still, there is no one else here. There should be. It's a beautiful day. There must be a phone around somewhere. If any place in town would still have a pay phone, it would be Jimmy's. It would probably only cost a dime, too.

No phones on the wall. I step behind the bar and stupidly move bottles around, nothing helpful there. Behind my head now I can hear the channels flying through. I'm tempted to wrench the remote from Roger's grip, but the thought of unpeeling those curled fingers…under the farther television there is a door and I walk through.

It's cold, real cold, and there is beer everywhere, a tangle of tubes for the keg lines cover the wall to my left and ahead are stacks and stacks of cases, a few crates of Slim Jims among them. I'm moving things around like there's going to be a phone in the walk-in, but I don't want to have to run outside screaming for help, stopping a stranger to use their cell phone. That seems excessive at this point. By the door is a pencil drawn chart, a work schedule covered with 'ROGER' at every shift.

I'm running through CPR procedures in my head, trying to remember the drill I had done to get my certification for some job years ago. Was it breath, 3 seconds, push, or breath, breath, wait? There is no remembering these things.

I push out through the walk-in door, back behind the bar, and I hear loud country music. There, behind his drink, Roger sits upright as possible, the remote aimed high at the screen. Credits roll over a semi driving into the distance. He doesn't seem disconcerted in the slightest to see me behind his bar.

"Roger?"

"Uhhhyeaaah." He doesn't even throw a glance in my direction. He's watching the Karate Kid balance on the beach. Christ, my heart is pounding. I lean against the cooler, the cold metal sticks against my hand.

"You okay, Roger? Shit, you had me."

"Mmmmuhhuh."

I turn to watch the TV with him. Leaning back against the inside of the bar, I reach behind me with an awkward twist for my beer. I take the last dregs. The Karate Kid gets ready for the big tournament. When I finish my beer I hold up my empty and crush it, showing it to Roger. He barely glances, only motions toward the cooler. I slide the top up and grab another, crack it and neatly arc my empty into the trash. By the time the day of the big karate tournament finally comes, I've made three baskets. I feel good. Roger doesn't respond much to my comments, but he's good company and generous with his drinks. I even enjoy a Slim

Jim.

Right after the brutal cheating of The Karate Kid's opponent, I hear a door open. A moment. Then the next door, like an airlock. I turn to see who it is, purely curious. I'm not even thinking about my presence behind the bar.

It's an older guy, dressed a little warmly for the weather. He's wearing a green baseball hat and looking down at something in his hands, checking his wallet maybe. Even looking down like that he walks right to us, casually skirting the table by the door.

At the bar now, he finally looks up, but past me, at the bottles, looking for the label that will catch his eye, trying to spot that particular shade of red against a whiskey brown background.

Roger raises his head. "Blake. Howyourdoin?"

"I'm just fine, Roger. How's things for you?"

"Aaah, goodyIguess."

"That's good." He turns to me. "And you, Norman?"

"Hi, Dad," I say.

# Chapter Fifteen

"And still your fingernails grow, Norm. That's what I figured out, they just keep growing."

"That's what got you?" I say.

"I got it, Norm, that's what I got. Don't you see?" He lays his hand on mine. "There was one day, weeks afterward, when I realized my fingernails were too long."

"I hate that feeling." My beer is empty, and I want a break in this conversation to get another one.

"No, it was a small thing, maybe, but it made me realize that my body had no idea she was dead. No idea. It just kept going."

He's looking at me, his gaze steadier than his hands, waiting for a response. He looks old. And tired. And too much at home here. One of the legions of old men who never used to be like this. It makes me sad, and nothing I can offer is going to make him better. I wait for him to continue.

"Do you see what I'm saying, Norman?"

"Sure. Totally," I say.

"Don't do that." He looks away.

"What?"

"What you always do. Dismiss. Make light of. Always."

"Christ, Dad, what am I making light of? I get what you're saying, that's all."

"When you were a baby, we could've looked at you all day. Just looked at you. Did you know that?"

"I guess I never thought about it."

"That is the truest thing I've heard all day."

"Dad, Jesus, let's just have a beer. I'm here, you know, I came back, so, let's just have a beer together." I stand, for the first time in a while. "I'll get you one."

He slides his empty towards me, but watches the door over my shoulder. A crowd is filing in. I have to turn sideways to get to the bar, PBR cans crushed in my hands. Roger tends bar at his own pace, which seems to be pissing off the younger crowd, queuing with cash in hand. A quiet row of mesh backed trucker caps and camouflage jackets sitting at the bar seem unperturbed by the pace of things, their heads down over their afternoon drinks or on the televisions. The waiting crowd is flashier, louder, cruder, out on the town after their day's work, not their life's. I realize I'm older than they are.

I regret talking to my dad with this teenaged abruptness. Being home, though, being home again—seeing these kids around me now, these drinkers in their first years, it's stirring. They're ordering drinks they've heard of. They probably still remember their home room and locker numbers. They're funny. They all know the same movie lines and treat them like their own witticisms. Now, though, I just want two more quiet beers, no reminders of what could have been me, had I stayed.

I use what cache I've earned by opening the place up this morning to slip to the front and order four beer. This elicits a quick flurry of swearing and derogatory comments about my PBR tallboys, $1.75 each.

138

Roger hands them to me unopened, dangling from a plastic six pack holder. I leave an oversized tip, a model for those behind me, and make sure Roger gets the bills before I leave.

It's earlyish still, and Jimmy's, apart from the bar area, is darkened. Only Dad sits in the big room. His back is turned, and I see his slouch, wonder if that's new. In all my memories, he is taller than me, even after junior high, when I shot up and over him. Late night sneaking in, I can see him nearly bent double over me, pointing. I see him kneeling to speak to me through a car window. Now he examines the yellowed ceiling tiles and bikini posters, waiting for his beer.

"Here you go, Garrison City's finest." I clank the four cans down, removing one, cracking it on the way down to my seat. "So, I was a good baby. You were saying something."

He smiles and nods, but only works his finger under the pull tab. It evades his grasp and takes his concentration. I watch the process, trying not to do it for him. It opens.

"Ah," he says. "There." He drinks.

"Listen, Dad, I'm—"

"You, you're more like your mother than you know," he says.

"That's probably true. Seeing as I don't think I'm like her at all."

"There, right there. You just did it."

"What?" I say.

"Made a joke."

"Everybody does that."

"True, but only your mother and you made, make, a joke any time anybody says something serious. It's like you're allergic. I should bless you after every joke."

139

"I can be serious, Dad." I wipe the rim of the can and drink. "Besides, Mom wasn't funny."

"No, most women aren't, to most men, but your mother made me laugh harder than any other woman, any person, alive. Hmmm. Or dead."

I almost say something, but just 'hmm' with interest. This is not the mother I remember, who seemed to be in constant motion. You couldn't watch a movie with her in the room, getting up adjusting things, bringing you blankets and opening windows. It was strange, but not funny. Drove me crazy. I would imitate her for my friends. That was funny.

"You used to piss her off so much," Dad says.

"That's what kids are for."

"See, there she is," he says.

"I guess."

The crowd from the bar drifts over, takes over pool tables, drops fives in the jukebox and breaks the silence. It occurs to me there is something I want to ask my mom about, but can't.

We drink our beers separately. People come and take our extra chairs. He asks nothing about why I was here this morning, and I return the favor. Nikki's name is never mentioned, though I'm curious. I want to hear about her in high school. Maybe it will help me remember.

The energy of the room crackles away from our table, leaving us in a reverse spotlight. Two men drinking in the silence of their thoughts. I know he wants to talk about Mom. There's a particular phrase he wants to get to. That's how he thinks. He'll let ideas linger and brew until a phrase appears to him, like that fingernail thing. I doubt he awoke one day, saw that his fingernails were long, and accepted his wife's death. Things don't happen like that. They become clear in the telling. There was probably a day when he realized he was thinking about Mom for the first time since waking, and he cut his fingernails. Or something. I don't know and don't ask. I let him have his epiphany and await my own.

I'm getting restless and suggest moving on, assuming from Dad's slouch that he'll opt to go home. He doesn't. He perks up and wants to continue, even tips his can straight back and opens the second, no problems this time. I'm already on my last and join in the quick sipping. Dad's excited at the prospect of bar hopping. He's curious to drink somewhere else. It's Saturday night.

"I don't know, Dad. Where do you want to go?"

"Oh, it doesn't matter. You choose. You're young." He waves a nonexistent disagreement away.

"It's your town," I say.

"You grew up here, same as me. Leaving doesn't take that away."

"Coming back does."

He's quiet. Sipping. His legs are double crossed, his ankle wrapped around his calf. I always hated when he sat like that.

"Are you glad you came back?" he says.

"Sure."

"Don't placate me. I know it's not for me that you're here. I know that."

"I wanted to be here for you."

"Oh, that's nice!" He laughs into his chest. "You're like a, I don't know, you're a- a roommate who needs a ride to work!"

"I'm glad I came back."

"Fine, don't answer. But think about it. What are you doing here? If you're just killing time, that's fine. But don't, don't Norman, pretend that it's for me that you're here. Don't confuse confusion with loyalty."

I'm silent.

"Or love. Don't confuse anything for love."

He drinks long from the tall red, white, and blue can, large in his old hands. Beer runs down the side as a funny thought hits him.

"Lust. You can confuse lust with love. There is a very long tradition of that. You'd be in high company!"

"Very funny."

"Thank you."

"Are we talking about last night?" I say.

"Do you want to talk about last night? We can."

"I'm sorry if we bothered you. It was kind of late, I know."

"Kind of late? It was this morning. If we're talking about anything, we're talking about this morning. Not last night."

"Well, I'm sorry. I got a little carried away."

He tries to slam the beer down, but it only makes a light hollow sound.

"You don't have to apologize. For Christ's sake, don't apologize for that. You're a young man, and Nicole Follansbee, whoa. I mean that."

"Were you always like this?"

"I've been here forever, young man, I haven't changed," he says.

"Young man. I knew I was in trouble when I heard that. I felt like I was in your class."

"Nicole was in my class."

"You guys made that clear. This morning."

142

"Norm." Dad stands, searches around for his jacket and works his body into it. He puts his hat on, pulling it down over one eye. "Fucking lighten up."

Then he walks out of the bar.

# Chapter Sixteen

The end of the day's sun shows brilliant on the bricks downtown. Looking down Bending St., the river reflects orange. Cars line up at crosswalks, allow a full flow of pedestrians to go by before creeping to the light, where they wait again. Dad looks around like a tourist. After catching up with him, I need to stop every ten feet, still in this morning's t-shirt, and shiver while he reunites with the dozen or so people he knows on each block.

"Mr. Mean?" they all begin. "Remember me?"

Every time he says, "Jonathon!" or "Cynthia!" or "Of course!"

And they have a few good laughs. Each one leaves with a smile, prideful from the quick exchange, assured they are remembered and missed. They all take his friendliness as the warmness of an old man, happy to see someone he had cared about, not a drunk widower out with his half-orphan son.

I hang back, throwing quick nods and tight smiles to Dad's greeters. Waiting. Ready to go. A full day's beer runs through me. Leaving Jimmy's, the last of the day's sunlight hit me hard. I'd staggered at the door, and smiled. Dad was already down the street, his admonition ringing in my head. He never used to swear. Maybe he's right. Fucking lighten up.

The main square, more of a wide Y where three streets spill into one, is flowing with people. We slip into the crowd's current, crossing the streets in packs, splitting at the sidewalks. We tag along like flotsam.

"Norman. Where are you taking me?" Dad stops suddenly, causing a backup in the flow. People course by, excited and loud, prepped for the evening ahead.

"Jeez Dad, I was following you."

"Well, that doesn't work," he says.

"Let's go to the Box. Maybe Riverdriver's," I say, leaning towards places away from a rowdy crowd.

"I've spent enough time drinking with an old man today. Let's go someplace new."

"I don't know Dad, you've been around. What's new?" I say.

"Where'd you go last night? Let's go there."

"The Lock Up? I don't know if that's really your scene. It's all frat boys and sports fans."

"Is that your 'scene'?" He smiles.

"Not really, I guess I decided to lighten up and try it out."

"That's the best fucking thing I've heard all day."

Tonight is a swearing night. I turn us back to the square, toward The Lock Up. The crowd seems to surge with us, to have made up its mind and redirected itself along our path. There is sure to be a line, and I need food and drink as quickly as possible. If I suggest somewhere else, though, it will be seen as an attempt to avoid The Lock Up. Dad clearly wants to see Nikki. Or for me to see Nikki. Or maybe he's forgotten completely and just wants to go somewhere new. He does seem jovial tonight.

There's a line outside The Lock Up, and Dad is greeted like a celebrity. It's as if the entire graduating class of three years ago has come out on the town, all waiting to see old teachers and prove their freedom through alcohol. Dad accepts their backslaps and light insults: "I hated your class!" "You failed me!" "You're still alive?" "The Mean one!" with good natured smiles and full reciprocation. I take our place in the back of the line.

None of Dad's greeters are yet my age. Freshly crowned legal drinkers, this place is as new to them as any other bar in town. They may not remember it as the police station, and assume it's all just a theme, a gimmick, confusing the whole time line, disregarding the actual progression of things. Nikki knows, she is aware, and she still has to wear that stupid shirt and badge. I don't know if I respect her more for that, or less.

Not that, I suppose, it's really my place to respect her or not. We don't have much of a tie: a few drinks, a few hours. One night. It is a bad idea to come here tonight. It's nearly desperate. Not that I'm not, but that doesn't mean I'm ready to appear that way.

There's a crowd of young sports fans pointing at me. I don't point back, and it takes me a moment to find Dad in the center of them, pointing right along. He waves. I raise a hand back.

He calls me over. I shake a 'no' with both hands, indicating something about our place in line, and rub my stomach indicating something about food. He waves me over again, the sports fans await my response. There's only a few people behind me, and we haven't moved an inch yet anyway. I go over.

"Boys, this is my son, Norman. You can call him that due to your status as graduates. I, however, will always be Mr. Mean!"

147

A chorus arises, "The Mean!"

He sounds like an auctioneer, rolling the crowd in his palm, selling them on what he's got.

"Hey," I say.

"Norm!" the choir shouts followed by a series of lame questions about being the son of a teacher, like it's something special. In their minds, old high school teachers still hold stature and probably some power. If Dad told them to take off their hats, they probably would.

There is nothing to say now that one-sided introductions have been made. Dad stands beaming, and they begin talking among themselves, growing bored with the exchange.

"Dad, come on, they're letting people in," I say.

"Goodbye, boys! I'm off for sustenance!" He waves, a few of them raise hands and drop nods before returning to their own conversation.

"Come on, Dad."

We take our place in line, a few back from our original spot. My drunk is becoming a hangover. Something needs to be done about that.

"Oh, it's good to be out, Norm. With you. It's a good thing."

"Yeah, Dad, it's cool."

"'It's cool.' That's what you can say, 'it's cool'? Come on, Son, I thought we were bonding. Lightening up."

"We are."

"So. Fucking enjoy it. This is good. You've been back for months. Months, Norm. This is the most we've talked. Today. We've talked more today than the rest of the year combined."

"It's been a tough year, Dad."

He doesn't seem satisfied with that.

"You know, with Mom and moving back and stuff," I say.

He scans me from the hair down, then looks away. We move a few steps toward the door, stepping with the line.

"Norm, there's something I want to tell you."

"Go ahead. I'm listening."

"I'm going to wait 'til that's true. Tonight we'll drink, more, and we'll go home to our separate rooms, pass out and wake up wondering what we said to each other. I'll have coffee going by the time you come down. We'll eat. And then we'll go outside and look for the stars."

"The stars, Dad? You got your itinerary mixed up. The stars are usually out at night."

"Good then, tonight. It's a plan," he says.

"What do you mean?" I say.

"Tonight. We'll look at the stars and enjoy outgrowing the cookies we used to enjoy."

"Mom made us those cookies."

"Mom's dead," he says.

"Doesn't change the fact she made a damn fine cookie," I say.

He laughs, turning heads toward us, and pats my back.

"Norman, it doesn't change a lot of things."

"I know. Your fingernails still grow. I'm not sure how I feel about that."

"It doesn't really matter how you feel about the truth. It just is. That's how it goes," he says.

We look at each other until it's natural to turn away. I find that I am enjoying this and that he should know that. I catch his eyes again.

"You sound like you're in class," I say.

149

"Do I? I don't remember feeling like this in class."

"You probably never drank this much before school."

"It's not the drink, Norman."

"That's always what drunks say," I say, thinking it may have come out wrong, but he laughs again.

"You're funny. Your mom was funny."

"You mentioned."

"I did? Well, that's what drunks do, I suppose."

We're at the door, and the bouncer seems about to ask me for my ID when Dad calls him by name and asks him for a hall pass. Another round of back claps, and we're ushered into the crowd. I can't see the bar from here. Dad makes a beeline through the crowd, squeezing between close-talking couples and bumping the guys deep into video golf challenges. I catch up and follow him, muttering apologies to each drinker he bumps on his way.

"Nicole!" he shouts.

Shit. I see her now, in the middle of trading a wad of crumpled bills for half a dozen drinks. She looks up, ready to be angry with whoever is interrupting. Then she's smiling, waving all that money at us. Nikki turns to the register, bumping into a waitress punching in an order. They speak briefly and both turn to look at me, more than us; they're looking at me. They return to the blue register screen.

Dad's beside me, pushing me forward, I realize, toward the bar, to Nikki. There's one seat at the bar.

He says, "I have to piss." And disappears.

Smooth, Dad. I take the seat, wondering how I didn't notice the bar top's decoration last night. Old photographs are laminated onto the cheap plywood of the bar. Old street scenes of Garrison City with dirt roads and horses, buildings now gone to rubble. Three neat rows of somber women in front of the old mill, looking like this photograph is cutting into their pay. I scan their faces for a cute one, for a smile. There are none.

I run my finger over the photos, knowing the possibility that these woman are some relation to me. There've been Means here forever. Mom was a Jersey girl, the joke being that Dad saved her by bringing her north. I was never sure. Whenever we went to visit, for holidays or weddings, she would meld into her big-haired, large-jeweled cousins as if she had never left. Her accent came out, and I would run through suburban lawns with my cousins, perceiving them to be infinitely more worldly, based solely on their proximity to New York City, where we never went, not once on all those trips. We'd see the buildings from a bridge, and Mom would say, "Oh, let's go in!" And Dad would say something about taking the girl out of the city, but—maybe Mom would have liked to go.

"Hey, stranger." Nikki's there with the same beer I drank last night.

"Am I that much of a regular already?"

"No, all the regulars say thank you."

"Regularly?" I take a sip.

"Every time," she says. "At least for the drinks."

"Thank you," I say.

"You're welcome. But don't get too comfy, the Clam's been cursing you all night."

"The Clam?"

"Sherry. Said you came to her house last night, tried to beat up Steve.

Why would you do that, Norman?"

I present my palms to her. "I didn't even—"

She touches my hand, holds it there. "Christ, just kidding. I don't believe a word that leaves her fucking mouth."

"It wasn't like that."

"I know. That's what I just said."

"What else did she say?" I take another drink, look around for a menu.

"She said you're an asshole and that you only work at the school to touch little girls."

"She didn't say that."

Nikki hands me a menu. "On the house, tonight. And, yes. Yes she did."

"That's fucking ridiculous."

"I don't know, Norm, you seemed pretty happy touching me...what am I supposed to think?"

"Come on. That's not even, that's completely fucking insane." Damn, she makes me nervous.

"Is it?"

"What?" I say.

"Insane."

"Can I get two burgers and another beer for my dad?"

"Like I'm just here to serve you? Christ, Norm Mean, Sherry was right about you."

"Shut up."

"See? You are an asshole." She takes my hand again, and still holding it, takes an order from a frat boy who looks at our twined hands while he orders.

When Nikki turns away, releasing me, to fill frat boy's order, he looks down at me in my stool, sipping my beer. I held the bartender's hand. I smile up at him. Man, bartenders and teachers hold such strange status. He blows air from his nose and stares through the bottles on the shelves into the far more interesting mirror. He looks at himself until Nikki returns with his tray of drinks and he leaves.

"Bye," I say.

"Friend of yours?" Nikki says.

"Best friends."

"Oh, that's weird, 'cause I went home with him last night, no two nights ago, last night was you. I forget." Nikki wipes at the bar top. The millworker women remain unperturbed by her scrubbing.

"What? You're lying." I think she's lying.

"It would just be weird if you two knew each other, that's all." She scrubs, leaning in closer.

I smile at the mill working women. "He told me about you. That's why I came in yesterday. He said you were easy."

"Well," she says, our noses almost touching, I can feel her breath on my chin. "I guess he was right."

"And good. He said you were good." I tilt one more degree forward until our lips touch. She doesn't quite kiss, but she allows my mouth to remain.

"I need to work." She stands up straight.

"You meeting someone new tonight?" I ask her as she walks to the end of the bar.

"Naw, sometimes it's the same guy twice."

153

Then she's gone, taking orders from the crowd stacked in layers at the bar. I watch her work for a while. She's very good. Moves quickly without rushing and adds the orders in her head, pulls up bottles without looking down, pouring and making chit chat all at the same time. When Dad slides into the now empty stool beside me, he asks why I'm smiling, and I don't even know I am.

Our burgers come. At this point in the evening, they're delicious, though I don't know if that means they're really good, or just that I'm starving. I think the only thing I've had to eat today was a few Slim Jims. That may have been days ago.

Dad is fading a bit, head dropping to his ketchupy plate. But I'm feeling better, rejuvenated by the burger and draught beer. He's quiet, watching the baseball game on TV, raising his mug every time something good happens, at a funny commercial, or whenever he gets the urge. He's into drinking-at-home mode, examining the top of his beer closely, chin on his chest.

"You still with us, Dad?" I say, and throw an awkward arm on his shoulder, then take it away.

"I'm going home," he says to his beer.

"I'll walk you."

He pushes himself up, drops his legs to the floor. "Don't worry about me. You have fun for both of us."

"You sure? I don't mind…" I say without any real conviction.

He leans into me, his head on my shoulder. It seems miniature. Dad puts his arm around me, one around the back of the stool. "No, I'm going."

I laugh and give the hand on my belly a pat. "If you're sure."

He stands quickly. "Nicole Follansbee!"

"What are you doing?" I say.

"One the for road, son. Surely, you've heard of that tradition. I haven't raised my only son to not have one more for the road."

I look at him. His eyes are glassy, focused on something a foot behind my head.

"Surely, one road more is fine with you, son, my Norm, one road."

"No, Dad, one road more would be fine."

"You'll join me?" He finds my eyes.

"For the drink? Or do you want me to come home?"

"You do what you want. That's clear." He's waving an arm loosely in the air.

"What are you talking about?"

"One more. Whiskey. Finally, whiskey." He slides his beer roughly down the bar to me, some spills down the side of his glass mug.

He attempts to retake his stool again, misses and catches himself with his arms in my lap.

"Nikki! Whiskey!" He calls into my chest.

She's standing by us, on this side of the bar. "Is he okay?"

"Oh yeah, I think, he's just a little drunk, that's all. He'll be fine, I'm going to walk him home in a—"

"I'm not going anywhere. Whiskey." He rights himself, and we're all watching it happen, puts his hands on Nikki's shoulders, missing the first few attempts so it seems he's grabbing at her chest.

"I'm sorry," I say.

"Are you okay, Mr. Mean?" she asks.

He points at her nose, an inch away. "Blake."

155

"Are you okay? Blake. I can call a cab for you guys."

"Can you call a whiskey?" Dad's very serious, looking her right in the face, squeezing her shoulders.

"I got him, Nikki," I say. "We'll go home. I'm sorry."

"It's fine, Norm, stay. I'll get him some whiskey."

"Really?" Dad and I say together.

She laughs. Dad and I look at each other. He shrugs himself together, stuffs his shirt tails into his pants top, really only tucking them under his stomach.

"Thank you," I mouth at Nikki as she takes her place around the bar again.

There are two large rocks glasses, minus rocks, in front of us, filled with whiskey. Dad looks as surprised as I feel. He slides his over to clink against mine and makes a pretend drinking motion with his real glass, spilling some whiskey down his shirt front. He doesn't seem to notice. I lift mine, inches off the counter, careful not to spill so I'm not associated with him.

"Here's to you, Dad. Drink up."

He lifts his glass to his lips, but before he drinks, he says, "The tables have turned, Norm. How do you feel?"

"I'm fine. I feel good."

"I bet you do. She's a pretty girl."

"Nikki? Yeah, she seems great."

"Your mother and I slept naked. Bet you didn't know that. Did you?"

I laugh, blowing a tiny brown wave across the top of my glass before I drink. It's harsh. "Actually, Dad, I did know that."

He looks over, ready with his prepared response to my presumed answer, his mouth angry, and he mutters something, but then turns, laughing into his drink.

"Yes. Yes, I guess you would."

"Let's drink and head home."

"You're staying. Stop pretending."

This is getting old. "If you want to go home, that's fine. I'll stay. But, if you want to stay, also, with me, I don't think that'll work."

He drains his glass, I see his open mouth expanded through the bottom. "That doesn't make any sense. Christ, it's like talking to your mother."

"Dad, I have to pee. If you're here when I get back, I'll assume you're okay."

"I'll be here." He settles his arms out proprietorially across the bar, looking over his shoulder, following my path through the crowd.

The bathroom is quiet. I focus on getting my piss in the toilet and on the lightened weight of my bladder. Dad needs to pull it together. In all our recent time together, it hasn't gotten to this point. Or maybe I've been there with him, but we've just been at home, where it doesn't matter. Maybe I crossed some unspoken barrier by leaving home last night. I zip up, watching myself in the mirror, remembering our street this morning and the light and thinking of getting the paper with him and how I haven't thought of that in years.

Every Sunday, Dad and I would walk to town and get the paper, a chore at the time, often an hour gone for what should've been a twenty minute walk, but we'd take detours off the quickest path, returning to a big breakfast and that show tune music I hated on the radio. I inhale,

157

run through my hair a few times, and wash my hands. This'll be fine. We'll pay up and go home. It'll give an excuse for an easy goodbye to Nikki. I don't know what is expected of me with her tonight and what is rude presumption. Helping your drunk dad home can only be seen as a good-guy bonus, unless that whole sins of the father thing holds true. She doesn't seem the type to hold a grudge. But Christ, I wouldn't mind taking her home again.

On the trip from bathroom to bar seat, I hear my name, but can't find the source. I ignore it, keep my head down until I reach the spot at the bar where my and Dad's seats used to be but are now filled by two pairs of very low cut shirts with blonde hair.

"I'm over here, Norm." It's Nikki, from the end of the bar. "He left."

"Dammit. Shit. I hate this shit. Am I supposed to follow him now?"

There's a crowd gathering at the bar. They want their drinks, not their father. Nikki actually looks a little worried, and that makes me somewhat less willing to blow this off and assume that he made it home just fine. Though I'm happy to stay and want to be okay with that assumption. "Was he all right?"

"Is he normally like that?" Nikki says, rushed, holding a finger up to ward off increasingly angry drinkers.

"Like what?"

"Hammered."

"Sometimes," I say.

"Well, then, I guess he was fine."

"Good."

"Good," she says.

"Can I get another one?"

"Christ." Nikki sets off behind the bar, taking more orders even as she pours mine.

This most recent beer jitters before me as it comes to a sliding rest. I calm it and lift it directly to my mouth. Maybe I am smooth. It's crazy in here tonight. Should I go home and check on Dad? I'd just leave, look for him everywhere on the way home, probably convince myself something terrible happened, fly into the house and find him, head back, mouth open, passed out on his chair with whiskey spilling from his tilted glass into his lap. Probably, anyway. I might as well just stay here. That would only make me annoyed that I had to give up my seat at the bar, which is a pretty hot commodity at this point in the evening.

Nikki's flat out for a while. After about half an hour, I wonder if she's really worried, or just joking, or just busy. She's the only thing making me at home here, which is strange, we met maybe a little over 24 hours ago. There's the feeling that the past months have added up to this, and I want to be happy about that, until I remember Dad. If the recent past for him has only equaled a blind stumble home, then it seems we're headed on different trajectories. And even if that was the one I wanted to head on when I left home yesterday, I've done my own stumbling onto something else.

"Hey." Nikki slides me another beer. "Smoke in a minute?"

"I'll be here when you're ready."

"See, that's why I like you."

"Thanks." I raise my beer.

I realize I haven't smoked today and that also makes me feel good. And also makes me want one desperately. Patting my pockets, I remember that last night destroyed my cigarettes and that I would need to bum another one from Nikki, and I know that that won't be a problem and that is also good. I'm sure Dad's fine. He always is. I comfort myself for a moment assuming that he's faking his drunkenness. He's taking a quick goodbye so as not to interfere with me and Nikki. That's a possibility. But so is an impending drunken Dad breakdown.

When we're outside, in the alley, Nikki has two cigarettes out. She lights them both at once, hands me one. She's smoking hers with the voracity of someone on a quick break. I'm enjoying mine, looking up at the memorable windows of the Orchard Apartment and Rooming house.

"Fuck, it's busy," she says.

"It is, yeah."

"I'm tired."

"Did I wear you out?" I reach over and rest my hand on her shoulder, give it a quick squeeze. I think it's our first private touch with clothes on, and it somehow seems more intimate, that I suddenly have the right to do this.

Nikki absently reaches up and pats my hand, smoking with her other. "That's it, baby. You're an animal. I gotta go."

She stretches onto her toes and kisses me quickly on the cheek before turning and heading back to the door. As I'm watching her walk away, thinking, 'she called me baby,' the door opens and there is Sherry. Shit.

"Are we paying you to smoke?" Sherry shouts from the door, leaning far out, balancing herself with one arm on the frame, only feet from

Nikki.

"Apparently you were," Nikki says, and I laugh. "For a minute." She continues forward without pause, angling her body past Sherry, back into the packed bar.

Sherry doesn't move. I smoke. Think about what to say. She appears to do the same.

"Don't think you're coming back in here. Not for one second. Don't think that," she says.

"That's actually not what I was thinking at all, Sherry," I say and inspect my butt for a last drag. I take it and stamp it out.

"Fuck you," she says.

"Listen. Last night got a little messed up and I'm sorry. I think maybe you—"

"I didn't do shit."

"I was just saying, I thought maybe—"

"I didn't do fucking shit, Norm. You have no fucking idea what I do."

I reflect on that for a moment. In essence, I guess, she's right. "What are you talking about?"

"Fuck you and your little girlfriend."

Sherry lets the door close. I'm alone in the alley. It's very dark. No stars on in town. Yelling from the apartments drifts down. Something shatters and the screaming inches up a notch. I watch the bar's door stay closed and wonder if I'll go back through. Above me another door slams and a man screams, "SHIT." Yeah, buddy, there's a lot of that going on tonight. A baby begins what is sure to be a lifetime of crying.

Well, I'm with the guy in the apartment, shit. There are some options and repercussions to run through. If I just walk back in through the side alley door, Sherry is sure to be lurking, perched to catch me and throw me out, which could make things unnecessarily difficult for Nikki. I could go back in the front door, thwarting Sherry through pure wit and gumption. Again, that could put Nikki in a bad spot. Going home is an option. Maybe that's what the world, this town, is trying to tell me. Go home. Call it a night. I should have done that this morning after I couldn't even handle a simple run-in with a student downtown. I should have done that twelve years ago. I can't shake the feeling that there is shame in calling it a night when there is more night left.

Turning to leave the alley, I remember that I don't have to listen to what the world is telling me. I'm sure Nikki wouldn't take any of these thoughts seriously. She seems to do what she wants, and the fact that I got to be a part of that for even a day forces me back towards the side door, which, at the moment, looks unguarded.

It's not. The door flies open, and I focus on the hand on my chest and I'm surprised at how strong Sherry is as I'm pushed backwards into the alley. Then I hear a voice, and it's not hers, it's Steve. Oh, he's here, too. No wonder Destiny does whatever the hell she wants.

"Norm. Go home," Steve says.

"Steve. Long time, man."

"What don't you get?" he says, his arms crossed over his chest.

"What are you? The bouncer?" I hold my ground.

Steve lets his arms drop and gives his head a quick swipe under his ball cap. He looks up at the Orchard Apartments, where the argument has continued. "F'ing Christ, they never stop up there."

"Some things don't change, I guess."

162

"I guess. I don't remember seeing babies up there when we were kids."

I double his gaze at the window. "No. No, me neither."

"Just give her a week, Norm. Come back next weekend. Or go somewhere else, I don't care."

But, you do, I think. You certainly do. "I still have a beer on the bar."

"We'll save it for you. Put it in a glass case above the pool table."

"Wouldn't that mean I retired?"

"Everyone's got to hang it up sometime." He's smiling.

"Why do you put up with her shit?" That should take care of the smile.

"Christ, Norm, didn't we go through this last night? What more do you need to know?"

"Everything," I say.

Steve moves to push me again, but pulls back a bit, and just rests his palm against my chest. "Go home. Sober up. Go home to your dad."

"Dad's just fine. Stay the fuck out of it." He takes his hand away, and I stumble forward a step, not a great argument for me coming back in.

He smiles again. Fucker. "See? Let's all stay out of it, it'll be forgotten in a week and I'll buy you and your girlfriend a beer."

I stand, wondering if there's anything I should say about the girlfriend.

Finally, I say, "Goodnight, Steve. I'll take you up on that beer." I stick my hand out, he takes it.

"You got it, Norm. Hey…"

"What?" We're still shaking hands.

"Nikki. Be careful," he says.

I take my hand back.

"I'm fine. I thought we were all staying out of it?"

"We are, we are." He holds his hands up, surrendering.

"Good," I say. "Why?"

"So you don't end up bloody again, I guess."

"No, I mean, careful. Why be careful? With Nikki?"

"Not for her sake. Nothing. Forget it," he says.

"You can't do that."

"What do you know about her? That's all."

"Good night, Steve."

He raises a wave. "Next week."

The only reason I look back is to try to catch a glimpse of Nikki, but the windows are full of rowdy drinkers and I can't see the bar. The asphalt from the alley leads to the brick sidewalks of town, and I follow it over several crosswalks, intending to continue onto the cement sidewalks. Instead, I curve around the nearest buildings, my footsteps tracing a haphazard square back to The Lock-Up. Sherry is at the door now, checking IDs. She's deeply involved in an argument over why she can't let some kid in until midnight, even if it is real close until he's twenty-one. Even if he's been drinking all day.

Sherry spies me in mid-shout and pauses, her eyes follow me until I toss her a friendly wave, big smile, and cross the street. This time I don't look back. I keep walking, wishing I could just let Nikki know what happened, and where I went. I'm sure she'll hear about it. Sherry's not one to keep something like this quiet.

Things, circumstances and feelings, flip so quickly. Last night was only moments ago. I left the house, getting away from home, like years ago, trying to avoid the past, and I returned to it.

The buildings of town disappear beneath the low rising roads toward home. I daydream of Nikki being in my bed. Maybe she quit when she heard about the outrage of not letting me back in. She'll be there, naked.

At my front door, I rummage around in and pat my pockets. No keys. I breathe in and rub my eyes with my palms. One more pocket check. Nothing. I knock a tentative three beat. Two more, louder. Listen, there's nothing. Dammit, now I'm sure Dad is dead inside, crumpled at the bottom of the stairs. Flat on his recliner, his lungs full of vomit. If Mom were alive, she'd fucking kill me, letting him go like this. For all I know, they're both laughing at me right now. Sharing a spyglass, and sip of something real nice, whatever they'd serve up there, on the nighttime clouds. They laugh at my predicament. She knows that I could have performed better. He just enjoys my panic.

I knock ridiculously loudly now. Not even the sound of a TV inside. I walk around to the side door, the mudroom going into the kitchen. It's locked, no matter how hard I shake it. I'm still not out of options. I'm no stranger to breaking into this house after hours, even if it's been a while.

All the windows are dark as I move around to the deck. There's no way to get onto the deck from the yard without scaling the low railing on the side. Dad has always bitched about that, but it was too expensive to put on stairs back when he put on the deck. He always meant to get to it.

I grasp the thin posts of the deck fencing, pulling gently, then harder, to test their strength. They'll hold. I heft myself up, slipping my toes beneath the railing and practically fall back when I see Dad curled up in his deck chair.

"Jesus, you scared me," I say.

He doesn't move an inch, doesn't even stir. It's dark back here, and I throw my legs over the railing and catch my breath from the scare. I hold my hand flat against my chest in the same manner, I realize, as my mother used to when I did something to truly upset her. I pull my hand down.

"Dad?"

"Dad?"

He has his knees pulled up to his chest, childlike and young. He looks hurt. On the deck, under his chair, is a now empty bottle of whiskey, drained down between the slats. His chin is tucked into a wine glass, which still holds a cone of whiskey above the stem. I look down, still breathing hard. He's not going anywhere, and I brush some wisps of hair behind his ears. His breath is so ragged that I lean in to listen to his chest.

My face hits the wine glass. Working carefully, so as not to disturb him, I raise his head from the glass and hold it up to the weak starlight. It's the same one. There's still a lipstick mark on the rim, and I'm reminded of the old legendary maps, the Elvish Tolkien maps I used to read about, the ones you could only read under a certain moon, at a specific time of year. I sip softly from the remaining whiskey and strangely taste Dad's breath on the glass.

I shift his shoulders around, only producing a loud snore. He shifts in the chair; I go inside. Flipping every light on the way to the closet, I pull out the two heaviest blankets, the green wool ones with the black stripes on the ends, and turn back to the deck.

I tuck one blanket around Dad's body, wrapping him like a child, pushing it in under his chin and under his thighs, lifting his feet and tightening the blanket under his shoes. The other, I drape over myself, leaving my hand out to hold the wineglass. Sneaking one last sip, I rest my head on the white plastic frame of the chair and look up, seeking a constellation among the clouds, finding Orion's belt as every thing goes dark.

# Chapter Seventeen

Monday morning, slumped at my desk, I wonder if I'd ever gotten Nikki's number, or where she lived, or anything. Six more fifty-minute periods to go, and this place has the feeling of a sick bay. I swear every kid is hungover, every adult remorseful. The halls are quiet.

I expect at any moment to be ushered into the principal's office, where a crowd will already be waiting for me. The principal will angle her computer screen so everyone can gather around to watch a grainy cell phone video of me drinking in Destiny's kitchen. We'll watch in silence until it cuts to the painfully long scene of Sherry kicking at me until I stumble away. Bleeding. Appropriate measures will be discussed. Then taken.

This keeps not happening. When the routine morning nonsense of The Learning Center continues unabated, I thank Destiny by allowing her to sit at my desk rather than go to class.

She's tapping her rings on my desk. A tiny shirt squeezes the skin of her upper arms, her scowling little face almost as pale as her forced blonde hair. She appears to be waiting for a response. From me, I assume.

"What?" I say.

"God! You don't listen to me either!"

"Well, what?"

"Can I go home?" she says, tilting her head and forcing a smile.

"Why?"

"Cause I don't want to fucking be here."

"Neither do I. But I am."

"Why don't you just go home? You're a teacher."

I laugh into my hands, lean on my elbows. "It doesn't work that way."

"Whatever."

"Exactly," I say.

Yesterday was a slow, cold waking. I found myself alone on the deck, barely under a blanket and hardly into Sunday. I awoke again in bed, cocooned under the same blanket, slightly further into the morning. Dad was gone.

When he returned, I was back on the deck in the same clothes as the night before, and the day before that, wondering if I'd done all the right things. Dad dropped a couple paper-wrapped egg sandwiches and two extra large coffees on the small table. We watched the morning's condensation drip from the deck railing in silence. I folded back the plastic flap on my Styrofoam coffee and shrunk away from the heat.

"If she could see us now, huh?" he said.

"I know."

"I guess we don't have to worry about her walking in on us."

"I don't know. Maybe she'll come by for breakfast again."

He was quiet. Then, "I meant Mom."

"Right," I said.

Destiny goes back to tapping my desk, and I continue pretending that I don't know exactly where it is she's supposed to be. It's certainly not here.

"So," she says. "Your face looks all right."

"Thanks," I say, trying to avoid any acknowledgment of anything at all.

She snorts, blows some of that hair out of her eyes. "You know what I mean."

I avoid looking at her.

"My mom fucking hates you."

"You've mentioned that."

"Steve is sick of talking about it," Destiny says.

"I bet."

"Maybe you shouldn't have done it." She sits up very straight, scrunches her pointed eyebrows together. "It's important to think about the consequences of our actions prior to acting." She slumps back down. Her neck reaches across my desk, and I look away from her cleavage.

"Where'd you hear that?" I say.

"Every teacher ever."

"Ever?"

"Yep."

"Well, they're all right. Every single one ever."

"Fuck that. You guys don't know shit." She snorts again, louder, growing into this role of having one up on me. She leans forward to jab her finger into my desktop. "You all think you're so much better."

"I'm not any of your other teachers except me." I know it doesn't make any sense. But I leave it out there, hope it slips by her.

"What did you say?"

"Don't you have a class to go to?"

Destiny's head turns very slightly to her left. She looks as demure as devious when she says, "I don't have to do anything you tell me to."

Maybe a video viewing in the principal's office wouldn't be that bad. At least I would know where I stood when it was over. I say, "I guess nobody really has to do anything. But you know you have a class right now."

"So do you. Know I have a class, I mean."

"But it's your class," I say, sounding more like every other teacher ever, preaching responsibility with every breath. Anything I can do to deflect the conversation from me. "You're the one who needs to be there. I don't have anything to do with your responsibilities."

She looks so disgusted, just done with me. I see her lips move a few times before she speaks. "Then what the fuck do you do here?"

I don't know. "Help you figure out what you need to do. I guess."

"Uh!"

Destiny gathers her stuff, checking her phone before forcing it into a skintight pocket practically at her thigh, her pants are so low. I feign indifference to her outburst and our conversation. She huffs her way out, screaming that she may as well go to her fucking class. So, I guess I win, sort of. With only hours to go.

Every moment since Eric's entrance, I've feared fourth period. On this eternal Monday, when the whole school seems to have agreed to just get through this, I'm especially dreading it. Scared of what Iceguy and Manfire have in store for me.

A week ago today, Eric walked into The Learning Center and flashed the requisite paperwork. He asked me whose side I was on, Manfire's or

Iceguy's.

"I don't know. I've never seen that show," I replied, all smiling and welcoming.

"They're in here!" He stood on a chair and spread his chopped at bowl-cut hair to reveal pink scars crisscrossing his skull. Eric went on to compare and contrast the two: Iceguy makes him shit ice cream, and Manfire burns his hair off. Classroom loyalty to either side is split pretty much down the middle, with the only girl in the room abstaining.

Eric walks in wearing a Budweiser cap, which breaks two dress code rules at once. I ask him to take it off, which he does, revealing a shimmering bare scalp hacked at with a three blade razor. This surprises me, given their cost, but the dried blood in triple rows clearly reveals the damage was inflicted with a three blade.

"It looks like Manfire is winning," I say and realize that today no pretense of classroom control is going to control all three of him. I may still have a shot at that visit to the principal's office.

Class discussion turns to old cartoons. When Eric can't think how Jabberjaw the Shark's theme song went, he becomes more agitated than usual. I repeat "Jabberjaw" to a few different tunes until he starts poking Ollie hard in the arm. Ollie, who is amazed by Eric, starts laughing and poking him back. I'm tired. I reach over and kind of slap Eric's hand away.

His abandoned chair flies back into my knees. He's up and gone, into the hall, screaming, "You hit me!"

With a plea for silence to the half dozen delinquents in the room, I leave to chase Eric. The hallway is empty. I can't decide whether to be grateful, or if I desperately want another adult involved in this. At least to block an exit, create a diversion. We could catch him up in some sort of schizophrenic game of pickle, volleying pleas over his bloody head until we get close enough to grab him. But then what? I regret skipping out on my Crisis Prevention Intervention training.

I pick a hallway direction at random and hurry past classrooms, slowing my steps at their rectangle doorway windows. Coming around a corner, I see him by a side door. He's punching a fire alarm.

"Come back to class, Eric," I say.

"You hit me! I don't have to!"

"How about you just stop punching the fire alarm?"

"Manfire!" he says. "Iceguy!"

I don't know why the alarm didn't go off. He seems to be done punching it; maybe Iceguy's better nature has prevailed. This needs to stop before someone sees me battling a pudgy bald psychotic and his imaginary nemeses in the hallway and losing. I beg, knowing it's the wrong tactic.

"Please, Eric. Come back to class. We don't even have to work."

"Iceguy! Shit ice cream."

I take a few steps toward him; he squeals and makes a break for the exit. He's outside. We've entered a whole new level of bureaucracy, I think. My knowledge is a little hazy here, but I think this has become a police issue. The school resource officer is down the hall; by the time I could reach him, red-faced and panicky, stammering half-sentences about Jabberjaw the Shark and three blade razors, Eric might be long gone. Or worse, back in the building, roaming free. I wish Dad would pop around the corner, smile at seeing me, and use his old man authority to get this under control. We'd keep it hush-hush until he quietly scolded me over late night drinks and television.

I jog ten feet behind Eric through the door to catch a glimpse of him rounding the corner to the front of the school. I say his name, not even loud enough for him to hear. There are plenty of open windows up the walls of our building, and the last thing I want are rows of jeering teenage faces cheering Eric's prison break. I don't see him. Behind me, nothing. Sunshine. Clouds. Hedges. Then there he is, on the bike rack.

"Eric! Get off that bike, it's not yours!" Like that's the point. "Eric, let's get back to class."

He rocks back and forth on the bike. I feel momentarily hopeful; rocking is good, it's soothing. Babies rock. The closer I get, the more maniacal he appears, eyes wide with a white grip on the handlebars. I'm next to him, murmuring calming things, as he shakes the entire bike rack. I must look like an impatient parent unwilling to cough up another quarter for my demented little son's ride.

"Come on. Let's get back to class. They probably miss you."

"Iceguy. Manfire."

"I know. I'm sorry for hitting you. Can we get back to class? Please, they're all alone in there."

Eric is off, actively ignoring my pleas. He makes a break across the bus lane toward the parking lot without a glance for oncoming traffic. I need to wait for a short bus to rumble past before I can follow. He's not fast with his saggy belly and thick legs, but he's unpredictable, and crazy always wins. It's never the size of the fight in the crazy, it's the size of the crazy in the fight. Or something like that. Folksy wisdom doesn't seem to offer anything I can grasp and put to use at the moment. Eric is careening back toward the school.

175

Of the row of glass doors fronting the building, only the door at the far right is ever unlocked. Which is odd, as it makes it harder for students to enter the school. Eric starts at the wrong end and uses both hands to rattle and slam the doors on their hinges, frustration building, yelling nonsense or possibly genius insights into Iceguy's nature. I approach him from behind and reach out, thinking it may calm him. I touch his shoulders and say his name.

He throws a blind elbow back, jabbing me square on the cuts across my cheek. Eric goes right back to the doors, working his way to the one that actually opens. I cradle my jaw, try to get a handle on this. Eric's opened the door. He's back in the building. I'm bleeding slightly from the cheek.

In the front hall, there is a little glassed-in booth they call the kiosk. By policy, it's always manned, our supposed first defense against school shootings. Today it is empty. Even the oddly aggressive old lady who's always there is absent. Everyone is treating today as an extended weekend. I see Eric take the six steps up to the mezzanine in three leaps. At the top of those stairs, he'll be directly in front of the administrative offices. I follow, expecting him to veer down the only path available, the hall. But as I round the corner after the stairs, he's nowhere.

I turn to look back down the stairs, where he couldn't possibly be. Halfway through my turn, I see him. Eric is balanced on the edge of the mezzanine, a story and a half above the cafeteria. He's standing on the round metal railing they've installed. It runs along the top all the way around, like the copper railings at some bars.

He wavers dangerously, his arms above his head. His legs are unsteady, and his upper body is suddenly over the empty air, suddenly over the hallway floor between us. Eric stands, raised four feet above me, an easy twenty feet above the cafeteria floor. He's smiling, looking at something above his left eye. Both his hands perform slow circles, holding his precarious balance. His worn sneakers skitter on the smooth metal.

Only my stare holds him up. If I lean back, I think, I can ease him toward me. Just float him down to the tiled floor at my feet. I repeat the useless nothings you murmur at these times, and still the halls are empty. I envision his impossibly slow, slow fall back until just his toes show above the rail, then they don't, and I'll have to bring myself to finally look over that edge.

I take a few steps back and go silent. Eric totters. I feel the floor through my shoes, solid and immovable. I ask him to get down. He echoes, "Down," and cackles. One foot off the bar, he's held in place by some sort of psychic magnetism I take credit for, my stare holding him in place.

A voice full of swears comes from behind me and crackles through the connected air between Eric and me. I don't dare turn my head. Eric will drop the moment I do. The voice is up the stairs, close, to my left. "Eric! Get the fuck down! What are you going?" It's Destiny.

She's beside me, her cell phone, for the moment, a foot from her ear. This is when it will all happen. Everything.

Eric lifts himself lightly from the rail and is next to Destiny. In the hall. On the floor. Walking. Destiny's attention is back on her phone, and he talks at her, shiny head bobbing, arms drawing arcs in the air between them.

I deflate. Adrenaline pools in my shoes. I watch Eric, down the hall, pull his Budweiser hat from his back pocket and shake it into shape before covering his mangled head.

A toilet flushes and a door opens. Sullivan emerges clasping his belt just as they pass the bathroom door.

"Hey, Mister! Let's take that hat off in the hall. And Destiny, I need to see you! Now."

Sullivan looks at me leaning against the wall. It crosses his mind to shake his head in disgust. "We need to work together, Norm, if these kids are ever going to get it."

I say nothing. Eric shoves the hat back in to his pocket and continues talking circles around Destiny while she talks into her phone, completely ignoring Sullivan.

Sullivan checks me over and begins to speak, but decides against it. I've used up everything I have in the last, what, ten minutes? It feels like a day. I can't say a thing. Sullivan seems grateful to turn from me and cajole Destiny into his office.

# Chapter Eighteen

## Sherry

"You think I can just leave work and run over? That I'm not doing anything?" Sherry speaks into her phone and works a cherry up the side of her glass. "I'll be there when I can."

She clicks the phone shut and presses the smooth plastic to her cheek, looks up at the daytime talk show on one of the two TVs above the bar. A large woman, crying into a tissue, is being held in a comforting hug by the host, who speaks into his microphone. Sherry pops the cherry in her mouth and wonders what the hell that school wants with her this time. What more do they need from her? Destiny is at school. It's up to them after that. If they can't even handle six and a half hours, what do they expect from her?

She dredges another sip from the bottom of her glass, moving ice and one last cherry around with her straw. She looks at her phone, dares it to ring again. "Assholes," she mutters.

From a few stools down, a man says, "Who got the shit end of your stick?" He's dressed for work in tan boots, dirty jeans, and a paint-stained sweatshirt, but he was here before Sherry. She doubts much is getting painted this Monday afternoon.

She looks him over, deciding whether to even answer. Maybe she will. Maybe she'll let him take her home. She gives her head a little twitch, knocking her earrings against her neck.

"The fucking school. They want me to come get my kid."

"Fucking schools. Can't just do their job."

Sherry sucks through her straw until it makes noise. The man reaches over, right up to her lips, and pulls the straw out. The sudden pop then silence surprises Sherry, and she turns away. "Yeah. I gotta go. Roger!"

An ancient at the end of the bar glances over. He waves his arm vaguely toward her, eyes on a TV, his hand on a brown drink.

Sherry puts down a twenty and yells, "Keep it." She takes a couple steps, then turns back, until she is right beside the painter. Meeting his eyes, Sherry reaches two fingers into her mouth, holds them there a moment. When she removes them, shiny and wet, one has a cherry stem knotted around it like a ring. The man reaches over, slides it off her finger, and tosses it into his mouth, Sherry raises her eyebrows, impressed, and walks out.

In the car, Sherry throws her purse on the passenger seat, wrenches the rear view to her eyes, touches her hair and kisses together her lips. She breathes into her hand. Rummaging for gum in her purse, and finding her keys first, she says, "Fuck it," and cranks the car to running. She pulls out of Jimmy's gravel parking lot, around the grocery/video store/tanning parlor and is on Central, bumper to bumper.

The high school is on the other side of a busy downtown, people out for lunch or delivering things or whatever people do. She doesn't know. It gives her a minute to pull herself together. She exhales, turns up the radio, and absently sings along with Bruce Springsteen. She pats the outer limits of her hair, then smacks her rearview reflection away. Shit. Her horn sounds into the traffic. Steve is going to kill her; at least the school called her cell and not his. Maybe he will never know. Always saying she is too soft on the girl, that she'll end up pregnant and dropped out. Sherry always demanded to know just what that was supposed to mean, though she knew. It meant just that.

What the hell has happened this time? she wonders. All the same old teachers, handing out the same shit that had been handed to her. They all know whose kid Destiny is. They do. That's why she gets hassled all the time. Sherry is sure. Stupid fucking small town bullshit is what it is.

Pulling into the school parking lot, she feels the old everything all over again. Sherry stops the engine, straightens the mirror, and grabs her purse. Walking across the bus lane, she can make out the silhouette of gym teacher Sullivan, sorry, 'Dean of Students Sullivan', behind the glass door. Goddamit Destiny, she thinks.

Sherry lets Sullivan's handshake linger in the air until he lowers it along with his smile.

"Why don't we just step into my office, then?"

"Why don't we hear what this is about?"

Sullivan runs a hand from his forehead to his chin. He says, "I thought we'd let Destiny tell you herself."

"Is that what we thought?" she says under her breath, allowing Sullivan to lead her up the stairs. He directs her to his office as if she doesn't know where it is, like she didn't know it when a different man sat behind the desk.

Destiny is on her phone when they walk in. She gives Sherry a quick once over without breaking conversation, the only acknowledgment of their entrance. Destiny chats lightly into the small phone as she twists hair around a finger. "It's bullshit, right? Yeah. I know. Yeah, I gotta go.

She's here. Cool. I'll be at my house."

Sullivan indicates an old wooden chair for Sherry and sits in his high-backed padded one, green and bearing the school logo: an angry face on a wave holding a spear or something. He leans back, touches his fingertips together, and waits quietly.

Sherry adjusts herself in the chair and holds her purse on her lap, then puts it down. She picks it up again, holds it with both hands. She thinks to tell Destiny to put her goddam phone away, then looks at Sullivan, smug in his big chair, and says nothing. Sherry doesn't even look at her. Sullivan leans back, clears his throat.

"Why don't I start?" he says.

Destiny snorts. Snaps the phone shut. Sherry uncrosses her legs, rummages through her purse, pulls out some gum and hands a piece to Destiny, who grabs it from her hand, opens it, and tosses the wrapper. Sullivan looks at it on the floor, opens his mouth, closes it, and leans forward.

"Destiny. Would you like to say anything before I begin?"

She snaps her gum around, looking everywhere but him or her mom.

"Destiny!" Sherry says.

"What?"

"What the hell am I doing here leaving work? Wasting this man's time. What do you think everyone thinks?"

Destiny turns to the wall. "Yeah, right."

Sullivan leans away from them.

"Destiny!" Sherry says.

"What?!" She wipes the corners of her mouth. "Fine. Whatever. Me and Josh were fooling around."

"And?" Sherry says, flipping her hair back.

"And what? We were fooling around."

Sherry begins to gather her shit and stands. She says, "I'm sorry. I'm sorry, but why don't you people do your job and deal with this? A couple high school kids making out in the halls and I need to drag my ass down here? I'm sorry."

Sullivan stands and waves his hands. "Please, Mrs. Stone, let's calm down. Please, have a seat. Please."

She does, her denim stretching at the crossing and uncrossing of her legs. All the decorative key chains rattling on her purse.

"Please. Thank you. Now, Mrs. Stone, I think there's a little more Destiny needs to tell you." He sits down. "Destiny. Go on."

Destiny's phone clicks open, shut, open. She looks around the office. Sherry can't take any more of this bullshit. "Des! What? Tell me. What else do I have to listen to today?"

"We were fucking fooling around! Under the stairs. Everyone does."

"Were you skipping class again?"

Sullivan says, "That's part of the problem. But I don't think Destiny is being completely honest with us."

"No? Where's Josh? He goes back to class? It's always her fault?"

"Of course not. We take these situations very seriously on both sides. Mrs. Stone—"

"Fine. I was giving Josh a blowjob! All right? I was sucking his dick. That's why they're so pissed."

"Destiny Elliot! You watch your mouth!" Sherry stands, takes a step toward Destiny, who flinches. Sherry sits, thinking only that she doesn't want this to be happening. She feels her eyes building tears and sniffles back a sob. Sullivan reaches across his desk, grabbing the opposite side, as if he's pulling it closer. It's quiet except for Sherry's sniffing and Destiny's snapping gum. The repeated closing click of her phone.

"Mrs. Stone. Please, help yourself." Sullivan hands her a box of tissues.

"Thanks." Sherry wipes carefully under her eyes and blows her nose.

"We take these situations very seriously."

"No shit."

"Well, yeah." He laughs. "But I was saying, we understand these are teenagers, and at this time in their life, well..."

"They're sluts?"

"Mom! If Steve would let Josh stay over, I wouldn't even be suspended!"

"He never said you're suspended, Destiny. He never said that."

Destiny looks away, at a wall of photographs, all showing Sullivan with his arm around a student. Sherry hears her mumble something that sounds like, "Maybe if Steve got a blowjob."

Sherry leans to her, pointing. "Steve has nothing to do with this!"

Destiny mumbles in to her lap, pushing buttons on her phone.

"Alright, alright. I think we need to calm down. Destiny is correct, Mrs. Stone. She is being suspended."

"Great. More school gone."

"And she will have to go before the board for an expulsion hearing."

Sherry brings a handful of tissues to her face, leaning down to her lap. She glances up at Destiny, seeing only disgust on her face. Sherry doesn't want to tell Steve. She feels a tremendous guilt, though for what? She doesn't know. She doesn't want Steve to be right.

Leaving Sullivan's small office, they pass a closed door. Through the window, Sherry recognizes Josh's mom with her goddam Burberry plaid scarf and sunglasses resting on her blonde head. Sherry bangs on the door before Sullivan can usher her away. Josh's Mom turns, and Sherry sees running mascara and tissues.

At the main desk a secretary delivers all the details for the expulsion hearing: date, time, who is allowed to be there. Destiny ignores everything. Sherry stuffs all the papers into her purse in silence. She grabs Destiny's arm and begins to walk out when the office door swings open.

"Hey, Sher, what are you doing here?"

Great, Sherry thinks, turning to look for Destiny, whose arm she still has clenched, it's Norm Mean. Sherry eyes the cuts on his face with something like pride. He looks like hell.

"Norm. We were just leaving."

"Destiny in trouble?"

Sherry can't believe this shit. "No. She made the goddam honor roll."

"Congratulations, Destiny. I'm sure you worked really hard."

Destiny snorts, looks past him into the hall. It's packed with kids switching classes.

"Nice talking to you, Norm. But we have some mother-daughter talking to do."

"No one better than you."

"How's your face feel?"

"Tell Steve I said hi. We should all get together again some time," Norm says, and Sherry can't tell if he's joking.

She yanks Destiny's arm, and they enter the pack of high school kids, all of them looking at her, knowing something happened. Parents aren't ever at the high school for anything good. As Sherry turns her body to angle through the crowd, she sees Destiny turn and give Norm a wink. Sherry pulls Destiny's arm hard enough to make her stumble. Destiny says hi to somebody, and they're out the glass doors, straight to the car, where they will drive directly home.

# Chapter Nineteen

"So when are you going to stop moping and call her, Norm?" Dad says from his chair.

"Why would I call her Norm? Her name's Nikki."

"You're at your funniest when you mope. I guess it's working for you."

I've gained control of the remote this week, and I change the channel.

"Yep," I say.

"Yep," he mimics. "I'm getting another one. You in?"

I'm only half empty, but I agree to a top-off. He talks to me from the kitchen, his head in the fridge, laying out dinner options from our meager selection. No combination of the condiments we have available sounds appetizing. He says he's going to order pizza, which works fine for me. I nod my acceptance, assuming that with or without hearing my confirmation, he'll go ahead and do it anyway. Which is also fine.

I hear drawers sliding open and shut, papers rustling and muffled phone conversation. There's nothing of interest on TV. I haven't even called her yet. Nor have I been back to the bar. Maybe I've taken Steve's invitation about returning in a week to heart. It could have been a warning. I know I don't want to bump into Sherry after hearing the lurid details of Destiny's 'incident' at school. Why I was such a prick to Sherry in school yesterday is certainly on my mind. Though, at this point, an apology is not.

"Pizza will be here in an hour!" Dad announces, and plops down on his recliner with ice clinking drinks in each hand. He sniffs them both and hands one to me. I motion for him to put it on the table.

"An hour? On a Tuesday night?"

"I guess they're busy." He bends, balancing his drink, and takes the remote from my hand.

"I thought it was half hour or less or free," I say.

"They stopped doing that years ago, jeez. Some kid got ran over or something."

"That sucks."

"I'm hungry, too."

"I meant the kid that got ran over," I say.

"I know, son, I know. You're going to love the service from this place. Best in town."

On the screen a couple reaches for each other. Then a man sits behind a well-lit desk. Then a soldier dies. I watch each two second selection with equal interest and drink my whiskey, waiting for the feel of ice cubes against my front teeth to know when to stop. In a while Dad gets up and returns with a different shirt, which I think is odd, but I ignore it, assume he's slipping into some sort of earlyish onset senility. Nothing I want to deal with tonight.

I don't think anyone got blowjobs under the stairs when I was in school, not that I knew about anyway. I would not have said no to the offer back then. I don't know if any high school boy worth his hormones could. Consequences would not have been on my mind in the slightest.

The whole school knows about it. It was tough, or maybe merely awkward, talking to the other kids about Destiny and the blowjob situation. There was lots of "what's wrong with her" and "what a slut" talk, mostly coming from these boys who would fall over themselves at the opportunity for a real live blowjob. After useless attempts at pointing out that we should mind our own business and just possibly take the test in front of us, I cut to the chase. "Like you guys wouldn't have done it." They fell back, claiming to disagree with me. At least their embarrassment at the proposition quieted them for a good chunk of a period.

Dad checks his watch again.

"They said an hour," I say.

"Just hungry," he says, checking his watch again and laughing.

The doorbell rings, and Dad begins a leap from his chair, but sits quickly back down. "You want to get that?"

There's no reason why I would, but I get up anyway, bringing my drink with me. At the door I grab Dad's wallet from the little bowl and take out a twenty. That's what he gets for being too lazy to get the door.

It takes me a moment to realize that it is Nikki holding the pizzas on the front step. She's wearing a ball cap with her hair hanging loose over an unbuttoned flannel that can't be keeping her very warm; her cleavage rises nicely from above the pizza boxes. She must see me looking.

"When you work on tips, you know how it is." She cocks her hips in a quick modeling pose, then says, "Can I come in? Or do you just want the pizza? Cause I already paid for it."

"No, I think I'll take the delivery girl, too. No wonder this is the

189

most popular pizza in town."

"Can I come in? It's not summer anymore, you know."

I move aside, knowing this was Dad's doing, but also realizing Nikki's complicity and feeling good about that. I trade my drink to Nikki for the two boxes as she squeezes past. I stare the whole time, barely making way for her. Dad is here, beside me, hugging Nikki hello. They greet each other and chit chat for a moment, sipping from their drinks, before turning to me. She is a head shorter, leaning against his shoulder. He's standing straighter than I've seen in a month.

"This is a nice surprise. For me. It doesn't seem like anyone else is surprised."

"Norman," Dad says. "Let's just have a nice night."

"Yeah, Norman, fucking lighten up."

"It seems like you two have been doing a lot of talking." I attempt to remove any hint of a tone from my voice, because I'm not mad. In fact I think the tone I'm trying to hide is giggly school boy nervousness. "That's nice."

Nikki and Dad look at each other and laugh. She says to him, "You were right!"

"I know, look at him!"

I blush and bring the pizzas to the kitchen. Dad returns to his recliner and settles in, thereby announcing that we'll be eating in front of the television tonight. He's in that chair so often, I expect to see his reflection hiding behind everything on the TV's screen.

At the stove, Nikki's arms wrap around me from behind. I cover her hands with mine.

"I like your shirt," I say.

"This old thing? I like your Dad."

"That old thing?"

"Be nice." She whispers in my ear before giving it a quick bite. That drives me wild. Always has.

Nikki helps me gather plates, napkins and fresh drinks. The talk is light, unassuming, as if this happens every night. Nikki takes a cross-legged seat on the couch, Mom's seat, and dangles a slice of pizza before biting off the end, catching the falling cheese with a napkin. She looks up to see who saw that, and I smile at her. We all eat.

Dad tosses the remote to Nikki who tosses it to me. I throw it back to Dad. With a grumble, he settles on some murder mystery comedy action thriller. It's fine, I'm not paying attention to it anyway.

I lean forward and say, "How'd you get her number?"

"A little technique left from my bachelor days."

"I'm in the phone book, Norm," Nikki says. I can't believe that never occurred to me.

Dad asks his usual roundabout series of questions about the actors on TV, all in search of another actor's name. Nikki turns out to be his saving grace; she knows every name he's looking for. Every time she comes up with one, Dad tips his glass towards me and shakes his head.

After the pizza, after the movie, Dad announces that he's an old man who has to work in the morning and stands. Nikki rises with him. On her way to give him a hug, she stops. Her eyes flutter and she reaches to her neck, touching the spot behind her ear again, her other hand to her chest. She looks about to faint, and I half stand as Dad puts his hand on her back. He asks if she's all right, and she doesn't answer right away. When she sits back down, her face returns to us, looking sheepish, but flushed, aglow, her eyes bright and moving, focused directly on us.

She over apologizes, and assures Dad that she's fine, and waves me to sit down. Then Dad's gone, and we're sitting across the couch from each other. It feels like junior high, parents gone to bed, and, hey, there's plenty of room on that couch. I make my move and rise so I can sit next to her.

With one hand on her shoulder and one on her knee, I ask if she's sure she's all right and say I could drive her home or anything. She says, "Actually, everything is great now, even clearer." And she kisses me, great deep, searching kisses, right on the old couch. We fumble and move our plates to the floor to free up couch space, and after some initial adjusting and whispering, apologies at pulled hair and squirming out of jeans, everything goes very smoothly.

Nikki's body is tiny beneath mine. The other morning I was too busy appreciating sex to appreciate Nikki. I feel inexperienced above her. She moves smoothly, and I just move until her eyes open, her hands hard on my back. Then we smile and I allow my weight to fall on her.

Afterward, I walk naked through the house to get the same blankets Dad and I slept under on the deck just days ago. Before returning to the couch, I run upstairs to grab a pillow from my bed. Back down the hall, arms full, but just as naked, I hear the toilet flush, the water run, and Dad steps out into the hall, at the top of the stairs, naked as me. We appraise each other briefly. He covers his eyes.

"I don't see a thing."

"Goodnight, Dad."

"Goodnight."

I remain there, trying to get the words out as he closes the door to his room. I hear his TV come on. "Thank you," I say to the blankets and empty hallway.

Nikki is also naked, eating pizza on the couch. I laugh when I drop the blankets next to her, and take a seat and a slice. We eat in silence, smiling through bites. I blanket our laps when we're done. She pulls the top of the blanket up, to cover her chest, and I pull it back down. She gives me a look, but lets it be.

"Norm," she says, bringing my attention back to her face. "Do you believe in accidents?"

"Oh sure, I've seen them. They're real."

"That's not what I mean," she whispers. Then louder, "Let me try this, then. Do you believe in coincidences?"

"Like, do I think they happen? Or that they're not really coincidences?"

"Like they're not really coincidences."

"Well, if I agreed to that, then wouldn't that mean I don't believe in coincidences?"

"You're such a pain in the ass." She leans back against the couch, pulling the blanket over her, and I let it be this time.

"Okay. I guess I believe that sometimes things are meant to happen."

She leans forward, though she clutches the blanket to herself. "Right! That's what I mean, but is it every time? Is everything that happens meant to?"

"You're asking if we have any control over our own lives." I'm not sure I like where this is going, Steve's jab at Nikki the other night rings in my head. What if she's about to announce a life long love for me? I

193

barely know her.

"Maybe I am. Do we?" she says.

"Have control over our lives? Christ, I'd like to think so. Nothing is set in stone and we certainly don't have control over anybody else."

"But we have influence? Right? Can't you influence kids in your class?"

"I can't even get them to be quiet." I pause, feeling the rough wool against my skin. "Are you trying to get me to do something? Just say it, how strange could it be?"

"You have no idea."

"Come on, tell me, I'm a man of the world. I've seen things."

She laughs, letting the blanket drop all the way to the floor. "Shit. You have no idea what I've seen."

Then she pushes my shoulders down until I'm flat, and she kneels beautifully above me, her hair in my face, the smooth, soft opposite of the couch beneath me. She hangs her head low, moving slowly back and forth, thoughtfully pulling her hair across my face, my chest, my stomach. I feel the muscles in her arms moving to balance her weight.

I say, "Like what? What have you seen?" Then I stop caring.

# Chapter Twenty

I'm taking a cue from the ladies today and decorating my desk. They all have cheerily framed photos and inspirational posters on their walls, every surface covered with what they view as quirky, fun things for the kids to fidget with while bitching. My desk has been covered with nothing but paper scraps and incomplete to-do lists, the green walls bare and cracked behind me. This morning, after waking up on the couch with Nikki, everything seemed too dull at school to even show up. So when Dad was coasting through coffee and toast, I went searching through my room and the basement.

Ollie was kicked out of class immediately this morning. He's kneeling in the pile beside my desk, searching through old family boxes and plastic grocery bags filled with stuff, adding his personal touch. I figure he spends nearly as much time here as me, so he should get a say.

"What's this?" he asks, a record sleeve in one hand and a photograph in the other.

"Which one?"

"The square one."

I assume that he's talking about the larger square. "That's a record, Ollie. You've never seen one?"

"You mean like what DJs use?"

"Yeah. That used to be how people listened to music."

"What do you mean? On this fucking thing? That's queer."

"Yeah?" I say, hanging up an old poster I had taken down from my bedroom wall when I was in junior high. It's a huge photograph of an astronaut on the moon with the Earth in the background. "Why's that?"

"Cause it's so fucking big. You can't take it anywhere."

"Well, it didn't really matter, you had to play it on a record player, like at someone's house."

"What'd you do in the car?"

"I don't know, listened to the radio, I guess. Talked."

He bends it back and forth, so it wobbles, faster, until we hear the crack of the record in the middle.

"Shit," he says. "It's broken."

"You broke it, man, it wasn't broken before."

"Before what? This thing sucks."

"Just put it down and pass me some of those thumbtacks in my desk."

He drops the record and hops into my chair. My neck is craned down at him as I hold up the top half of the poster with the palms of my hand. Ollie yanks on the drawer, rattling the whole desk. When it doesn't open immediately, he begins a flurry of yanking, crashing, and swearing. It turns the heads of the few students assigned to be here and their deeply concerned paraprofessionals who are only trying to help. Really, they just want these kids to succeed, and, well, with all this noise...I try to instruct Ollie that he has to open one of the side drawers and then open the middle one, but it's tricky over the sound of his crashing struggle, with my back to him and trying to hold up the poster.

"It's fucking stuck!"

"Ollie, Ollie! Just open that other drawer and then open that one!"

"I can't! It's stuck!"

"Come on, just listen for a second, open the side drawer first."

He crawls across the floor to the side of the desk, where clearly, there are no drawers.

"There's no fucking drawer here! You don't know what you're talking about!"

"No! Not there, on the front."

"You said the side!"

"Not that side! The front."

"Wait, I figured it out. It's stuck."

I mutter, "No shit," and try to turn, so my back can hold the poster while I do the drawer trick. All pretense of work in the rest of the room has ceased. Every eye is on this debacle. There are even some signs of movement from behind Deidre's lace-curtained office door. Dammit. I bend over, the poster draping my back, and try to work the drawers. It still won't open, even with the side drawer. I try a few more times, slamming things around myself.

"Oh, I got it. Shit," Ollie says from the floor and skitters beneath my desk to mess with the sliders on the drawer.

"Ollie! Get out from under there! I got it!" No I don't, but I don't want anyone to see him crawling around like an animal.

"Stop fucking slamming it around! I got it!" Ollie says, his little voice muffled from under the desk.

Deidre's curtains slide aside. Oh, man. And today was going to be a great day. A little shooting the shit with the kids, a little decorating. Some reinvigoration.

I try to alternate pulling the middle drawer open while simultaneously slamming the side one shut. Nothing but noise.

"You almost cut my goddam finger off! Stop it!"

"Get out of there! Will you please get up here?" I say.

"I can do it!"

"Dammit, Ollie."

Deidre's door creeps open. She's afraid to actually make an entrance and simply ask what the hell I'm doing.

"Ollie, just crawl out. I'll figure it out later." Then, in a forced whisper, "Ollie, get the hell out here. Now."

"I almost got it."

The paraprofessionals are staring. The kids don't know if they can laugh. One of the nice ones is ambling over to offer her assistance, and I can't tell her to sit back down without sounding like a complete asshole.

I kick my rolling chair out of the way to get at the drawer better. Ollie is working something under the desk, keeping a constant river of swears flowing. Deidre appears in her doorway, a question on her face. I look at her, the poster hanging over my forehead.

"Hello." I smile at her. "Drawer's stuck."

"I see." One of her hands massages the other.

Ollie must have successfully worked something free. When I try one final attempt at the old side drawer slam, middle drawer yank it, comes smashing into my crotch, doubling me over so I hit my forehead off the edge of the desk, and end up crouched, looking at Ollie. Who is triumphantly grinning under my desk.

"I got it," he says.

This is all too much for Deidre, and after a quick glance around the room to make sure there is someone else who is surely going to handle this situation, she retreats behind her lace barricade. I can half stand, but after that blow I need to bend. I'm fighting a natural urge, for fear of appearing unseemly, to cradle my nuts.

Ollie scrabbles out to sit in the rolling chair and performs a spin. "Yes! I got it!"

"You certainly did," I say.

"Break them out!"

I have only bad ideas about what Ollie's asking me to break out. "What?"

"The thumbtacks. Break 'em out!"

Right. I'd forgotten that what's what we were looking for. A few deep inhales, and I can stand upright again. I pick out two red thumbtacks and hang the poster, stepping back to admire it.

"That's gay."

"Thanks, Ollie. For everything."

"No problem."

He turns his attention back to the box o' stuff and pulls out a few framed photographs. One is my graduation picture. I look uncomfortable, stoned, and awkward. When I threw it in the crate of potential decorations, I thought it would be a funny thing to have on my desk, now, though, I can't imagine having to look at that version of myself everyday. It probably wouldn't be healthy for the children, either. Ollie tosses it on my desk, wondering who that guy is, and that hurts a little bit. The next photograph is the one Dad stole. Ollie holds it out at the end of his arms. Fitzy and I smile back at him. It gets tossed on top of my graduation photo. Number one, our fingers proclaim. I pick it up and sit on top of my desk, facing the astronaut and his moon.

That would've been our sophomore year. We both made varsity and were introduced to the world of the fake ID. I don't think I've even held a stick since high school. Suddenly it seems as if it would be fun again, and I try to picture where in the house my old gear would be. Maybe I sold it in the spirit of dedication to my new life, one that certainly didn't involve Lacrosse practice or running around or punishment for laziness.

Watching Ollie, his smallness exaggerated by baggy clothes, it occurs to me how we are formed by a series of small decisions. Ollie is oblivious to this, I know, and he may remain so. The thought of that raises a deep pity and sadness. I wonder what he will look back on with happiness or regret and if he will ever recognize his role in either.

Nikki asked about my theory concerning coincidence, and I blew it off with attempts to see her naked. Now, watching the Earth rise over the moon, it occurs to me that there may be only two possible answers to her questions. Yes, there are coincidences, and everything in this world is a huge tangled web of them, overlaid on top of each other in invisible infinite layers, forming unbreakable sheets in which every thread crosses another. Or, no. Just no. How in this unfathomably complicated universe can one thing have to do with another? How can whatever is in charge (and if there is something in control, wouldn't that negate the entire question?) possibly give each of us the individual attention that such coincidences would require? The paperwork alone would be crushing.

I imagine all the people on the blue planet before me as red dots, individual and separate, some babies and lucky children with 360 degrees of options moving around, dropping a degree with each decision. Every accident and incident eating away at their circle until they're a single red line from their start to finish. These lines follow them, splitting at their feet into arcs until they have used every option possible. Red stripes continue to their endpoint, everyone's lines intersecting in infinite latitudes and longitudes.

I want to remember to ask Nikki if this is what she was talking about. Or the exact opposite.

# Chapter Twenty-One

## Steve

"Sherry, I don't see why we both need to be there tonight," Steve says.

Sherry is watching herself in the small hallway mirror; she lifts twists of wild hair from one side of her head to the other. Steve rests his hands on Sherry's shoulders, watches himself squeeze them and move up her neck. She straightens, and for a moment Steve thinks her body is pushing into his. He can feel her shoulder blades against his chest, her ass in the middle of his thighs, but she's only backing away from the mirror, looking at more of herself. She pulls her hair down, and presses it to her shoulders, making sure it's even. Steve lets go of her, saying again, "I don't see why we both need to be there tonight."

"Because they need the help, it's fucking Friday night," Sherry says, turning her reflection side to side. "And because Timmy doesn't know what he's doing."

"He's your brother, Sher, and the place is doing fine. It's busy every night."

"That," Sherry says, turning to face Steve, "is exactly why we both need to be there."

Sherry is already patting her pockets for keys, but pauses and puts her hands on Steve's cheeks, gently roughing him up and smiling at him.

"Thank you for helping us out at the bar. I appreciate it."

Steve feels his face warm beneath her hands, his little beard hairs standing on end. He wraps his dangling arms around her and realizes that he's given in, that she has just won. He smiles at her tenderness and accepts his loss. Again.

He says to the top of her head. "You're welcome." When she removes her hands and turns away, he says, "What about Destiny?"

"What about her?"

"Should she be home alone? I thought she was grounded."

"She is. She said she'd stay in all night."

"I'm just saying, you know, shouldn't one of us be here?"

Now Sherry stands just beyond an arm's length from him. "You mean me. You mean I should stay home, again, to watch her."

"It's just, I think one of us should."

"Well, we have to work, she's going to have to deal with it. She's a big girl, Steve."

"It's not that I think she'll miss us." Steve tries out a laugh. "You know? Besides, it's not like we're getting paid."

"She's a big girl, she can stay home alone, Steve. I can handle her."

Steve knows that's not true, and this is exactly the issue he's skirting around: She can not handle this. No, it's not that she can't handle it, she just won't. He knows it, and Destiny definitely knows it.

"I know you can, okay?" he says.

"Okay." She has her hands on her hips, head cocked.

Steve exhales, and worries the line where his beard meets his mouth, wishing he had kept it shut, but knowing it's going to open again. Because he's right.

"We fucking grounded her," he says.

"Yeah?"

"And now she's going to do whatever she fucking wants."

Sherry offers nothing.

"That's all." He turns to pull his keys off the hook. "I'll drive."

Sherry yanks her keys free from her purse. "Me too."

"F'ing Christ, Sherry, what do you want me to do here?"

"I'm not going to be like my father. I'm not going to do that to her."

"Sher, that's not what I meant."

"I'll see you at work." The door closes behind her, and he hears Destiny's phone go off, playing some song, probably about blowjobs. Destiny's laugh mixes with the sound of Sherry revving out of the driveway. He can hear the big car round the cul-de-sac and roar past the houses, all of them quietly lit. Steve listens to Destiny make plans for the night; each snicker yanks a small piece of caring from him.

He takes the long way through the house, thinking to give Des the common courtesy of a goodbye, maybe an estimated time of return. Maybe a reminder that she is not to go anywhere or have anybody over. She has the phone stuck against her shoulder, her hands busy opening a frozen cheesy something to put in the microwave. Steve doesn't even know where she gets that shit; he does the shopping and makes a point of buying ingredients for meals, not the meals themselves. But when he comes home from work, Sherry and Destiny are always eating something recently unfrozen in front of the TV. He waits until she looks up at him, still talking into the phone.

Steve waves his arms in front of her face, smiling, to get her attention for moment. She says, "Hold on," into the phone and slightly tilts her face toward him. "What?"

"I'm leaving, your mom had to be there early, so she left."

"Yep." She moves around, pushes buttons on the microwave.

"We'll be back late."

"Uh-huh."

"Remember, no going out or having friends over."

"Whatever."

"Your mom and I are serious about this."

"I said I know."

"No, you didn't. You said, 'whatever.'"

"Whatever."

"See?" Steve smiles at her again and is about to say something else about how he can pick up a movie for her or something before he goes to The Lock Up. She's still talking into her phone, making plans. Steve watches until she raises her hands and scrinches her face up at him. The thought, "this isn't my fucking problem" passes through his mind, and he goes out through the deck door to find Lacey panting at his feet.

"Hey, girl." He rubs her head as she slaps her tail against the deck and pushes into his leg. "How long you been out here? At least one of you ladies is happy to see me."

He moves aside and Lacey runs in. Steve shouts through the opening for Destiny to feed Lacey. The door closes, and he is in the early dark silence of fall. All the lawn lights are off, as he likes it; they're always leaving them on, uselessly illuminating the night. Steve looks out over his large yard, the slow slide down to the pond, circled with leaf-covered pavement. Before last weekend he never would have looked for any life out there, but now he scans the pond's edge for Norm Mean, or anything. He thinks of last weekend's debacle, remembering Norm appearing like swamp thing.

The pond is silent. The peepers apparently have grown to frogs, now hibernating or something, he doesn't know. But that sounds like a reasonable explanation for this silence. Steve doesn't know a lot about what goes on directly outside his house, or, he's beginning to realize, inside, but he feels there may be some connection. Before Norm's return, he truthfully hadn't given more than a moment's thought to the pond, beyond its simple presence. But lately he's felt it out there. Out here. He senses it as much as sees it tonight.

The pond rests, its surface broken only by whatever small creatures still inhabit it in tonight's chill. Fallen leaves spread undisturbed from the lawn to the water and gather at the edge like a lifted skirt, exposing a center. Steve feels a foreboding as he walks down the twisting levels of stairs to the yard. He can see his breath and hear Lacey bark inside. Destiny better feed her. But she won't, he knows that. And he's not going to do a thing about this, beside let it stew in him all night.

Steve doesn't mind the actual work at The Lock Up, but he doesn't like having to do it. The work itself is actually kind of fun, a reminder of the rest of the world, the one outside his office and home. Ever since he got the promotion to the office at the distributors, he's missed the driving around from bar to bar, dropping off kegs and taking orders for new ones, having a beer with the regular clients. He loved running up ridiculous tabs during the beer promos. Now he just speaks to bar owners on the phone, every once in a while keeping a promise to meet up with them for a beer.

Sherry had been working in the office when he met her, that's how he got the job. It's also, he fears, how he got the promotion. Her family built these houses. It's an underlying theme; how is he beholden to her today? He's sure she keeps a checklist in her closet or her side of the bathroom, someplace he's not supposed to look. If only, he felt, if only she'd give him a little something back, more than a passing softness or momentary bedtime comfort, then it wouldn't matter to him at all. Steve's never felt he had to be the man in charge who did everything, who provided the paycheck for the family and treated it like a mammoth he'd speared. Would a little kindness, a little camaraderie in all this hurt?

Well shit, he thinks, looking at the pond. Maybe Norm's right. Maybe there was something greater here before all this pavement, before the concrete foundations were set. Being here could be a disservice. To what, exactly, Steve isn't sure. If this is a disservice, then there must be somebody pissed off about the whole thing. Somebody more than Norm, who is just generally pissed off. and focuses it here, on the pond. And thereby on Steve. And his house, and his wife. Well, maybe he's right on with that one, but the rest of it—Norm just feels guilty over Fitzy. And maybe he should, Steve's always felt that Norm was complicit somehow. More than the rest of them, himself included, who were there that night. Only Fitzy and Norm were awake. Then Norm's shouting, much too late, woke them all. He'd been so drunk.

This last line of thought reminds Steve of where he should be—at The Lock Up with its vainglorious hordes, vying for drinks and physical contact. His house behind him, Steve crunches leaves under his feet. They extend over the water's surface, and he imagines he could just keep walking over them, that the pond would hold him. Steve gazes at a surface that holds no reflection, watching for movement as if it's a screen, as if the images of his thoughts could play out before his eyes.

Steve envisions a healthy Norm walking from the muck, carrying Fitzy like a sleeping princess, waking him with a sacred sip from a rusty can, the fateful last one before that midnight swim. A swim Steve had completed countless times. Maybe they would walk dripping through the house, escorting out Sherry, Destiny, and the dog. Each carrying the end of a couch, a fridge, a small suitcase, until the whole house was emptied into the street. Would they all stand together and watch as the water swelled to contain the yard? Staring as it seeped under the door frames, finally pouring through the windows, the sunroofs, until it ceded, running in rivulets Steve could block with his boots, back into its natural state? Erased, all of it erased, returned to its original being.

# Chapter Twenty-Two

He's laughing as we round onto our street. After all these years, Dad has memorized each spin of the steering wheel, and barely needs to watch the road. Today we stopped for smokes on the way home from school, deciding that this Friday called for self indulgence. Neither of us wanted to feel as if we were lacking anything. The unfamiliar grip of holding a cigarette in one of his driving hands may have thrown off his steering a bit. Maybe I'm not paying attention either, but we come within millimeters of hitting Nikki's car in our driveway.

"We have a visitor!" Dad announces, and forgets to undo his seat belt in his rush to exit. He's barely embarrassed as he fumbles himself free, just anxious to greet Nikki. I wonder which one of us is more infatuated. I gather up my bag and the smokes and lighter, not hurrying, allowing Dad his greeting, knowing Nikki's welcome will make him happy. There are things I want to tell her, small things that happened today, and the realization of that is nice.

She smiles at me over Dad's shoulder. Her black hair is stuck in Dad's beard, pulled across her face. He's talking about a real dinner or just pizza, or maybe even taking us all out, it was payday after all, but first we should all go in for drinks, right? Nikki agrees, saying she has to be at work in a bit, but, sure, Blake, a drink would be great. She winks back at me as Dad escorts her into the house. He stops momentarily at the front door, after ushering Nikki in, to surreptitiously stomp out his cigarette.

Nikki and Dad retire to the living room; she takes what has become her regular seat on the couch. She looks comfortable there, in her sneakers and work shirt, her eyes done up. Dad is in his recliner, shifting himself around until he's settled on the old cushion. It's assumed, I guess, that drink responsibilities fall on me. I drop my stuff by the door, leaning back briefly to toss a butt onto the walkway, the closing door sucks in a last puff of smoke.

The windows are already darkening, making this immediate drink upon entering seem acceptable. I crack the cubes from their trays. The whiskey warms them. Ice cubes snap and pop in the glasses I balance into the living room. Dad and Nikki each accept their drinks with thanks, but with little break in conversation. I'm not sure where to jump in, they seem so comfortable and engrossed. I take my seat on the couch next to Nikki. She rests her hand on my thigh, chuckling at one of Dad's witticisms. I watch her hand. Her fingers arch and stretch, the tips absently rubbing. I hold her by the palm, allow her fingers to continue.

After moments of feeling left out, I decide to just sit back and enjoy the bumps on Nikki's spine with my fingertips as she talks. I'm not even listening and soon my hand is working itself under the back of her shirt, counting vertebrae and dropping occasionally to the very split of her ass under the rim of her jeans.

I'm not sure whether she thinks this is annoying or playful, and I'm not sure I care. Their talk has gone on for a full drink now. Finally Dad rises to change into his sitting-in-front-of-the-TV clothes, khakis that are more worn and a differently frayed plaid shirt. Apparently the offer of dinner out has expired. The moment he leaves the room Nikki throws a leg over my lap, and we're kissing, one of my hands feeling the silk weight of her breasts in her bra and the other balancing my drink. Both of Nikki's hands hold my face.

When we part, she smiles. "Hey. How was your day?"

"Educational."

"I wish I could say the same."

"I was thinking about you. Today, I mean, I thought about you a lot."

She leans back on my lap, away from me, and we hear noises coming down the stairs. She swings herself back to her seat, smoothly lifting her whiskey from the carpet.

Dad flops himself back into his chair. "So, what did you do today, Nicole?"

"Ran some errands. Tried to figure some stuff out."

"Trying to figure things out." Dad nods into his drink. "Is there a more noble way to spend your time?"

Nikki looks at me like she won. "Blake, I can't even figure out what it is I'm trying to figure out."

That cracks him up, and he points at me with his drinking hand. "That is the wisest thing I've heard all day."

Nikki offers to pour another round for me and Dad, for practice, she says, before she goes to work. I'm barely through my first, but Dad takes her up. He's quiet, seeming disappointed in her leaving, and searches through ice cubes and channels. Nikki and I walk out to her car.

"Can I kick the tires?" I say.

"Shut up. It's nicer than yours."

"What do I need a car for?"

"Because you're a grown up."

"Maybe," I say. I put an arm on either side of her, pinning her against the driver's door.

"Yeah, maybe. Listen. Don't come by work tonight." She's looking down.

"Why not? You think there's something here I might miss?"

"Don't make fun of him, Norm."

"What? I just wanted to come see you, that's all."

"That's why I came by." She hangs her hands from my shirt collar. "But it wouldn't be good for you to come by tonight. Sherry's going to be there. It's going to be wicked busy anyway, the weekend before Thanksgiving. Everyone rehearsing for reunion night."

"Sherry still hate me?"

Nikki laughs.

"Yeah?" I say.

She drops her hands, clearly uncomfortable with this, or with something.

"What's up?" I say.

"Just what I said."

"Okay," I say, not believing her. "Stay here tonight. After work."

"Yeah? Is that okay?"

"With me or him?" I say.

"Either. Both."

"We're both okay with anything."

"Can I use your toothbrush?"

"I don't think we know each other well enough for that."

"Your loss." She smiles. "You're the one kissing me."

"Not yet," I say and prove that wrong until she pushes me away. Nikki has to go, and I watch her car grow smaller. It turns at the stop sign and disappears. Standing at the edge of the pavement, I urge the sun further around the Earth, the stars to appear and solidify, and for her car to drive right back around that corner.

# Chapter Twenty-Three

## Nikki

Nikki smokes through town with every window down. The cold winds push in from all sides and swirl the smoke, center it over the dashboard; it clears her head of Blake's whiskey, but not of the vision. That always lurks behind every other thought. She doesn't know where her responsibilities lie. Does she control this future? Her role, is it to ensure that this scene of water and disaster happens? She's always assumed so.

Is she playing coy, keeping Norm wanting her? Or does she really think he should stay away tonight for his own good? Wouldn't that mean she genuinely wants him to keep wanting her? All these years of seeking answers, and she just pushed her one clue away. Nikki lights another smoke off the butt of the last, hoping for a little traffic to allow time for another after this one. At a red light she looks in the windows of the cars around her, making assumptions about the people behind the wheels. That woman is furious, and doesn't even know it. The way she's staring suggests an unfulfilled obsession. That man adjusting his hands on the wheel—he worries.

Nikki chastens herself, she doesn't know these people, and is in no position to judge. She could be wrong about so many things. She's always trusted her assumptions as they've occurred. Her trust in them became so strong that they became knowledge. Maybe that's how things worked. Is this how confident people move through life? She's thinking she should widen her trust, perhaps to include other people.

Nikki thought everything would fall into place the moment Norm appeared in person. She expected something upon first seeing him, that he would impart some knowledge. There would be a mutual recognition, "Oh, it's you. I've been looking for you. I know all about it," he would say. Something like that, leading to dark bar corner revelations. She never expected to be sleeping with him. Or chatting with his father over breakfast and drinks.

What she knows will happen, what is actually happening, and the distance between the two, takes up her thoughts as she circles the lot by The Lock Up. She parks as close as possible to shorten her pre-dawn walk after closing time. Nikki fights the urge to sit, smoking, in her car for another hour and let Sherry work the bar. Let her bitch about the service after having to provide it.

Her expectations for Norm were unfair, of course. This is something she tries to accept as she walks toward the smoking waitstaff by the dumpster. It's awful of her to assume her visions to be more important than reality. How disingenuous for her to allow Norm and Blake to think she appears without a purpose, one more than actual friendship. Sleeping with Norm, laughing with Blake, the whole time she runs blurry scenes through her head; she tries to force an epiphany that just won't come. At first, whether waking alone or beside Norm, she had to justify her actions each morning, needed to remind herself of the purpose behind all this pretense. The vision.

The other day, waking with Norm on the couch, she had forgotten his role in her head, that that was why she was there. She feared for a moment he had slipped down to her heart. Pushing him away, she dressed and walked through the house, looking for clues.

A couple cooks are lingering in the alley as she approaches, laughing and smoking. One climbs up on a bar stool, placed for this purpose, to peer in the window to see if any order slips have clicked out of the machine by the kitchen door. The kitchen crew changes on a bi-weekly basis, as soon as paychecks come, and she doesn't trust herself to say the right names. So she just smiles and stands outside their circle.

One cook she definitely doesn't know nods her way, his eyes openly dropping south to take in her low shirtfront and tight jeans. Other nights, Nikki would call him out on this. Tonight, it only confirms a fear she's been having—she's a slut. She has used sex to get something she wants from Norm. And it came so naturally. When Norm hadn't even remembered her, she immediately knew how to get him close, how to keep him there. Nikki turns away from the cooks, hears their barely stifled giggles as they dare the new cook to say something. "Just ask her..."

If these young cooks appear in her head, will she sleep with them, too? If more faces surface, if another voice becomes clear, asking something she can almost hear, what then? She just wants the future to be here. None exists beyond the one in her head.

The side door opens, and Sherry is there. "I just put an order in. Anyone here going to make it?"

The cooks exchange looks. The new one says, "Thinking about it."

"You want to 'think about it' in line at the unemployment office?" Sherry says, and the other cooks turn away, laughing.

"I got it," the cook says and sneaks in past Sherry.

"And you have customers waiting," Sherry says to Nikki. "Let's go."

"Thinking about it," Nikki says. But she drops her cigarette and walks through Sherry's raised arm into the bar. She hears Sherry castigating the remaining kitchen crew.

There actually are a couple guys at the bar, watching three different sports on TVs. Nikki drops her bag and takes their orders. As she arranges her bar, replacing bottles and cleaning up the sloppiness of the previous bartender, Steve walks over. He asks her for a Diet Coke. His stop sign red bouncer T-shirt clings to his gut as he seats himself at the corner stool to wait for some trouble to arise or for a crowd that needs to be carded. It could be another couple hours before he has to actually do anything and Nikki wonders why he gets here so early, or why he even comes in at all. She imagines that he could use a few hours alone.

There I go again, she thinks. Assuming she knows something about other people. There's a chance Steve is happy to be here, could be he looks forward to it all day. He looks at her, and Nikki realizes she's been staring.

"Hey," he says.

"Hey."

"So. You think it'll get busy tonight?" Steve searches for conversation.

"Usually does. Friday."

"Friday," he agrees.

They nod to each other, and Nikki moves away to find something that needs taking care of. She hears Steve again.

"Hey," he says.

She looks over and he's holding out his soda. He glances over his shoulder, then says, "Do you think I could get a little—"

"No problem." Nikki slides his glass under the bar and pours a third of it into the sink. She tops it off with rum, slides it back. The whole thing quick, both of them knowing enough to hide the act from Sherry.

"Thanks, I could use it."

"I bet," Nikki says.

He smiles at the drink and takes an interest in one of the games being played out behind the bar. Nikki feels somewhat justified, she was right about something. Steve doesn't want to be here. Timmy, Sherry's brother and the bar owner, could easily handle the job. Especially the sitting at the bar downing booze part.

Nikki relaxes into the routine of the evening ahead. With work to focus on, her mind can calm its wandering. Customers start trickling in. At first in pairs, then threes and fours, until there is just a crowd before her. She pours beers, makes change, and gives Steve another couple top offs of rum. He hasn't given up his seat. Even when Sherry comes to him through the crowd, furious about something, with purse in hand, he doesn't move. She throws up her arms and leaves him, he goes back to the televisions.

New customers dusted with snow approach the bar, laughing at their unpreparedness for the early weather. Nikki wonders if she shut her car windows. She imagines Norm at home looking past the TV, through the windows at the snowflakes. She pictures Blake, with his standard drink, in his usual chair. There's a smile on her face as she imagines Norm trying to decide if he should come to see her anyway, and she realizes that she can't wait to see him. She thinks this without a single thought beyond seeing his smile as she enters his kitchen, being quiet so as not to wake Blake, and envisioning how she will greet him.

# Chapter Twenty-Four

## Sherry

Two phone calls in a week, what is Destiny doing to her? Sherry thinks, driving through the dark from The Lock Up. She knows the cops are at her house, and she runs through the conversation that is about to happen. In her head, she is so goddam witty and understandably angry that her imaginary cop leaves laughing, assured that she will handle the whole thing. As she curves the big car slow under the stars, she sees flashing blue lights shining on a dozen crappy teenage cars. They're parked in front of her house, on her lawn. She realizes her next conversation is not going to go anything like the one in her head. Nor is the one she will have with Steve later tonight. She pulls behind a bumper-stickered mess of a station wagon and shuts the engine. Her red tail lights reflect off car chrome, mixing with the strobing blue lights, filling her car with purple. The season's first early snowflakes catch light and dance past her windshield. Sherry sits, holding the wheel, assessing.

There is one cop on the lawn, talking at a few kids around him, all of them hanging their heads. From around the side of the house another cop comes to a stumbling halt beside his partner. His face glistens and he crouches, hands on his knees, breathing heavily. The flashlight in his hand shines behind him, spotlights the broken ride-on mower.

"A bunch ran into the woods. Through the pond," the tired cop says.

His partner speaks, looking at Sherry. "I think Mom is finally here."

Sherry walks right up to him. "Thank you so much for calling me, officer. I just can't believe this. This is not like her. I'm so sorry."

"Ma'am, is this your house?" the cop from the lawn says. His partner is breathing too hard to ask any questions.

"Yes, it is, and I just can't believe this nonsense. I'm going to give her a piece of my...what?" Sherry says. The cop is eying her, shining his flashlight over her chest, stopping on the oversized fake badge pinned to her shirt.

"You work at The Lock Up."

"My brother owns it. I help out." Sherry is guarded, aware of the tension between local police and the new bar.

"Tim Elliot?"

"Timmy. Yeah."

"Timmy," the cop says.

"That a problem?"

"No, ma'am." He trades his flashlight for a notebook.

Sherry is good at sensing power shifts, and she feels a subtle rise of energy flow to her, away from this cop. She considers the best tactic to move in with next. Should she strike, take the offensive? Just to get them off the lawn and gone. Or should she continue playing demure, get them on her side? Then two of the hangdog teenagers, lurking on the outskirts of her and the cop's conversation, take off and split into the woods. It distracts all the adults, giving her a moment. The tired cop takes off huffing, showing no real hope of catching anyone. The cop with the notebook gives Sherry a quick look and follows his partner into the woods.

Sherry stands, smug for a second, under the flashing blues and takes a direct route over the lawn into her house. She follows the loud music spilling from her open front door. It's a wreck inside. Couch cushions are scattered, it reeks of cigarette smoke. Beer cans stand in loose pyramids on every surface, ash piled on their rims. What the fuck? she thinks.

"Destiny! Get your ass out here!" There is no response she can hear over the music.

Sherry walks to the stereo, its wood and glass case overflows onto the floor with unfamiliar CDs, and turns it off. The silence seems to increase the glow from the cruisers outside. They could at least turn their lights off, she thinks, everyone knows they're here. Something crashes in the next room. A lamp hitting the floor?

"Destiny?" Sherry moves toward the noise.

In the darkened den, she steps on a blanket that has spilled out the doorway. Sherry slides her hand up the wall until she finds the switch. In the quick glare, in the moment the light comes, Destiny rolls off a boy she'd been straddling on the leather couch, and quickly yanks down her shirt. Her pants are widely unbuttoned. The boy stretches out his legs, fumbles with his fly; he gives up and pulls his sweatshirt down low over his lap.

"I don't know what is going on here. Destiny! Can you please tell me what the fuck is going on here? Please?"

"They told me to wait in here." Destiny lifts a red plastic cup from the table beside the couch and takes a long sip, watching her mother

225

over the rim. The boy twitches between Destiny, Sherry, his lap, and back at Sherry. He looks terrified, and Sherry thinks it would do Destiny some good to show some of that fear herself. Just a little bit.

"Who told you what?" Sherry says.

"The cops. Obviously. To just wait here for them."

Sherry turns on the boy, who's again trying to zip himself in. "Get out."

He hops up, almost loses his pants, and runs, crouched, out of the room. Destiny adjusts herself on the couch, barely trying to cover her opened jeans.

Sherry looks out the door after him, watches him stumble over cushions and empty cans out the door. His empty spot on the couch is sunken, blankets shoved down between cushions. A red plastic cup lies overturned on the floor.

Destiny says, "Steve said I couldn't go out, so..."

"So...what?"

Destiny flips her head, encompassing the whole scene, waves an arm around the room. Sherry walks the length of the couch twice and opens her mouth to speak. She takes a lunging step toward Destiny, then backs away. "I can't think of one thing to say to you right now."

"Whatever. Good."

"You—" Sherry begins and tightens her fists. She exhales, then turns to the door and hangs from her hands at the top of the frame, her back to Destiny. She lifts her feet from the floor, so she dangles there, feeling her weight sway and looking over the trashed living room.

"We're screwing this up, Des. We're fucking it all up."

From the couch, Destiny offers nothing. Sherry lets her feet drop and walks out, thinking of her father with a hammer, building this house, and the neighbors', all of them.

On the lawn the two cops are bent over, their heads almost touching. They form a silhouetted 'M' before their blue lights. Apparently their run through the woods has been unsuccessful. Not even Destiny's couch partner is anywhere to be seen.

Sherry has lost her earlier advantage with the cops. She feels it the moment they rise in unison as she approaches. Putting on an apologetic smile, she prepares to get bitched at for a good long time. Even if she hasn't done shit.

Maybe the cops are embarrassed about the runaway teenagers, now hiding in the woods, shivering in the dark, waiting for the opportunity to sneak back out. Maybe they just lose interest, but after some strong warnings for Sherry, the cops climb into their shared patrol car, finally stop the blinding lights, and pull away.

Only the kid's cars parked all over the cul-de-sac circle reveal any sign of a disturbance here tonight. Sherry waits until the police are surely gone and turns to look at her house. It's nice, she thinks, so different than her childhood home. The word 'home' is a stretch, barely defining the taut fears of her childhood. There's a chance she thought this life, here, would fix everything. That idea seems pathetic now, looking through her front door to the post-party mess inside. She sees Destiny walk past the door, holding a handful of crushed beer cans, and bending to pick up another.

Destiny pauses, framed by the doorway, and looks out into the darkness. Sherry stands and watches, silent. They remain that way until Sherry releases a hissing puff of air, and turns away.

# Chapter Twenty-Six

I watch Dad sleep more than I watch the TV. The clock clicks slow minutes between glances. It's Friday, and it will be busy at the bar. Nikki will need a long time to close up before she gets here. But, of course, she really wants to be with me, so I work that into the equation. 2:30 seems reasonable. Maybe 3:00. I'll be here.

This thing with Nikki contains a sense of foregone conclusion. Part of me hopes that it's not simply because we have nothing else going for us; another part of me couldn't care less if that's the case. We don't talk about it. I'm in the middle of some lifelong conversation she has going on with the world, and I've been quiet. It's as if the pull I feel is not to Nikki, but from her. She's stuck herself into my and Dad's life, slipped into a voided spot, a shape left in the air while the rest of us blinked.

The late night weatherman on TV is the same guy who predicted storms during my childhood. I can't help but think he must be making it up by this point. He stands before an arrow-covered map of the country; reds and blues swoop in from West to East. Some circles sneak in from the South. We're about to be hit by something. The weatherman gestures over several thousand miles with his pointer; he appears to be directing a disaster, grand and wonderful. He seems excited about it. I feel at the center of it all, caught in a spiraling. Not downward, not a flush, more as if I'm at the bottom and being raised up.

I didn't realize I was standing to think about this. I look up at a noise, expecting to see the TV again, but I'm in the kitchen. The door opens, and Nikki is standing inside with snowflakes dotting her black hair. She's pale from the cold, the dusting of snow a natural extension of her skin.

Her jacket slides off, and we're together before it hits the floor. Her shirt is damp and catches up on her breasts as I lift it up and off. I spend more time than needed working it up and over. My shirt comes off. Her skin is smooth and freezing against mine; my hair and rough face seem cruelly unnatural against her. But she pulls me closer than possible, so her nipples slide back and forth across my chest. Her tongue is cold; the snowflakes melt and drip down my stomach. I taste them in my mouth. We don't say a thing.

Out of the kitchen, through the living room, and Nikki touches Dad's sleeping head on our way upstairs. The TV is still going, talking of snow and cold and Thanksgiving travel. We leave it be, our clothes left like stepping stones behind us. On the stairs I'm close enough to kiss the base of her naked spine while we walk. She pulls my hand ahead, and I hold her hip. She smells of cold and water and barroom smoke.

In my room, Nikki leans naked out an open window. She's watching the snow fall in the coned glow of the streetlights. The entire length of her bare legs are turned to the room. Naked behind her I feel the breeze everywhere. I'm almost afraid to touch her skin. Its softness could be too much.

She turns her head and pushes her hair back, her eyes quickly catching mine before turning back, away from me, to the night outside. Her hand rests on that spot behind her ear, and I reach out, rest my hand over hers, align my hips with hers. She moves forward, her head out the window, overlooking our darkened street, the snow silencing even my breath, as she moves back onto me.

The cold air lifts Nikki's hair, raising it in a dark cloud which billows between us. Leaning forward, into her, I can feel it brushing against me. We move together with the drifting motion of the snowflakes. Over her head, out the window, I see the snow beginning to fall faster, the wind picking up, shooting the flakes in horizontal lines. Tiny gusts swirl the snow in miniature versions of the larger storm softening our city. They pinwheel on their own trajectories, some scattering in the wind, others meeting and melding into great spouts too large for the street to contain. They rise up, beyond our view.

The wind raises the curtains, they brush over both our bodies until I can't tell what is her moving against me or me moving in her, and what is windblown fabric, and what is cold snow on my chest, melting in rivulets dripping over Nikki's back.

She turns to face me, resting her bare ass on the windowsill. She must be freezing. I imagine her body seen from outside, long and thin, mirroring the pale columns of the snow-covered trees. Kneeling on my floor, among the remnants of an old life and into a new one, I rest my head on Nikki's lap. She runs her fingertips through my hair, loosely twirling and scratching. She emanates heat, warming the side of my face, and it's so nice I could nearly fall asleep.

I may be actually dozing. Her voice surprises me out of something far from this room.

"Listen," she says.

"Okay." As long as she can stand the cold windowsill, I can lean here and listen.

"There's something more going on here."

"More than what?"

"Than this."

"This is good enough." I don't really want to talk about anything.

"It is, yeah," she says. "But, listen. Please. I need to tell you something. It's not fair."

Her hands move lower, they're gently dragging from my chin to my forehead, stopping to circle my closed eyes. I have to force myself away from the far place in my head, somewhere near an ocean. I drag my mind to waking, and say, "What? What's not fair?" The waves in my head grow calmer, but still hold me buoyant, my insides swaying to their motion. I barely hear Nikki as she talks.

Time has passed when Nikki raises my head, finally moving from the snowy window. She lowers me to the floor, standing naked over me. Softly waking, I look up at her body. She has her arms raised, hands clenched behind her head. It's not often I get a chance to look at a naked girl from this angle, and it brings me quickly out of sleep to admire. "Wow," I say.

"'Wow' I can't believe what you said? Or 'wow' look at that body?"

I sit up. "Which one would be better?"

"Usually the second one." She crouches on bent knees, one nearly touching both of my shoulders. "How long have you been sleeping?"

"How long have you been talking?"

"Too long for you to have been sleeping." She drops onto the carpet, sits cross-legged. "Can I smoke in here?"

From my position on the floor, I can't find a reason why not. It sounds lovely. I sit up and mirror her position, our knees touching. I reach up onto my desk and grab an empty beer can to use as an ashtray. She leans across me to grab her pants, where her cigarettes are. She lights one and hands it to me, lights another.

"I'm sorry I fell asleep. What were you saying?"

"I don't know if I can say it again."

"I'm awake."

"This has been going on for a long time. It's more than just you." She takes a long drag and opens a desk drawer at her shoulder. "Probably too long."

"What is it?"

"I'll figure it out. Or not. Where's that shoebox of photographs?"

"Next drawer up. You sure? I'm awake now."

Nikki stretches up, cigarette in her mouth, and pulls out a tattered Converse All Star box. It matches the one I just bought the other day. Photographs fall out the sides as she places it between us.

"There's more in there. Loose," I say.

She grabs a handful and drops them next to the box.

"Tell me about these," she says.

"There's not much to tell."

She picks one from the box and turns it to face me. "This one."

I smile at such a young me. "That's my first bike."

"This one."

"That's by the pond. Sophomore year, I think. That was a bad hair year."

"This one."

"I don't know who that is."

233

She flips the photograph over, so she can look at it. "I think that's you."

The heat clanks and rattles through the radiators, fighting the open window and the snow. By the time the sun replaces the dark, we've gone through all the loose photos and are almost done with the box. Nikki's smokes are done, and so am I. I need something softer beneath me than this carpet, and I stand, reaching down for her hand. She takes it and rises, leaning her body against mine. Our kisses are parched and smokey, soft, in need of sleep.

We fall sideways onto the bed, still holding each other. I'm cold, but too tired to pull the blankets over us. It doesn't seem to bother Nikki. All those old memories, captured on paper, I hadn't thought about most of that in years. Not those people, not those times, and most of them occurred within a three mile radius of this spot. Nikki's eyes are closed, her breathing almost that of sleep.

"Did you want to tell me what you said before?" I say.

"Not now."

"Tomorrow?"

"Maybe I won't have to."

"Okay," I say, and watch as the sun crosses the windowsill.

# Chapter Twenty-Seven

## Blake

Blake doesn't know what the hell to do with Thanksgiving. He's avoided the few phone calls which have trickled in and erased their messages before Norm can hear them. Nothing has been mentioned between the two of them about the upcoming holiday. Besides some regular teacher talk about needing the break and the genius of our forefathers in providing one just when the kids are completely losing it, they've said nothing.

Blake looks back on their night out on the town together with a strong nostalgia as if years have passed, rather than weeks. Since then, only Nikki's appearances break his routine of watching television in Norm's presence, or as now, by himself. Still, Blake feels himself and his son to be closer than at any other point in their lives, and that's including Norm's baby and childhood. A small boy had seemed Pat's domain. That's just how things were then, he comforts himself with, feeling the lie within that thought, even as it rises in his mind. He understands now that he had felt trapped in fatherhood and maybe even husbandhood. This realization is shameful to Blake. But he thinks it often, out of some sort of self-flagellation, repeatedly making the guilty twinge turn his heart in its cage.

Maybe it's the whiskey, all the evening whiskeys. The drinks and that one other idea. The one which he has only briefly allowed himself, before briskly tucking it somewhere behind his liver. That recognition is this: he feels a certain freedom at his wife's death. The thought is repugnant to Blake. Of course, he has been mournful and somewhat broken, and again he has to comfort himself with these half truths. Of course.

Shock, that's what he feels. He is in shock. And the sudden loss—a fellow widower at school had told him to expect strange things. If Blake is guilty about the quick elation he feels at some new found freedom, isn't that fine? Fine, healthy even, he thinks with a nod and a sip. Blake tells himself he has just moved through the stages of grief faster than most. He is a realist. A well-adjusted one at that, and certainly not the cold-hearted bastard he suspects himself of being.

None of this, enlightening as it is, answers the Thanksgiving Day question. Blake knows Norm will be out tonight, leaving the house empty. Norm has left home to buy a shirt, of all things. This is not a Norman whom Blake recognizes. He arrived at the airport with one suitcase, stolen from Blake over a decade ago. There hadn't been enough clothes to last through two days, and now he suddenly needs a new shirt for Reunion Night.

Reunion Night is the busiest bar night of the year. Blake is proud to be one of the founders of this peculiar to Garrison City annual event. Everyone who has left is back for the long weekend. If the next day, Thanksgiving, is dedicated to family, Reunion Night is reserved for a type of debauchery that only returning home as a visitor can conjure up. Reuniting drinkers share made up memories and lie about keeping in touch. It is a night of last shot, maybe-this-would-have-changed-everything one night stands and infidelities. Soldiers have gone AWOL to be back in Garrison for Reunion Night. It is an evening Norm would've avoided like a rash in August, but is now giddy, getting ready to go to The Lock Up, where, Blake reminded him on the drive home, he had been kicked out of not very long ago.

"Sherry's got bigger things to worry about than me tonight. She's got a love child running wild and it'll be so crowded, she won't even notice me," Norm said.

"That's not the Sherry Elliot I remember."

"Sherry Stone now, Dad."

"Isn't that a clam?"

Norm just laughed and drummed his fingers on the dash, anxious to get home. They pulled in, and Norm walked around the car, before Blake had even gotten out. He grabbed the car keys to leave and get a new shirt, and then go out drinking. His assumption, clearly, was that Blake would stay home alone, drinking.

Norm took the driver's seat, and started the engine, arm over the passenger seat. He even looked over his shoulder before turning to Blake and saying, "Did you want to come with me tonight?"

"Oh no, you don't want me hanging around."

"Nikki would be happy to see you."

"She'll be so busy, she'll barely even see you," Blake said.

"I'll just say hi."

Who am I talking to? Blake thought. "Have fun," he said.

"I'll come back before I go out," Norm said and pulled out to go shirt shopping.

Blake supposes that despite this evident happiness, Norm is still the

Norm he's known forever— more interested in debauchery than family. This is something of a comfort.

Maybe there is a chance that Norm feels the same sort of freedom Blake does. A freedom which certainly feels waning and wasted here on the doorstep. Then Blake thinks of his whiskey, sitting out in the open on the counter, and he lightens, before feeling that guilty pull in his chest.

# Chapter Twenty-Eight

## Nikki

Nikki grew up with half the sweaty crowd in the bar. But tonight she knows them not by their faces and shared histories, but by their drinks. She chooses the orders to fill based on their drinks, not their place in line. The quick round of shots, the draught beers, they come first. That tray of margaritas, and who orders margaritas at this place, really? That guy goes last.

Tonight, of all nights, Sherry has parked her kid at the end of the bar with a stack of dollars for the stupid trivia machine. One less seat free to hold someone who might actually pay for a drink, or at least throw a tip her way. Destiny taps the screen, downing cola mixed with every available non-alcoholic syrup. She's driving Nikki nuts trying to trick her into pouring booze into her drinks. Nikki can't muster any true hatred for the girl, she can only feel bad for her. It's clear that this girl's problem is her mother. Nikki considers sneaking her some rum. Nothing can hurt the girl more than what's already happened.

The bar is packed deep, but it's calm enough. Everyone's busy slapping each other on the back, playing "who's doing what now" and evaluating the ex-cheerleader's asses. Nikki feels confident, smug even, with her tight jeans and cleavage, unafraid to give the old prom queen a quick once over before taking her order.

She works quickly, keeping the drinks and cash flowing. It feels a little off-putting serving drinks when she has every right to be reuniting like everyone else, though she likes busy nights like this. Nikki is a confident bartender, adding prices complete with tax. She knows all the obscure tropical drinks the young guys order. Nikki knows what makes a dry Manhattan dry. It's four steps from one end of the bar to the register. Behind her bar, the bottles always stay in the same order. She never has to check a label. She likes watching customers sign off on ridiculous tips, feeling generous in old company, and being in constant movement, looking forward to, finally, that cigarette.

A group of guys from high school sit clustered at the bar. She vaguely remembers them sitting in the same order at a cafeteria table. She evaluates how the years have weighed on them: that one bald, that one fat, that one unhappy. They are drunk, forcing the old camaraderie; their conversation practically flips through a yearbook. One thinks of a name, another a derisive comment to go with it, another name, another insult. It makes Nikki glad she's lived more in the future than the past.

During a lull when the room has reached some sort of boozy equilibrium, she overhears the cafeteria table trio bring up Norm's name, and what has likely become of him.

"He disappeared," the bald one says.

"Wouldn't you? After that," the unhappy one says, fidgeting his beer.

"You're right, something happened to him. I think," the one who got fat says.

"Nothing happened to him. He was with that other kid. Who died."

"Norm's not dead. At least he wasn't."

"No, no. Not Norm dead. Fitzy. Fitzy died," the bald one, who seems to hold the most clout, says.

"Fitzy was a good kid," says the unhappy guy.

They nodded at that, quiet with their beers.

One of them says, "What was his real name?"

"Norman, I guess, right?"

"No shit. I mean Fitzy."

"Henry FitzGerald. Fitzy. He drownded at the pond," Sad Guy says.

Nikki cringes. She hates when people say drownded. Nikki stands close, ostensibly to wash glasses, but is eavesdropping. People tend to ignore bartenders until they're needed, treating them simply as part of the bar.

"You don't remember? Norm and Fitzy were at the pond and Fitzy drownded."

"Shit."

"He let him drownd?"

"He fucking killed him. Pretty much, anyway. He was just fucking lay there and Fitzy —"

"Shit. What a bastard. I bet he's still a drunk. Probably worse."

"I heard they were doing the swim. The Dawn Cross-Pond Challenge."

Nikki scrubs harder at the already clean enough glasses in her bar sink, rubbing the metal scrubbie against her hand to keep quiet. They're looking in their beers. The bald one smiles.

"I made that swim. Once."

The fat guy snorts, "Once more than Fitzy."

"I never went to the pond," Sad Guy says.

"We never invited you? The pond was awesome."

"I never got to go."

"To the pond!" Bald Guy raises his glass, followed by the fat one. They clink glasses. The sad guy sips without clinking.

They drink and drink, and Nikki doesn't say a goddam thing. It hurts, to hear all that. Of course, she knows the whole story, ten different versions, in fact. She'd heard it over and over again, in the halls, in class; it was everywhere. Norm and Fitzy were the last ones conscious at the pond, the sun coming up. Norm challenged Fitzy, his most loyal drinking companion, his friend, to the traditional dawn swim—a tradition Norm had started the previous summer, and sat down to watch. Then he passed out.

At least, that's the version Nikki believes. Every one knows the story. They all just translate it differently. Even in high school, Nikki realized that each person's interpretation of the events revealed more about that person than the actual tragedy. They all wrenched a new truth to fit their own ideas of the truth. Nikki found this to be the case at her hospital. She sees it at the bar night after night. Drunks twine strands of realities around fictions until they're indistinguishable, until they can't tell which came first. Until they find one which suits what they wanted in the first place.

It twists her heart around, keeping silent before these three men. She slams a couple glasses around the sink, trying to end their talk. They look up with six bleary eyes. Red faced.

"Hey, can we get three more?" the unhappy one says.

"We're out. Sorry," Nikki says.

"Of Bud? We'll take three whatevers." They laugh and share another round of back pats.

"We're out of that, too." Nikki's hands are on her hips, unbudging.

"What the fuck?" the fat one says.

"We're definitely out of that," Nikki says and walks down the bar to take an order of five rum and cokes from the old bad girl clique.

"Fuck you!"

"Fucking bitch!"

She looks back only when she hears the sound of their stools scraping. They are gone, replaced by three women, deep into sangrias, which is just a vat of crap red wine, fruit punch, and a few limes. She pours them three more and forgets to charge them as a silent thanks for filling that space. They don't even notice, just continue talking.

New crowds enter, shaking their jackets and hair free of snow. It's getting bad out there. There are sure to be automotive assaults on telephone poles all over town tonight. She quietly hopes, before sucking the thought back, that at least one of them, possibly three, involve those assholes.

The crowd's drinking balance tips to empty, and they swarm the bar. Nikki has to force herself to do the math correctly; her head swims. Her ears sweat. Not now, Nikki thinks, hurriedly taking orders. She tries to force the vision away. This doesn't feel like the full bodied wave of vision, just the rippling surface. Something new. A hint that she should be paying something some attention. The little she can make out clearly in her vision is dreamlike in the way that she knows something without knowing how she knows it. But it is definitely so. There is water. In her head, there is lots of swirling water.

It baffles her, as she pours four bottles, two in each hand, into six glasses, how she has never made the connection between Norm and water. Norm and water and the pond. She has been too stuck on trying to clear up the moments within the vision, too focused on the details. Nikki feels the scalp ends of her hair tingle, then stop. She has been going about this all wrong.

# Chapter Twenty-Nine

On the walk over, I'm nervous that Sherry will be working the door. She'd definitely block me. Steve probably would, too, but only from a deep-set fear of Sherry and her bottomless capacity for angry grudges. When I reach the door, it isn't either Sherry or Steve. It's some young guy, from out of town probably. Bars famously have guys from other towns working security on reunion night. It's an attempt to keep old rivalries from surfacing and exploding. He glances over my ID and packs me into the crowd.

There's a cop by the door. There's cops all over town tonight. I must have passed a dozen, their slow crawling cars sliding like sharks through the snow. This cop has a huge coffee mug, surely spiked, the way he laughs and mingles. The high ceilings, the brick walls with their cursive neons glowing, the windows with long shades pulled down—it all glares down on the crammed mass. People shout to each other over the heads of other people shouting along to jukebox memories. A glass breaks. A couple rolls on one of the couches by the window, heavily making out to the cheers of the paired off drunks on the opposite couch. Way in the back someone hangs off the bars of the old jail cell, accepting cheers and screaming back in raucous reply.

It's instantly too much and I want to turn, head out the door. I don't remember what I was thinking when this seemed like a good idea. I'm already planning where I can find a quiet bar that doesn't give a shit about the Garrison Green Wave's bygone glory days. That would be Jimmy's. After seeing this crowd, quiet drinks followed by a drunk trudge home through the new snow sounds appealing. But it's too packed, I can't turn back. The general stream pushes to the bar. I give in, allow myself to be carried through the noise and green clad crowd. This is clearly not for me.

My new shirt is stupid. I shouldn't have left Dad. All my memories are blurry and stupid, the only face from the past I care to see is the one that definitely won't be here. He's buried. No chance for reunion there. Fitzy is where I should be tonight, kneeling in the falling snow, hanging a warmer jacket on his stone grave. What have the past months been for, if not for me to do exactly that? Dad's drunk. Mom's dead. Garrison City hates me for all I've done and all that I continue not to do. I should be mourning for us all. Paying my penitence.

Before it occurs to me how to do that properly, Nikki appears through a slit in the crowd. From behind the bar, she raises my courage. She looks furious, though, with hands on her hips, and I'm glad her look is not for me, but some guys at the bar. Three of them. She's denying them something they apparently don't want denied.

Nikki turns away from the trio to take an order. I can see the corner of the bar, with the touch screen trivia box. Is that Destiny? At the bar? Dammit, Sherry. Just because your daughter is a drunken slut who can't be trusted to stay home alone doesn't mean you should take her to the bar. In fact, I think it means the opposite. I realize I should go.

The guys at the bar shout a few swears at Nikki, their reunion night maybe not as merry as planned. They push their way from the bar into the crowd and head my way.

There's a quick drop in the crowd's collective volume, and a slight path away from the bar splits open. The cop's laugh over the blaring music is the only voice for a moment. The room absorbs all three. Noise returns, and the trio is replaced at the bar by another group.

The three push by me, still bitching about Nikki. In the inches available, I move over to block them, not really thinking to do anything, just show them the disapproval they deserve.

"What the fuck was that about?" one says, shrugging into his jacket, carelessly elbowing a fat girl in a Garrison football jersey.

"Just a bitch. She always has been," another says.

"Who is she?" the heaviest one says.

"Can't remember her name. Went to the crazy hospital up north."

"Should've kept her!" They all laugh over that one, and the fat one bumps me with his shoulder. I don't move. He's looking down, doesn't even see me, adjusting his jacket and pushing forward. I don't move. Again.

He looks up and his face spills into drunken recognition. "Well. Shit. Guys, look!"

The other two chirp in. "Norm Mean."

"No fuckin' way!"

"Hey," I say. Their faces retain something recognizable under the years, but I can't place them and don't have the energy for this conversation. "Leaving?"

They squeeze themselves into a tight semi-circle. "We were just talking about you."

"What a coincidence," I say.

"The good ol' days."

"There's a lot of that going around," I say.

"Yeah," two of them say together.

The bald one, their apparent leader, says, "Reunion night. Shit. I can't believe you're here."

"Why not? Right? You're here. That guy's here." I point off to the left. "It's reunion night."

They're silent, but only because smarmy shitbag grins keep their mouths slammed shut.

Finally, the fat one says, "Yep, but we didn't kill anybody."

Their grins give way to a hacking laughter, and they pass by me.

"Where's Fitzy? You dick," one of them says from behind me.

Nobody moves in to share the spotlight shining on me. I feel on display, but also somewhat justified. I was right; this is what Garrison thinks of me. Prior to my return, and I've barely offered anything else, this is what a whole city, a collective people, has been thinking of me as I wasted time in California. Which is as far away as I could get without burdensome paperwork. I have made no effort at redemption, unless returning counts as effort. Maybe simply being here counts for something.

Tonight everyone is here for their own redemption. The fat unpopular girls have dragged out their new out-of-town husbands, their new too short overly dressy outfits, and are busy proving their happiness. The sagging jocks wear their faded college sweatshirts, evidence of washed out hope. The old dorks, now somewhat successful in some computer something, keep close eyes on their new trophy wives to ensure they don't get groped by the old jocks. These new entrepreneurs glance around, terrified of the jocks forcing a reenactment of old high school nightmares. Because, of course, they've remade themselves. And here I am in my new shirt, for what?

Probably my own shot at redemption. Nikki? She knows almost everything and still seems to see some hope. I step out of my circle, into the crowd, and approach the bar.

Maybe this is what draws me to Nikki—she provides drinks. It seems like I can trace the trajectory of my life back to a particular beginning, not signaled by a starting gun, but by the crack and whoosh of an opening beer can.

That initial thrill of illicit alcohol, of the adult, lasted too long. Until, in fact, I was an adult and had shot right by any opportunity to veer onto a different course. Everything has turned out much more circular than I ever expected. I've been in this building when it was the police station. I've been next door, in the Orchard St. apartments, when it was thrilling. I've been in love only when it seemed to be the best mixer. And now I think I've been in this town the whole time, that my whole life has been spent sitting, shivering with a beer can on the dam, waiting for a dead boy to surface.

Destiny sits at the bar, surrounded by empty glasses with varying heights of melting ice, maraschino cherry stems piled in front of her. At the moment she is too absorbed in the video trivia screen to notice me or anything else. It's funny how out of place she looks here, crowded in by these drinkers, by exactly the type of adult she wants to be. Her cheap necklaces dripping into girlish cleavage, desperately pushed together, have the opposite effect than they intend. Everything works together to accentuate her inexperience. It's almost tender. Until she speaks. "Mr. Mean! Buy me a drink!"

It's loud enough in here, I think, that I can plausibly pretend not to hear her. I'm halfway around a full bar. She knows nothing of barroom etiquette and continues calling to me over the thrown back heads of laughing drunks and the waving arms of a group of women shouting along to what, I think, was our prom song.

"Hey! Mean! Over here, I'm at the bar!"

No shit, Destiny.

She's standing on the rungs of her stool, leaning over the video machine so her necklaces scrape the top and her bracelets slide down to her elbows. I have to respond.

I give her a wave and flash a friendly smile, a quick acknowledgment, and hope to leave it at that. But I know she's going to require more of my time. She takes it as encouragement, and I just wish she would go away. She has no right to be here; it's not my fault she gives blowjobs under the stairs or gets busted for parties at her house. The whole school knows. And this is the punishment she gets? To be out at a bar, which is all she really hopes to achieve in life anyway? Shit. I wonder where Nikki is.

She's serving shots a few drinkers down. I'm squeezed in on a stool between two separate chatting groups, one of which is a group of girls consisting of friends' older sisters' whom I used to fantasize over. Knowing there's no time to chat, or get great service, I plan on ordering two drinks. A big beer and a monstrous whiskey. I watch Nikki turn from her customer, in constant smooth motion. She's bent low over the cooler, reaching in deep. She looks great, which a couple guys around me also notice. The knowledge that none of them get to help her out of

250

those jeans in a few hours buoys my mood. I can already feel the skin of her leg, cold from being outside, slide against my own rougher leg. It's almost enough to ignore Destiny as she clambers down from her stool and works her way over to me.

I need to order quick. Or leave. At this point, I'd rather order. Nikki's gone from the cooler, but glancing toward the taps, I see her walking over with a big beer and monstrous whiskey. She may be the best bartender ever.

"God, thank you," I say, when she sets them down.

"I thought you could use two." She ignores calls from down the bar.

"It's a hell of a start."

"Hey," she says.

"Hey."

"Don't worry about those guys, okay?" She looks concerned, trying to read my face.

"You heard that?" My heart switches sides in my chest.

"It was hard not to. Assholes."

"Huge ones."

"Gaping." She smiles. "I need to go. Looks like you've attracted an admirer."

I don't turn around. "Destiny?"

"You can't escape it." Nikki manages to rush to the end of bar without hurrying. The beer goes down so smoothly that I need the whiskey just for the sharp cut, an exclamation point to my sip.

I feel two hands on my shoulders, like somebody trying to climb up. "Mean!" Destiny shouts in my ear. "What are you doing here?"

The level of disgust I feel surprises me. I twitch her hands off me and speak without looking. I know any attempt at subtlety will be useless. "Hello, Destiny."

"This is crazy, huh? I can't believe you're here."

"I usually sleep at my desk," I say.

"I mean my mom."

"What do you mean, 'your mom'?" I want her to go away, just disappear. Go play with your cell phone, I silently order her. I can't even drink in front of her, though it's clearly she who is in the wrong just by being here. I shouldn't need to control myself.

"My mom said you couldn't come in. But that I could."

Still without looking at her, I say, "Isn't that illegal?"

"She pretty much owns the place, she doesn't have to let anybody in if she doesn't want to."

I don't want to be having this conversation. I'd rather watch Dad toast the television. Or maybe look at the bottom of my glass.

"Whatever. No one cares. They're all hammered," she says.

I brave a glance sideways, at the group to my left. Three women sitting, talking to a standing man wearing a tie and cuff links stare openly at me and Destiny.

"Even Sullivan. He's trashed. He's such a dick," she says.

There's no point in facing away. I turn on my stool, reaching back for my whiskey, but almost grab the beer, then leave them both at the last moment, out of some sense of decorum. What a role model.

"Sullivan's here?" I say, my knees nearly touching her belly.

"Yeah he is! And he's fucking trashed! Look." She puts her hands on my bent knees. I can't move; this feels terrible. Destiny hops onto the bottom rungs of my stool. I hear laughs and breathy inhales from the group next to me.

She takes a second to balance herself, using my lap for support, her hair brushes against my face, and I get a whiff of chemical hairspray and something fruity. I hate that it instantly reminds me of every girl I kissed in high school. She steadies herself and rises up, so her chest is in my face. I can see all the dangling designs on her necklaces.

Her legs are pushed together in between mine, and she looks like such a child, thrilled with the view above her normal height, as if this is how the rest of the world sees.

"See him? Over there." She points, her arm out straight. "Douchebag. He's talking to, like, a whole football team or something."

"Destiny. Get down."

"That one's cute. Do you think he's cute, Mr. Mean?"

"Destiny. You need to get down. Don't do this, please."

She flings her hair around and almost loses her balance, her hands jamming into my shoulders to catch herself, her face right in mine. She laughs, much too close, her breath sickly from soda. The people around me are all watching, whether horrified or amused, I can't tell, but there's no way this looks good. If she actually catches Sullivan's eye over all this noise, it's going to get a lot worse.

"Get off me, Destiny. You shouldn't even be here."

She speaks from above me, without looking down. "Whatever, we're not in school, so you can't tell me what to do. My mom said I could come. Sullivan! Over here!"

I hear whispers beside me. At this point I can't decide who would be the worst person to be coming to stop this. Is Nikki watching? Is she laughing? Will we make fun of this late tonight, how awkward it was, and what was I supposed to do, really? I can't do anything.

"Oh, he sees me! Hi! Fucker won't even wave back. God, he's such a prick."

I raise my hands to my shoulders, palms facing out, almost ready to push Destiny off me, onto the goddam floor, but I hear a woman shout, "Stop!" beside me, and I think I shouldn't push her, but then realize that it must look like I'm about to grab her tits. I drop my hands.

Destiny slaps her arms to her sides, balancing with jerky motions on my stool and says, "You probably don't even like him either, do you, Mr. Mean? You're, like, the coolest teacher."

"Stop this, please, get off."

Too loudly and plainly meant for the audience, she says, "You want me to get off?"

"Be quiet!" Shit, that was the wrong thing to shout.

"Can you get me a drink? I'll get down if you get me a drink."

"Just get down, Des, please, get off." My voice sounds desperate, pathetic in my ears.

"And you'll get me a drink?" she says and lifts her arms straight out, knocking the cuff-linked man in the head. He swears and says something about this being enough.

He grabs her arm, and she tries to pull away, which throws her off balance so she falls into me. The metal of her necklaces digs into my nose, and her weight pushes me back against the bar. I hear a glass break and my back is wet, beer dripping onto the floor. There are shouts. I can't see a thing, and finally, as Destiny moves against me, her foot off the stool, her knee shooting into my thigh, I push her off me, hard, a full strength shove. Away from me. I'm standing in a straddle over her, a foot by each of her hips. I'm shouting something as Sherry starts to get up from the floor, from behind the wall of watching people, and that's surprising. I must have pushed Destiny right into her, throwing her against the crowd.

The sharp-dressed man takes hold of my arm, holding me back from doing something he assumes I'm doing. I struggle a moment against him, but stop, realizing it can only make things worse. Then another guy, this one in a baseball hat and jersey, grabs hold of my other arm.

"I'm fine! I didn't mean to, let me go! I'm leaving, I'll leave!" I say 100 times in the seconds it takes Sherry to reach me. Without saying a word, she punches me right in the face, right above my lip. I feel it in my neck and still my arms are held. I hear yelling around me, swears and hurried explanations to newly arriving onlookers.

"Fuck!"

"That was her daughter, the guy just shoved her!"

"He was hitting on her."

"Is that Norm Mean? I thought he died."

I open my eyes to see another Sherry punch come at me. I turn just enough not to take this one square on the nose. Her ring rips down my cheek. Teeth slam against each other. A clump of something flies from my mouth.

Bottles break behind me and one of my arms is freed. The man beside me is replaced by Nikki, who must've come right over the bar. Nikki steps between me and Sherry. I watch her trying to hold Sherry back, but Sherry's crazed, jumping right off the floor, trying to get at me over Nikki.

I break my other arm free and try to get Sherry off Nikki. I can't tell whose arms are whose or which fists hit me, with all the long hair everywhere. They're both wearing the same goddam blue shirts, so it's even harder to tell which one I'm protecting from the other. The jukebox is silent between songs, and Sherry's solid screaming fills the space. My head lights up against something hard in my eye. There's an arm around my throat, buckling me down, and I fall hard. For just a second I see Destiny's face against the floor, even with mine. It's a tangled mess of hair and tears. She looks terrified, surrounded by winter boots and ridiculously high heels. I reach towards her, to maybe help get her up or to have her help me get up, but a boot hits me hard in the stomach, curling me. Another one. I hear Nikki scream, "Stop!"

My nose breaks. I hear it and choke on the blood. I rush to cover it, but someone steps on my hand. I leave the ground and fall back, my legs are being held down, twisted. I twist back, but they're slammed down, and my back takes the brunt of the next blow. I hear, more than see or feel, Nikki on top of me, covering me. Then she's gone.

I can't distinguish one blow or shout from another. The next face I see is Sullivan's. His arms outstretched, a referee calling me done, down and done. The legs around me seem to back off. My attackers are still trained to respond to the assistant principal, and if it wasn't for the blood, I'd laugh. He takes me by my new shirt collar, and I'm lifted from the floor. He's shouting in my face. I hear nothing but a high droning buzz, every mouth is open, but I hear nothing.

A different blue arm comes between us. I get a shoulder in my face, and I cling to it, knocking free a cop microphone, pouring blood down his uniform. I take in a searching breath; it feels like surfacing. I gush blood and bile down his uniform onto the floor. Now he's shouting

256

something, his face twisted red. I hold tight to his shoulders, and we move through the crowd this way, him dragging me, walking backwards, the crowd parting.

I turn my head back and see Sullivan dragging Nikki away from Sherry, who's still clinging to a handful of hair. The cop twists my head away, saying something, something, until I feel a sudden cold, and we're outside, my deep breaths burning. He drops me against the curb. I stuff a handful of snow against my face, and it drips through my fingers, melted by the blood. Strobing blue lights flash, and gray snow fills the space between the bricks. Snowflakes melt into darkening pools of blood. The cold begins to work through my pants, burning my skin. More cops are pushing their way through the door, stepping over me. I'm thankful not to be disturbed. For a moment, it occurs to me that maybe I can just work my way up and wander off, avoid any repercussions. If I can only make it to my bed, I'll eventually wake up unbroken.

Nikki falls beside me, dumped by Sullivan. She scrambles on the slick sidewalk to get up, I see her screaming lips move, as if she were very far away. Sullivan races back in with the cops. He should have a whistle clamped in his lips. I imagine watching this scene from the couch. Dad would toast the actress playing Nikki, admiring her tenacity and cleavage, still buoyant beneath the blood stains.

Nikki pushes herself up, takes a step, but her foot fails to touch the ground. She wavers on one leg. I try to connect my muscles with my brain and think my arms to moving, but they don't. I'm nearly slumped on the ground and can only watch as Nikki's hands go to the sides of her neck. She cups her ears. Her head nods between her shoulders, and her legs go out. Nikki folds into herself and hits the sidewalk in a heap. Silent. Her hair has come free and spreads, dark against the snow.

I spend seconds trying to will my body closer to hers. I watch snowflakes build whitely in her hair, specks, then a smooth sheet until there is a light brighter than all these flashing ones and then nothing.

Light begins to creep in from the edges of my vision. I can begin to peripherally make out walls. Something is mashed against my mouth, hard enough that I can barely breathe, but I don't have the ability to make my hands find my face to take it away. Beneath me it's soft, so I figure I've moved from the sidewalk. I wave my arms enough to make whatever is muffling me stop. I blink until the dark spot in the middle of my vision breaks up into smaller dark spots. They become white dots, darting across my eyes until I can see everything. I sit up.

My face hurts, and nausea throbs through me at the slightest movement. If I hold my head at one angle it seems better, but one degree to either side brings back the white dots. It's confusing. The street is in front of me, I can see it now. I'm facing down Orchard St., which means The Lock Up would be to my left, but I can't see it. I need to move my shoulders and twist gingerly at the waist to look right. I'm in an ambulance. An EMT kneels beside me, holding a blood soaked rag and ice pack in his gloved hands.

"You back with us, Norman?" he asks with official concern, formal and bored.

"I think," I say, maybe loud enough for him to hear. "What happened?"

"Seems like you've had a rough night, Norman."

I snort a laugh and pain rockets up between my eyes and releases a chunk of dried blood from my nose, which resumes bleeding. Oh, fuck. "Where's Nikki?"

"The bartender?" the EMT says.

I nod and reach over for him to hand me the bloody rag. He twitches his head toward my lap. I pat around until I feel the pile of clean cloths. It hurts too much to look down. I press a rag against my mouth to catch the blood. It quickly becomes hard to breathe, and I need to take it away again, patting at my nose until the bleeding slows.

"Hospital. She went down."

"Fuck," I say.

"It was a scene in there."

"Yeah?"

"Yeah," he says. "And I would've been there if I wasn't working."

He seems disappointed, almost mad at me, like it's only because of assholes like me that he needed to work tonight.

"Sorry."

"If it wasn't you..." He stands as much as he can beneath the low roof. "You okay?"

"Sure." That doesn't seem to satisfy him, so I motion at the cloths in my lap. "I'm fine. I'll be fine."

He looks me over. "Don't go anywhere, Norman, we'll be taking you somewhere in just a few."

He hops down into the accumulating snow and takes the few steps to a cluster of cops and EMTs, a couple firemen, all chatting. They quietly laugh, throw punches in the air and point in different directions, piecing together the night as best they can. Unfortunately, I don't have

259

to do that. I remember it all. I can't say who did what to whom, exactly, but I know enough to know how badly I've fucked up. At least two jobs have been lost tonight, Nikki's and mine. Who knows what charges will be filed once it all gets sorted out. I've let down Dad, and definitely Nikki.

I pushed a 14-year-old to the ground, after her cleavage was in my face, her hands on my lap. I got a lap dance from one of my students in front of the whole town. Possibly the worst Reunion Night performance in Garrison's history. The only thing that happened tonight was that I proved the whole town right. All these years, despite my return to work at the high school, the heart of small town pride, I'm still one of the biggest fuck-ups Garrison has ever produced. My new shirt covered in blood says it all. You can't escape, you can't change, you should have been mourning, but were too busy drinking and hurting children, you asshole, you fucker. You murderer.

# Chapter Thirty

## Nikki

Nikki knows she is in a large room; all she can see is the soft shower curtain surrounding and separating the hospital cot. Her finger is clipped into a white plastic thing. A curly cord stretches from the clip to a machine that beeps every second or so. The thin paper separating her bare skin from the bed sheets crinkles against her ass every time she moves. Her feet dangle. She doesn't feel badly hurt. Sore, bruised up a bit, cold, but fine. Not like Norm. He'd looked bad last she'd seen. Laid out on the sidewalk like that, gushing blood. She doesn't know if he saw her collapse. Nikki wonders where he is. Wonders if Blake is with him. Norm probably thinks she passed out from the fight, but no. It was all in her head. It was all that water.

She lost her shit, Nikki knows. She's always heard of bartenders leaping over the bar, just didn't think it actually happened. Well, damn.

Sherry never landed a solid punch on her, just lots of pushing and hair pulling. Nikki got more bruised up by being pulled off Norm so those assholes could kick him. She'd been felt up by whoever had been holding her back and thrown a few elbows blindly back. The drop on the icy sidewalk hurt her more than Sherry's flailing. Maybe they all should have jumped on Sullivan, finally finished him off in some high school revenge fantasy.

Nikki listens to the regular beeping of the machine, and tries to slow her heart. She concentrates on her breathing. The beeps only come faster.

Destiny, that stupid, naïve child. Oh, God, Norm. What the fuck happened?

She pulls at her hospital bracelet, thinking to rip it off and walk out, but it won't break, and that's enough to hold her in place. She satisfies herself by disconnecting her finger from the beeping machine. There is no way she still has a job, nor can she get another one bartending. Not in this town. Not after tonight, not after protecting a customer rather than the owner. Each bar in town is connected to the other by strange bonds, traced through generations and shifting, layered levels of loyalty. Nikki has no family or friend connections in the business to hook her up, and that's what it takes. She's neglected to make any real connections; she has been too busy working out the connections in her head.

And look how well that has worked out. This whole month, she feels so stupid now, working her way in with Norm and Blake. Showing up with pizza and pussy, all in some selfish attempt to make her imagined world become reality. She shakes her head, drops her chin to rub against the worn cotton of her hospital gown, covered with cutesy pictures of clouds and waterfalls. Nikki wonders if this, tonight's debacle, will break Blake. He's so lonely.

She was wrong to think that anything happening inside her head would ever truly occur outside. Sitting here with her work clothes piled uselessly on a chair, her back exposed, she sees the selfishness of the past years. Nikki sees how the past has led step by step to this moment, this present, this disaster—this which has never appeared in her head. Here, in the hospital where she was born, there are no trees, no sunshine, and no swirling water. There's only the wish that those had never appeared.

Exposed in this new light of selfishness and disaster, her life seems wasted. Nikki lies flat on the hospital bed, wishing someone would operate. She stares into the fluorescent lights until she's blinded. She wills doctors to arrive. Their paper covered mouths and hair would circle over her. Then a gas mask blocking her vision, softening the light until darkness. They could cut her open, remove some broken bit of brain and replace it with some more harmonious piece, folded into the proper curve of her brain. She would sit up, blink a few times, and move on.

During her time in the mental hospital, she'd been so sure that she could handle her vision, that she knew exactly what it was. She'd been disdainful of any doctor's attempt at swaying her. Or curing her. Her selfishness, as she now sees it, wouldn't allow them that. She'd thought the doctors small minded and manipulative, interlopers in a world they couldn't possibly understand. They performed plodding psychiatric probes with dull blades incomparable to the grace of her vision. She'd thought.

Then, she'd been proud of her deceit. She'd fooled them into granting her freedom. They'd cured her of nothing, because she wasn't crazy. Well, but of course she was. And still is. If she isn't, why hasn't she spoken of her vision to anyone?

She had convinced herself that everyone hides a similar secret from the world. We all walk around with our piece of future knowledge hidden in our heads, Nikki had thought. That it is, in fact, our shared deepest secret. That is how God, or whatever, showed himself, and we all keep it to ourselves. She thought other people as cowardly as she, to not share their personal vision with the world, and that is also an unacknowledged truth, Nikki had thought, that we are all cowards.

Nikki had even been delusional enough to worry that maybe she was doing a poor job with her bit of the future. She'd been so self-involved, she assumed everybody else even more so. Oh Christ, she thinks as she runs her hands back through her hair, trying to track down her elastic and fix her ponytail, clean herself up, either to walk right out of here, or check herself in. Maybe she would admit everything. "Listen, I'm crazy. Fucking nuthouse. Take me back. I'll listen this time. I swear."

A white-robed doctor walks in just as she stands. He doesn't take his eyes off his clipboard, just makes a couple quick motions with his pen. Nikki imagines him checking off a couple boxes. Nicole Follansbee. Check. Selfish bitch. Check. Shithouse crazy. Check.

She finally speaks, "Can I help you?"

"Hmm, what? Nicole? How are you doing this evening?"

That's how they do it, she thinks, they start with these innocuous questions, and you don't know how to answer them. Would it be better to say she was awful? Or should she say she's fine, because she's not hurt and that's all this wet-eyed man really cares about?

"Fine. You?" she says.

"How are we feeling?" He finally looks up from his clipboard. He actually has a very kind smile, and Nikki regrets her sudden anger. He hugs the clipboard to his chest, and Nikki glances down at his sensible doctor clogs before meeting his eyes. They both seem on the verge of tears.

"Got in a bit of a scuffle, did we?" He pulls a pen light from his pocket and, still hugging the clipboard with one hand, shines it into her eyes.

"You could say that." Nikki looks left. Right.

"Did you get any in?"

"Pardon me?"

"Hold your head up high, there, like that. Did you get a punch in?"

Nikki laughs. "A couple good ones. I'm not sure if they hit who they were supposed to, though."

"Hmm. It goes like that sometimes." He clicks the pen light on and off a couple times before clipping it to the pocket of his white coat. "Does anything hurt inside?"

"No."

"Headache?"

"No more than usual. No."

The doctor leans back on the heels of his clogs and smiles at her, writes something on his clipboard. "It says here you passed out. Is that correct?"

Nikki tugs at her hospital gown and scratches her neck. Now would be the time to fess up, she thinks, just say it. Tell him everything.

She says, "Yes. Yes, I think I did."

"Does that happen often?" The doctor moves his head back and forth, appraising her from slightly different angles.

"Sometimes. I guess. But no, I'm fine. I think I was just angry. Dehydrated, you know?"

"Reunion Night," he says.

"It gets very busy at the bar."

"Here, too." He looks at her for a moment longer, smiling.

Nikki finds herself smiling back.

"I recommend scheduling an appointment with your regular doctor, if you have one." He raises his eyebrows. Nikki nods. "And taking a couple aspirin. Go to bed and forget about this."

"That would be great."

"Your vitals are good. I think we'll be just fine here."

Nikki begins to step toward her clothes, then remembers her bare ass hanging out the back of her hospital gown and stops. The doctor stands, still watching her. Nikki stands back up straight. She says, "Thank you."

The doctor smiles and leaves, closing the curtain behind him. Nikki dresses, her jeans tight and cold against her skin. She wonders where she should go. Home? To sit, maybe sleep. Norm's? She doesn't know if she is ready for that conversation yet. Or if he is. It would be more confession, and she needs to brace herself for the weight of those revelations.

She realizes her car is still at The Lock Up. It's only a couple miles, but the snow had been building even when she passed out, and she has only her work shoes. Sneakers, not fit for a walk in a storm, but, and she pictures herself slipping over snowbanks and getting sloshed by the snow plow's spray, neither is she. Nikki isn't ready for a walk through the same old streets under a new light. She has spent her whole life under the idea of some sort of assumed greatness. It is terrifying to re-enter the world freed of the future.

If ever she had thought herself ready for a future she knew, Nikki knows for certain that she isn't ready for this, a world without hints, where she is free to follow anything she wants.

# Chapter Thirty-One

Bloody, sorry, and sober, I walk. I wonder what Dad knows, if anything, if he's awake yet. Town is silent. The deep snow reflects white bright, with more falling between the high red bricks of town. There's not a car, not a person going to work, walking a dog, nothing. Nothing but me and my bloodstains. I'm exhausted. Coffee is probably the best move, more for the time than the caffeine. I want to put off any explaining until I can understand it all myself. I may never get home.

The coffee shop looks empty, no crowd to deal with. As I approach, I see it's only empty because it's closed. The other coffee shop is also dark. They're supposed to be open early, when people need them, maybe it's too early, I don't know. I walk toward home, past the closed gas station, with its gas station coffee. After shivering around the pumps for a few minutes, Thanksgiving occurs to me.

The idea of turkey and stuffing and mashed potatoes disappears as quickly as it came. There'll be none of that without Mom. The Thanksgiving break from work seems less like a treat when I'm pretty well sure it's going to continue long past Sunday.

Last night, as I sat in the new police station, after being thrown out of the old one on my ass, I denied my right to a phone call—without even being offered one. I just told them I wasn't calling anyone. Like that showed them. As if I knew my rights so well that I could predict what they're going to offer me, rather than the reality of just having watched enough TV. They could've kept me forever, if they wanted, but Dad doesn't need this shit, so I told them I wasn't calling anyone. Nikki had been taken away in an ambulance. And who else would I call?

The cops, as a group, were unimpressed with my knowledge of Miranda rights. They responded to my refusal of phone privileges by relating horror stories from Dad's classroom, bad grades and impossible exams. I was allowed to walk out this morning with nothing but a blood covered shirt and a warning to expect official visitors in the next couple days. Oh yeah, and stay the hell out of The Lock Up. They would tell me nothing of Nikki and stopped speaking when I asked if Destiny was okay.

I never should have left the house last night. I should've imagined Mom's pleading in my head, don't go, don't go, you can see your friends anytime, and I would've appreciated the fact that Mom still thought I had friends, and maybe I would have stayed, drinking with Dad and enjoying cookies and whiskey. Of course, I wouldn't have come home if Mom were alive.

Half the houses I pass are lined with cars, half are darkened. Maybe they'll all be full in a few hours. Early riser chefs are awake and cooking turkey smell floats between the snowflakes. The homey feeling which that smell should instill is absent. The sky is solid gray, so much darker than the snow it creates. Even the road sides are pure white, not yet marred by slushy tires. I walk down the middle of the road, leaving knee deep tracks above the hidden yellow line. Then I'm standing before our silent house, not wanting to disturb what will surely be a temporary peace.

The kitchen is empty. Cheery TV voices from the living room laud parade floats and small town marching bands. None of those voices rise in greeting, or come into the kitchen bearing the perfumey hugs of visiting relatives. There's coffee in the maker and a few dishes on the counter. Not a noise from Dad. I consider telling him that I spent the night at Nikki's and saving the real story for later. That may retain whatever Thanksgiving cheeriness we have hanging around this old house. Against the small window above the sink, picture frames rest. They were carefully crafted from popsicle sticks and presented in newspaper wrapping during a different life. Mom watches me from these frames.

The TV is talking to no one; the room is empty. I walk around like a stranger, like a burglar, searching not for valuables, but significance. What, among these relics, holds the clue, the connection, the incriminating evidence that we all should have seen? There, the picture of me holding a lunchbox, maybe it hides a gun. The homemade pitcher shaped like a dog, maybe it was intended to pour sacrificial blood. Nothing gives itself up, and I think maybe the only hiding we do is not looking hard or honestly enough.

A toilet flushes upstairs. He's here. There's no way to cover this shirt or this shame, so I take a deep breath and stand up straight.

"Norman? Is that you?" His voice is quiet. I wonder what he knows, which good citizen called him to inform?

"It's me. I'm home," I say.

"I'm coming down. Hold on."

Where would I go? Water runs for a minute and eventually the footsteps move to the stairs, down around the landing, and there he is in

271

ironed khakis and a tucked in plaid shirt. His good one.

"Happy Thanksgiving," I say.

"Oh, Norman." Dad hurries over the rug, head down, and wraps around me, holding my arms at my sides, before stepping back. "Are you okay? You look terrible. Your nose." He reaches up to touch my face, but stops, and runs his hand down my bloody shirt.

"I'm fine, Dad, I'm okay." I can't look at him. "I guess you heard?"

"I can't believe that woman, bringing her child to that bar. She should've been the one in jail all night."

"It's not her fault."

"Norm. You would never..."

"What?"

"With a student. Never."

I take what is now Nikki's seat on the couch and run my hand over the rough fabric.

Dad says, "Nicole came by. Last night. Thank God."

I look up. "Nikki was here? Is she okay?"

"She's fine. She was worried. Told me what happened." He sits next to me and places his hand on my back, leaves it there. "She apologized."

"What does she have to apologize for?" I imagine she apologized for what is going to happen now. That she won't be around anymore, that she wanted Dad to know what happened and why she can't see me again. I imagine her hugging him as she stood to leave and him telling her to stay, just stay, have a drink and let's wait for Norm to come home.

Dad retrieves his hand, rubs his eyes and drags his fingers through his beard. "I don't know, exactly. I invited her to stay and wait with me.

But she left."

"Forever?"

Dad smiles. "She'll be back. It's Thanksgiving, Norman. She had to go be with her family."

"I'm sorry, Dad, I'm so sorry." I don't try to hide the tears when they come. I allow them to fall onto my shirt, willing each one to absorb a drop of blood, to replace it, and if I can keep crying long enough, it will all go away. That's all it will take: enough tears, and even the blood that can no longer be seen will become changed, cleansed. It will be this town's long-awaited transubstantiation of the past. Enough tears running torrents through the snow, and it will all melt away until everything will be back the way it was. I won't be here.

"It's okay, son, it's okay, you don't have to be sorry." Dad seems taken aback by my reaction. His hand returns to its repetitive circle on my back. "It sounds like you got kind of screwed on this one."

"I don't mean last night, not just last night...for it all."

"You're here now, it's okay."

"I'm here? That doesn't make anything okay, or better." I'm standing, wiping at my face.

"It certainly helps," he says, looking up at me, eyes wide between his hair and his beard.

I can't tell if Dad thinks that's wisdom or simply something to say. He doesn't seem to grasp that there is more going on here than last night. I don't have the words to catch him up on everything he should know. "It certainly hasn't helped me much."

"Your mother would be happy that you're back."

"Mom is dead, Dad. She's not happy about anything."

273

"I disagree, Norm. I think you do, too." He's quiet. "She was never upset with you."

"Everyone was upset with me." I hate the whine in my voice, that high squeal behind tears.

Dad doesn't look up at me from the couch. "Are we talking about Fitzy?"

"Shouldn't we be? Always?"

"We never really did, did we?"

"Everybody else did. But not us."

He stands. "I didn't know what to do, Norm. Neither of us did."

"Christ, Dad, what did I do? I should've stayed away, forever. Or I never should've left. Maybe both."

"Well, you couldn't do that. I could have done so much more." He holds his head.

"Like what? I feel like it just keeps happening."

"What? What keeps happening?" He's close to me, smelling of soap.

"All of it. People are dying and..."

He looks at me, his hands on my shoulders, until I return his gaze. My snot is mixed with the last chunks of dried blood, and I'm sniffling like crazy to hold it in. He watches me with filling eyes. I want him to wipe my nose, clap me in an awkward hug, and tell me to clean my room. Scold me and tell me what I need to do. Hit me. Tell me to never leave the house again. Send me out in the snow. Let me call Fitzy and laugh about the craziness at the bar last night. Let Fitzy pick up Nikki and come over. We'll all cook a turkey together, laughing as Mom lies through each bite, telling us it's perfect, perfect, what a good job! How can anything be wrong with all of us here? How could anything go wrong?

"People die, Norman," Dad says. "They just do."

"I know. I know that."

He sits, hands together in his lap. "We had a wonderful night together. Her last night."

I wipe at my nose, check my hand for blood. There's a small streak, and I press my shirt tails to my face. I inspect the scrapes dragged up the backs of my hands.

"She drank wine that night. Hadn't touched the stuff in months." He laughs.

"You never told me."

"About the wine? It was just the one night."

"About Mom. About how sick she was."

He turns his body toward me, followed by his head, and looks about to speak before his face breaks. He covers it with his hands. "I know."

"It's okay," I say, because what else can it be now?

"We talked about it. She said tell you, I said no, let you live your life. Then I decided we should tell you, she said no."

"It's okay."

"We should have told you as soon as we knew. She didn't want to make you feel like you had to come back."

"And you?"

"Oh, Norman." He turns away, and I rest my hands on his. "I didn't, I couldn't..."

"What, Dad? It doesn't matter now."

He looks at me, his eyes as red as my shirtfront. "I didn't want it to hurt her when you wouldn't come home. I'm sorry, I'm sorry."

I laugh. At his reasoning, at the truth behind it, at all of it. The past—it's ridiculous. And it makes me laugh. He looks so small, huddled into himself. His back is shaking, and I can't see his face.

"Oh, Jesus, Dad. You were probably right. It's okay."

"You would've come home. You're here now."

"Yeah. It's worked out well, right?"

"I'm sorry, Norm."

"What did you talk about? Over the wine?"

He tries out a laugh, wipes at his nose, forces his face to relax, to stop the tears. "What did we talk about? Nothing. The same things we always talked about. We talked about you."

"I should've been there." My hand is twitching over his. He straightens, wipes away tears.

"No. We were right. If you were there we would've talked to you, not about you. And it was nice. It was just so nice."

Dad stands and heads to the kitchen in silence. Out the window, the snow falls harder. Small flakes, sure to last all day. Each little speck is so insubstantial, a nothing that melts away with the slightest touch. But they add up, they pile on top of each other, building until everything is hidden and silenced. I follow Dad into the kitchen, finding him in the refrigerator. I gently turn him into my arms, hold him in the light of our empty fridge.

# Chapter Thirty-Two

## Nikki

Nikki breathes deep before walking through the door. Her father greets her in sweatpants and offers his standard soft hug, afraid of further breaking his fragile daughter. He asks how she's doing, and Nikki knows this is not a general question. It's a check-in on her current mental status. She lies and says everything is fine. He brings her a glass of water from the display of pitchers, mixers, and bottles of cheap pink wine.

From the kitchen, her mother offers loaded questions about her work hours, sleeping habits, and whether Nikki was involved in that commotion downtown last night. Nikki doesn't answer anything, only yells "hello" from the front hall. Her father apologizes with his eyes, and they settle into the living room, moving laundry aside to uncover the couch. They drink water and watch the televised parade. Marching bands trudge their instruments through the snow, and cartoon balloons float above it all. The TV personalities shiver between earmuffs and smile behind misty breath.

Blake's offer to stay the night had been so tempting. The couch was all hers, he said. She could wait in Norm's bed. Stay, please. Nikki wished she could have told him more. She wanted to tell him why she was sorry and in exactly how many ways she has been wrong. She wanted him to take comfort in the fact that Norm was fine. He'll be home soon, she almost told him. Then she remembered that she has no idea what the future holds, and she left.

After last night's blood and revelations, Nikki thinks that her family's Thanksgiving will be calming. A breeze. She realizes, again, that just because something is true in her head doesn't mean it actually is.

There are several clattering crashes from the kitchen, during which her father stares at the door until he's assured Nikki's mother isn't coming in. Nikki watches the snow on TV, falling in a city hours away, and marvels at how it matches the scene through the window. Her father looks at her for a few moments; he asks her again how she's doing. She answers with another lie.

"Getting there," she says.

"That's good," he says, afraid to ask anything deeper.

Another hour and Nikki's brother, with the tribe he'd married into, enters and explodes the silence. A horde of children run rampant, grabbing morning cookies from the several trays scattered through the house. They jump on her Dad's lap, spilling cranberry juice. He smiles beatifically and accepts them all. Nikki's brother and wife pour drinks for themselves, jackets still on, and go outside to smoke.

Nikki watches the children watch TV. Their dolls and the pictures on their t-shirts are machined copies of the characters floating through the sky on TV. Her mother's voice demands help from the kitchen, and Nikki works her way around the children. They never seem to know quite how to handle her. She's an aunt by marriage whom they never see. Nikki is sure they hear her badmouthed at home. The youngest one clings to Nikki's leg as she walks stiffly into the kitchen, where her mother immediately dismisses the child back to the TV.

"Bye, honey," Nikki says. She can never keep their ages or names straight.

"So," her mother says. "What are you doing?"

"I came in to help."

"You know what I mean."

"I'm doing fine."

Her mother turns her head, her body still working mashed potatoes around a huge pot. "I doubt that."

"I'm fine, Mom." Nikki lifts a lid from a dish and reaches in for stuffing before her mother smacks the back of her hand with a wooden spoon.

"That's your brother's stuffing. I put sausage in it. The kind you like is in the bird."

"Thanks," Nikki says and takes a bite of it anyway.

"Are you seeing anyone?"

Nikki doesn't want to have this conversation. There's no answer that's going to satisfy. She runs through a few fictions. Maybe she could be seeing a doctor, or a wealthy Canadian. "Actually, yes. I guess I am."

"You guess?"

"I am. He went to Garrison High with me."

"A local boy?" her mother says, not bothering to hide the disdain.

"Norm Mean."

Her mother turns from the stove, the same old apron stretched and tiny over her belly. "What the hell, Nicole? Is he out of jail?"

"He never went to jail, Mom."

"There was something. Can't you do better than that?"

"I don't think I can," Nikki says and turns from the kitchen. She angles past her brother and his wife, who carry drinks and frown.

In the bathroom she stares at her reflection, checking the makeup over her black eye. It's turning a sickly green-yellow. She looks around the bathroom, the one she shared for years with her family, and it looks foreign. The dirt between the cracked tiles, the stained towels, and the wire basket of outdated magazines beside the toilet disgust her. This is not where she is going to be today.

Nikki crosses through the living room, her father sits surrounded by children, all entranced by the TV. She puts her jacket on by the door and goes to the kitchen. The three of them, her mother, brother, and his wife, stand in a tight circle and cradle drinks. They all turn at her entrance.

"Leaving?" the wife says.

Nikki claims sickness. They all assume that to be true, anyway, she thinks. Her apologies go unacknowledged as the three of them exchange looks.

"Did you want to wait for the turkey? You could take some with you. Maybe have a real meal," her mother says.

"I think I just need to go. I'll come by soon, though."

"We're always here."

Nikki works her way through all the nieces and nephews, buttoning her jacket. She says goodbye to her Dad, who looks confused and guilty over her departure. She assures him she'll be fine. Then she leaves.

She watches the snow fall through swipes of the wipers and smokes with the radio off. Snowflakes twist through her open window. Hers is the only car on the road, a lonely speck between destinations. She has been seeing Norm to make sure he's there in her future. Because she knew he would, he had to be. She'd seen it. Now what pulls her to him? A need to explain, perhaps. Or something greater.

Seeing Blake's car in the driveway, Nikki feels lighter, knowing she has arrived at the proper place. She is comforted with knowing what's on the other side of that door without the need to know any further. It feels honest. This is the difference between wanting a future and wanting the future. Nikki knows she will have to explain this at some point. She will need to tell Norm she understands this difference. She will tell him she's here now because she wants to be, not because she needs to be, and that is the difference.

The door is unlocked, the house empty. She takes a walk through, touching surfaces, feeling the cold porcelain knick-knacks and picture frames. She pauses at their life's memorabilia. Back on the front step, smoking in the snow, she spots a double-row of footprints over the lawn and follows them. No one else has been out, and their tracks are easy to spot down the street, around a corner. At first it's a fun game through the empty white town. She wonders which way they will turn next and what they were talking about, who chose the path. Then she doesn't need the footprints anymore. She knows where they lead.

# Chapter Thirty-Three

Graveyards are beautiful beneath snow. The headstones appear as orderly drifts, their purpose softened, the lives they mark hidden, their stories mingled. It's silent, the snow too soft for our steps to sound. Dad and I walk a row apart. I lead, ahead by a few stones. He's quietly given me the choice of whose grave we see first. There are no birds; even they are nestled away this day with their families.

More snow is falling, large decorative flakes. Earlier, Dad made eggs and toast, sipping coffee while I ate. He spoke of the days following Fitzy's death. How I had come home, babbling and crying, muddy, wet, until they could calm me enough to sit and tell them what had happened. A flurry of phone calls, then Dad at the police station. Mom making me breakfast. He says I didn't leave my room until the funeral. I don't remember that. My memory begins at the funeral, high on enough substances to make the whole day float, and then, back at school, where friends passed in the halls. Then a world of memories, in a different color, with different air. Then yesterday. Then today.

My jacket is gone from Fitzy's grave. I hope it blew away, and his mother didn't have to wonder who'd been visiting her son's grave. Would she have thought of me?

Dad stands back, pretending to check his watch and blow his nose; he's leaving me be. I can't even read the gravestone, the snow is so high.

I reach to brush the snow off, but then let it rest. It's so pretty, I can't disturb it. I figured I'd cry once I was here, standing above Fitzy, but I don't. Instead, I think practical thoughts. I imagine the workers with red bandanas tucked into their back pockets leaning on shovels, watching the backhoe dig the classic six feet down. I imagine the stone being placed and wonder how far down it goes. I picture a family, comforting a wailing mother on her knees, but stop that stop that, that is an imagined scene, that isn't my memory. Fitzy's grave. It's here, and I was there when he was buried. I was there, and there's no need to imagine. I was there, and the truth is: it was awkward and blurry. Corny held me upright and walked me through a suspicious crowd, many of them believing I killed the dead boy. It was fucking terrible and still I don't cry. But I stop pretending I don't remember, because I do.

I wonder if Fitzy ever got to grow up, wherever he is, or if he's forever that drunken seventeen-year-old boy, ecstatic with the beer and the stars, swimming for the pure joy and pride of it in our little pond. I wonder if I ever got to grow up or if that's what I'm doing now, or if any of us get to grow up. And if so, how did we get there?

Dad clears his throat. I've been staring at the gravestone for a long time. I turn and he smiles. The snow is lovely. He turns away, hands shoved into his long wool coat, and I see his bald spot hidden up among all that gray hair, and I want that. It says a certain something about age and knowledge. Or at least experience, and maybe there isn't a difference between knowledge and experience.

"Is this our Thanksgiving, Dad?"

"I wouldn't know what else to do. Your mother always took care of the cooking." He looks at the sky. "Now that I think about it, your mother always took care of everything."

"You're doing fine, Dad."

"Thank you. Imagine what we would be doing if she were here."

I laugh and kick some snow, watch the arc it makes. "We can go see her now. Let's go see her now."

On this path, I let Dad lead the way. Maybe he sees the woman ahead of us before I do. He's bearing straight for her when I look up from our snowy footprints; if so, he shows no indication of seeing her. The woman is out of focus, blurred by the snowflakes.

As we get closer, I see she is standing at Mom's gravestone, looking down, her back to us. She has long hair that blows gently with the wind. It seems wrong to say anything to Dad, as absorbed as he appears to be in his thoughts. So I follow behind, silent, matching my footfalls with his, placing my feet in the shapes he leaves in the snow. Ghost, I think. She's a ghost. He doesn't see her, I think. It's only me. It's my mind and this graveyard, one of those flashbacks I've heard so much about. I'm afraid to look directly at her.

I watch Dad's bald spot bob ahead of me. The walking is slow through all of last night's snow. Today it falls softly, just a finishing touch. I see that the woman at the grave is Nikki. I try not to appear too gleeful.

She turns and raises her arm in a stiff right angle, holding it there until I mirror the gesture. Dad keeps trudging, right on until we're beside her, lined up like a parade. Nikki, Dad, me, all standing before Mom's grave, trying to read her name under the snow. For a moment, I think it may melt under the heat of our collective gaze. I realize that there is now a gravestone. Dad has been doing something more than drinking.

Nikki says, "I followed your footprints. From home." She points down in explanation.

Dad reaches out with his arms, heavy under the wool. Nikki and I slide in beneath, our heads tucking instinctively into his shoulders. We stand like that, together, for a very long time.

Finally, Dad speaks, "Happy Thanksgiving, Pat."

"Happy Thanksgiving, Mom."

"Happy Thanksgiving, Mrs. Mean."

"Pat," Dad says. "She'd want you to call her Pat."

"Pat. I never knew her."

"No," I say.

And Dad says, "Neither did I."

# Chapter Thirty-Four

"Do you remember if we had a good time?" I ask when Nikki begins
to stir. Sunlight creeps across the floor, promising the end of the storm.

She pulls sweaty lengths of hair from her face, then leans on an
elbow and eyes me.

I reach over the piled blankets to tuck her hair behind her ear. My
hand lingers there, and she pushes against it, rolling her face around to
kiss my palm before dropping back on the pillow.

"I remember laughing," she says.

"I remember crying."

She says, "That too," and pushes me flat, so she can rest on my
chest. Our bodies relax into each other until we sleep again.

When I wake up, the sun is high enough to fill the room and I'm
alone. It's late, closer to lunch than breakfast. A truck drives by,
momentarily drowning out birdsong. My head aches, my lungs feel
scratched, and last night reappears in small flashes. Standing in the yard,
staring up at the snow, laughing, our tongues out to catch the spiraling
flakes. I remember touching my tongue to Nikki's, our bodies hidden
under jackets and gloves. Dad watched, then turned away. There was
TV, there was a board game. There were many phone calls to many
closed pizza places. There were declarations that this was the best
Thanksgiving ever. There were tears declaiming this to be the worst

Thanksgiving possible. There was tearing clothes off, Nikki talking too much to kiss, talking and crying, nearly babbling through tears about something, the future. Me. Then there was waking up.

Dad and Nikki are watching the weather channel when I come downstairs, bowls of cereal on their laps. Dad is disheveled, his hair sticking up in front and matted down in back, nearly covering his bald spot. He's wearing the same clothes as yesterday, with more wrinkles.

"Morning," I say, dropping beside Nikki. I lean back and feel around my nose. There's definitely more of it. If I look down hard enough, I can see the bridge is swollen and bruised. I can't really breathe through it. I touch it gingerly, checking all around my face for sore spots. It's taken some time for my injuries to fully appear. I look to Nikki for sympathy.

She looks back. "You snore now."

Dad laughs and talks through his cereal, "He's just been too polite to do it around you. They say it's going to be hot today."

"I'm starving," I say, trying to remember if we ever got dinner last night. It seems impolite to ask. I pat Nikki's knee, and she taps my nose.

"Ouch. I need food." I push myself from the couch, gently feeling my ribs and neck to see what else still hurts. Turns out to be pretty much everything. I've never been beat up like this before.

I'm rummaging through the dregs of cereal boxes, contemplating which two to combine to get a full bowl, when I feel Nikki's hand on my back.

"Are you okay?" she says, more tenderly now that we're alone.

"Wonderful. Do you think Cheerios with Corn Flakes or the bran stuff?"

"Definitely Corn Flakes. You're all right?" Her hand is still on my back. I stop mixing cereals and turn around.

"I'll be fine," I say. Her eyes don't meet mine, but tick off the bruises and cuts on my face. "This will all go away. How about you?"

"Will I go away?"

"Sure. That, too."

She looks to the window, at the branches dripping themselves clean of last night's storm. "No."

"No, you won't go away, or, no, you're not okay?"

"It's going to be warm today." She turns to the fridge, gets out the milk.

"Okay."

She puts the milk down next to my cereal bowl, mixes the Cheerios and Corn Flakes, pours the milk, and hands me the bowl. "Both. I'm here. And I'm not okay."

"I'm glad. About the first thing. I'm glad."

Nikki nods and I eat, too hungry to continue without even this meager breakfast. I don't know if there's something I should remember from last night, but don't, and she does, or what. After a couple bites I say, "So, it's going to be warm today?"

"That's what they say. Some sort of record. Snowfall and then high temperature or something. A differential. They seemed very excited about it. On TV. Black Friday and shopping. They were very excited about shopping."

"They were? Did we make the news? The other night?"

Nikki snorts, watching me eat. "I don't think another fight at The Lock Up gets a headline anymore. But maybe. I haven't read the paper in days."

"Can we hide from it as long as possible?"

"I want to go walk around."

I'm not ready for that much activity yet. I need coffee. And a couch. Probably a shower. I moan and rock my head back and forth, as if I'm weighing her walking option, but thinking, no, that sounds terrible.

I say, "I vote for hiding out."

"Walk. It's beautiful out there."

Balancing my bowl, I reach out to touch her breast, but she moves subtly enough out of reach. "It's beautiful in here."

"I'm going for a walk. You have fifteen minutes. If you want to come."

She walks out of the kitchen, through the living room and up the stairs. I pour coffee and return to the couch. Dad's dozing, and I gently move a coffee cup from his lap to the table.

There's nothing about another walk through town that sounds appetizing. I can't imagine what out there could surprise or please. I'll go, I'll go. But I'm taking another fourteen minutes to get ready.

Nikki is sitting on the front steps when I come out with my boots untied. I'm holding my jacket and silver coffee travel mug, but leave them on the steps. It is warm, almost hot. A city plow truck buzzes past, orange plow raised. There's nothing left for it to push. Water streams down into gutters, and birds land everywhere, poking their heads into the patches of grass.

"It's like spring out here," I say and decide to just hold my jacket.

"I told you," Nikki says, reaching over to tie my boots. "Thanks for coming."

"Thanks for tying my shoes. It hurts to bend down."

She heads to the sidewalk and I follow, stepping a bit to keep up. The trees are clear of snow, and the sun beams down. Steam rises from the back of Nikki's jeans, where she was sitting on the steps. I think up some 'hot ass' joke, but don't say it.

We pass kids in t-shirts rolling up the last dregs of the heavy, wet snow into tiny snowmen, laughing at their own failure. Large cars full of women returning from shopping missions pull into driveways. A few men talk, leaning their tall roof rakes against trees. They seem happy to let the sun do their work. I'm glad I came. Nikki was right, it is beautiful. I can't believe the change.

After minutes of silence, I offer coffee. She declines.

I offer observations. Nikki nods her agreements, yes, it is beautiful. She stays silent. I want her to say so many things. Yes, it's amazing how that storm amounted to nothing, how it led to this. How, really, everything goes away doesn't it? And we have no say in it, most of the time, it's like these things just keep happening, constantly, then fade away until only the idea remains. Yes, it's easy to forget, and it happens all over again. Doesn't it sometimes seem, doesn't it, that it's as if these things happen in the world, like this storm, we all saw this storm, felt its cold and wind, but that it's only for you, or me, or whoever needs it the most, that it's actually happening. That it's all for very specific reasons or people, Norm, doesn't it? But she says nothing and I keep talking, trying to piece together last night and fit it together with this beautiful morning.

She says, "Shut up. We need to talk."

"We are."

"I need to talk."

"Okay. Talk, then."

"You need to shut up. I don't know where to start. Norm. I don't know." She turns on her heels, stopping me, her hand held up flat. "I was in the hospital."

"Yesterday? I know."

She looks at the sun. "Yes, but before that, too. I was in the hospital..."

"Up north?"

Her gaze leaves the sky. "You know?"

"I know now. Maybe I already did," I say and reach for her hands. They're given, but without any intent or affection.

"I was in the crazy hospital, Norm."

"I get it. Are you crazy?" But I say it with a smile, like I know she's not, but if she is, I'll be okay. What else can I be, after everything, under today's sun?

Her face twists for a moment, her hands twitch in mine, maybe she's been asked that too many times. But you know what? Not by me. There seems to be too much going on today for any subtlety. She smiles at the ground, then at me.

She says, "No..."

"Good, then."

"No. I don't think I am anymore. But I never thought I was. But now, maybe, I think that I was. Once. Maybe. But not anymore."

"Crazy about me?" I wink my black eye. That draws a sigh.

"I think so. It's different, now. Now that I'm not crazy."

"Were you nuts yesterday?"

Her brown eyes look up to the right, as if she really has to think about that one, run over some dates in her head. She laughs, her first real one of our walk. "No, yesterday I was not crazy."

"That's a good start. How about the day before?"

"For most of it, yeah, I was shithouse crazy."

"Wow. Did you ever kill anybody?"

"Not that I know of." Still smiling.

"Looks like I've got one up on you, then."

And there goes that smile. "I'm being serious."

"So am I."

I am being serious, for the first time in anytime. The madness of the past couple days seems to have melted with the snow, revealing something new. At least the hope of it. A line has reached its endpoint. Or perhaps several lines have met at an intersection, and it's here where there's change.

Every ending is also a beginning. It just depends on your direction. Today has the bite of the past. Last night's storm swirled everything up, from winter storm back to summer day, times have switched around us. We, Nikki and I, are in the eye of our lives, the future behind us and the past all around.

"You didn't kill him. You know that," she says.

"Maybe. I certainly didn't save him."

"Nobody is responsible for anyone else. I don't think." Nikki swings her hair behind her and takes my arm to move me along. We're on a sidewalk in front of houses emptying themselves of children, parents moving curtains aside to gauge our level of suspiciousness. "C'mon, let's walk."

It's getting even warmer, there are animals everywhere. Squirrels freeze and scatter at our approach, the sparrows are braver, or just more oblivious. They're landing around us, searching the cracks in the sidewalks until we're past the sidewalks, done with the neighborhoods. The houses are further apart. Snowmobiles, pulled hopefully out of garages, rest idle on the grass in front of these houses.

Finally I say, "So what were you crazy about?"

She walks the white line at the road's edge, and doesn't answer. I watch her place one foot in front of the other, carefully pressing her heel against the toes of her other foot, walking over the line like a tightrope. "Everything, but I guess it was one thing that affected everything else. Made it all crazy, you know?"

"I think so."

She stops balancing and stands straight. "I have visions, Norm."

I say nothing.

"Had visions. Well, just one really."

"That's not bad. Just one."

"It happened a lot."

"Don't you need three before they make you a saint?" I say.

"That's miracles. I'm still a ways off."

"What were your visions of? Fire?"

She glances away. "Close. Water. There was lots of water and noise. And people."

"Anybody I know?"

"That's the thing. For years there was nothing. Blurs and motion, but they would knock me out. I'd be down for an hour after they left. And beat."

I nod and reach over to rub the back of her neck. I don't doubt a word, only listen. She's getting animated, her hands moving up from her waist, acting out the strange movements from her mind.

"Always behind my ears, it would get sweaty and tingly and I'd know it was coming. I'd be covered in sweat after it passed. And all those years, I could never make out any more than water, or the awareness of water. Maybe the smell, like a dream, it was just there without knowing how, everywhere, and there were people shouting."

Her hands float in front of her, swinging in synch at the elbows, like she's moving boxes from an assembly line. Her fingers clench and she stops. "And then, one day, I was at work when it came. I had to go sit in my car, one day—and there you were. Your face right there. Sticking out from everything."

"Really?" I'm proud for a second, and complimented, even though I've done nothing.

"Yeah," she says, looking up. "I didn't even recognize you."

"Ouch."

"That was before you came home. Before we met again."

"How'd you figure it out? That it was me?"

Nikki laughs and stretches out her arms, looking down at them as if she's surprised to see them moving before her. "Good old Garrison High. I looked through the yearbook."

"That picture? It's not my best."

"I began to remember you."

"Something like, 'Norm Mean, what the fuck?' maybe?"

"Actually, yeah, it was a lot like that."

"I bet."

Nikki takes my hand, gently at first, but then harder the longer we walk in silence.

Then she says, "Thank you."

"For being your dream man?"

"That's not what I'm saying —"

"I know. I don't know what...you're welcome. You're more than welcome," I say.

"For not thinking I'm crazy."

"You don't know what I'm thinking."

We stop walking. She says, "Do you think that?"

"No. I don't. I'm in no position to judge."

"I thought that was your specialty. If it's gone, I'll miss it."

"Fine. You're crazy."

She hugs me then, and it feels good to be outside and to feel her without jackets or shivering and do I believe her? I believe she believes her. Walking again, I think of Nikki coming over to me outside the bar that first night, that night at Steve and Sherry's. I got beat up that night, too, and by the same family. I imagine Nikki outside smoking and seeing me, for real, outside her head that first time and walking over; what did she expect?

Did she hope for instant recognition and explanation? A quick reassuring speech, maybe followed by quiet drinks and a plan for the future drawn on a napkin. That's certainly not what I offered, and I feel an apology is required by one of us. For something.

"So," I say. "That first night..."

"Yes."

"Is that why you talked to me? Because of the visions?"

Nikki stops walking and tilts her head straight into the sun. She rubs her face, wiping it clean. "Yes."

"Oh," I say, turning away from her. "I always thought you just liked the cut of my jib."

"Norm. I'm sorry. I'm so sorry, I should've told you a long time ago. We should've talked about this earlier..."

"We should have?"

"I mean me, I should've. Me."

"This isn't something I thought we'd have to talk about. What's your favorite movie? Do like thin crust or Chicago style? Are you only talking to me to because of your vision?"

Nikki is quiet, looking off to her side, breathing deep. She covers her face before pulling her hair back and meeting my eyes. "I know. I'm sorry. I should have...something. It's hard."

"Being a prophet?"

"Don't make fun of me. You don't believe me."

Shit. I don't want to fight about this, nor do I want to really get into whether or not I believe her. And I think the truth is that I don't really care. I have my own secrets. I couldn't care less why she spoke to me, why she walked right up to me, how we came to be.

I say, "I'm sorry, Nikki. It's fine. I don't care. It's fine, come on."

She's crying, rubbing the back of her neck with one hand. I run through my hair, feeling the tender bruises. I drop my jacket on the wet dirt by the roadside to hold her. She lets me, eventually returning my hug.

"This is stupid," she says. "I don't know what to say."

"Nothing. You don't have to say anything."

"Yes. I was amazed to finally see you, for real, before me. That's why I wanted to talk to you. And go home with you, yes, that too. At first, but then, you know. I liked you. And Blake. I like you guys."

"I thought he was joking," I say.

"What?"

"I thought he was joking. We'd both swam across the pond a thousand times."

"Fitzy?"

I nod and look away. I've never spoken this aloud. "It was on his way back to me, it was dark and he started splashing around a lot." I smile at Nikki. "I thought he was fucking with me."

"Norm. Oh God."

"He wasn't under that long. And it was so dark, I couldn't find him. I was so drunk and I waited, then I went in and, and I couldn't find him. And I still thought he was fucking with me, had swum to the shore. Hiding, you know?"

She nods and takes my hands, but I pull them away to wipe my tears. She grabs them back from me, lets her tears run.

"It couldn't have been more than a few minutes until I figured it out. I kept going down, but it was so dark."

"It's not your fault. It's still not your fault."

"We were drunk, and I was so scared. I sat on the dam, went back in. Everyone else was passed out. I just kept thinking he'd pop back up. Come out of the woods. Laughing. I don't know."

"Norm."

"It was just me awake. I never told anyone."

"I know."

"Fuck, Nikki. I thought he was joking."

"I know. It's okay."

"No. It's not. It was just me. I should have...something."

"What?" she says, pulling me to her and holding me there. "What could you have done? How would anything be different?"

"I don't know. We were kids."

She steps back, onto the mud at the roadside, so she can look at me. "Exactly. You were kids. Listen to yourself. You tried to save him, Norm."

"Your shoes are getting all muddy."

"It's not your fault. Do you think it's your fault?"

"I don't know. No. Maybe."

"Stop it."

I look up, finally meeting her eyes. They're wide, with tears streaking her face.

"Thank you," I say.

"I didn't do anything. Nothing has changed, Norm. It's just as much an accident, a tragic accident, as it was five minutes ago."

"I believe you, you know."

"That it's not your fault?"

"That you're not crazy."

"Thank you."

I pull her from the mud onto the road. We lean into each other on the roadside, the pavement clear of snow. The painted white and yellow lines curve parallel into the distance. I can't think of one thing I have left to say.

She sighs and begins to speak, but it's drowned out by sirens. A fire truck goes screaming past, its wind buffeting us hard in its wake. I turn, and she watches over my shoulder as another, smaller one, follows, this one swerving well into the other lane to avoid us. I watch the blank faces of the firemen in the windows, their heads turning to track us as they fly by. I wonder if any of them were witness to the debacle at the bar the other night.

"Damn," I say. I pick up my jacket and we step back over the mud, off the road and onto someone's lawn.

A huge pick up flies by with one of those little stick-on lights on the roof and EMT plates. The driver's eyes meet mine over the CB at his mouth. A volunteer firefighter. He must be psyched. I imagine this is a moment he lives for, running from his family or job to answer a call where he may be needed. I remember those guys in high school, who had the first cell phones, the monstrous yellow ones, clipped to their belts. Two police cars, nearly bumper to bumper, shoot by us, their drivers intent.

"I wonder what's up?" Nikki says.

"Well, we're both here, so it can't be a drunken disturbance."

She laughs, a little too hard for such a joke. "Are you okay?"

"I think so. I'm better than I was."

"That's something."

"You? You okay?" I say.

"I'm something."

My fingertips meet behind her neck, and I pull her gently to my chest. She fits easily under my chin, and we hold each other until I give her a quick kiss on top of her head. She smells like smoke and evaporating water.

"You want to keep walking?" she says.

"Forever. I don't think I have anything else to do. For the rest of the school year."

"We sure fucked up, huh?" We hold hands and walk in the wake of the fire engines. Toward an emergency of some sort.

"Yes we did, Nicole Follansbee, yes we did. And you were always such a good student."

She laughs. "And you were always such a fuck up."

# Chapter Thirty-Five

## Steve

Steve is thankful to be alone in the house. Yesterday's Thanksgiving was a drawn-out hell, filled with arguments over the fight at The Lock Up. Sherry won't stop referring to Norm as either "that asshole" or, to Steve, as "your little friend." She woke Destiny at 4:00 am, without any warning, to go Black Friday shopping. Sherry just couldn't sleep and so decided to wake Destiny, to much swearing. She hadn't extended the offer to Steve, but, he knew, not out of any consideration or kindness.

What a beautiful day, Steve thinks, out on the deck with a mug full of coffee, the good mug. He'd used the expensive coffee he kept hidden in the cupboard.

He watches Lacey run around the lawn, which is quickly revealing itself through the melting snow. Even after the feet of snow accumulated over a couple days, there is nothing on the trees. The short-lived ice on the pond has melted. Under the morning sun a watery center is revealed, black and motionless, surrounded by muddy shards of ice. Steve watches the water while he sips. He keeps thinking he sees a subtle movement there, in the melted center, but maybe it's just the blur of the coffee cup as he lifts it. Steve raises the mug to eye level and glances at the pond. Nothing seems to move. He lowers the mug and glances real quick over at the melting ice. Maybe he sees something this time.

It is a beautiful day. It's a quiet, beautiful day. There's been nothing but trouble, it seems like, since the school year started. Destiny must have arrived at some age that brings trouble. That had been a good age, Steve thinks. Then he looks at the pond.

Fucking Norman. Crawling out of the muck at night, bringing doom. Coming into that goddam bar. Maybe that's when the trouble started. Steve decides that there is definitely something out in the pond.

Lacey stops scampering and points tail out, rifle-straight at the water. They both watch the water. Nothing. Silence. Then something.

Brown, almost black, a ball breaks the surface then descends again, followed by a tail. An animal, a big one. Lacey is going crazy, barking, running a tight circle through the mud, almost into the pond, stopping at the edge. She looks up at Steve, as if for permission.

"Go for it, Lace. I'm not gonna stop you," he says to himself and nods to the dog, who bolts. Taking another sip, he feels he has solved a problem.

Lacey runs into the pond, her splashing and barking breaking the silence. He watches, amazed at how naturally she becomes a predator even after years of housebreaking and domestication. The wild still lives in her muscles and nerves, right under the surface. She lies around all the time, watching TV with them and waiting to be fed. Yet she is an animal. The strangeness of keeping an animal for his own comfort and amusement suddenly strikes him.

Lacey holds her nose up in the air as she paddles toward the creature. Steve is impressed, she's really going after it. On the far shore, by the dam, a beaver, a huge one, flops onto shore. It runs in an odd waddle up the side of the dam, and pauses at the top to look down on Lacey. Steve laughs. If the beaver had a middle finger, it would be raised. It flops onto its belly and slides over the back of the stone dam, out of view.

Steve remembers a few years ago when he heard screams from the backyard. He rushed to the deck and saw a young Destiny in her penguin bathing suit, her favorite one. She wore it all summer, even under her clothes. She was standing, dripping, at the pond's edge and screaming. Steve followed her pointing finger to the edge of the dam, where a bloated dead muskrat floated. It had gotten stuck in the pipe through the dam, finally forced out. Destiny had been terrified, then distraught at the creature's death. They had to bury it in the yard, with a complete funeral service.

He checks his watch, then looks at the sun, pretending for a moment that he can tell the hour by its height in the sky. Still early. He figures he has a few more hours of solitude.

# Chapter Thirty-Six

There's nothing else to confess and we go in silence. Nikki wants to walk and I want to be with Nikki, so I walk. Past closed door houses, taking shortcuts over soggy lawns to straighten out the curves, we walk beneath today's new sun. Her hand feels comfortable in mine, and we walk like teenagers, avoiding each others eyes with fingers intertwined. We've been out so long that I'm hungry again. This morning's mix of cereal couldn't cut the whiskey hangover edge.

We're solidly in the outskirts, and every other house is ramshackle. Each feeling free to leave its hobbies on the lawn: snowmobiles, four-wheelers, and veritable monster trucks. The other houses have paid for all that horsepower. They're new and square, built on those extra acres the ramshackles sold off. Smooth lawns run straight up against a property line of unkempt grass poking through the wheels of forgotten boat trailers which haven't seen water in a decade.

Nikki squeezes my hand, I squeeze back. She's far into her head, lost in thought. I can't pretend to know what she is experiencing, but I can sympathize. My past and future haven't mixed well; my swollen face a monument to their collision. The darkest secret I owned is no longer mine alone. What is going to fill all this new found space in my soul? I don't know what to think about it, yet.

Nikki brushes my chin, pulling me into the present.

"Are we okay?" she says.

"We better be. Neither of us seem to have much else going for us."

"Is that why you're here?"

I smile. "No. There are stranger reasons why people are together."

A boy in The Learning Center the other day had one of those water cycle charts with arrows and cartoon clouds. It showed how water evaporates into clouds, falls, is absorbed and repeats the process unceasingly. Wash, rinse, repeat was how I tried to explain it to the kid, but he hadn't gotten the reference and one look at his hair explained why. The whole little failed lesson reinforced the old scientific platitude that nothing can be created or destroyed. Things don't go away; they just change.

I think of this as we walk, surrounded by water in transition. How true is that, I wonder. Can nothing be new, or forever gone? What of emotions? Any love we feel once belonged to somebody else. Lost through betrayal, death, or boredom, it moved on. Floated around, until it eventually lighted on another's soul. Where have Nikki's visions fluttered off to?

With each new person on the planet, love must lose strength, divvied up as it has to be between the growing billions. We have a fraction of the feeling our forefathers had, each generation thinking they've reached a pinnacle, when, really, they've dropped a notch. We can never be as sad as our fathers, or theirs, or theirs.

"Look," Nikki says. "Another one. And a cop car."

I follow her gaze to a fire truck taking a sharp corner, almost knocking the large sign naming a cul-de-sac development. I haven't realized how far we have walked. "Barbados Pond Estates: An Elliot

Development" the sign reads.

"Shit. I bet it's Destiny."

"Isn't everything? I don't even know if I believe that anymore," Nikki says.

"No. Destiny. She lives here, with Steve and Sherry. By the pond."

Nikki nods. "The pond. Is it on fire? What's with all the trucks?"

"If the pond is on fire, I bet Destiny did it. Or maybe Sherry berated it until it burst."

"Maybe Steve killed her," Nikki says, immediately taking it back. "That's not funny."

"But possible, even reasonable." I stop walking, not wanting to go any further. I'm perfectly content to read about whatever emergency is going down in tomorrow's paper. Then I'll check the classifieds.

Nikki keeps walking until my arm runs out, then she tugs it, like a child, urging me to come check out the scene.

"Nothing good ever happens down there. Who knows what this is?"

"No," I say.

"Oh, come on. We're over everything, remember? I thought that's what we've been talking about..."

"Really?"

"Really. It'll be romantic." She sidles up to me and rubs her hip against mine. "We were here together years ago, even if you don't remember. I have the picture to prove it. Come on, we'll sneak in the woods and have teenage sex."

"You want two-second sex? Besides, the woods are gone. It's all paved back there now."

"Wait here then. I want to see." She walks off, looking back only to waggle a finger at me, rolling her eyes when I shake my head.

She looks both ways down the empty road, beneath the glaring sun, and crosses. Dammit. I'll go. We'll see a man in a bathrobe crying over a burnt microwave, then go home. I cross without looking and get blared at by a city sand truck taking the corner into Barbados Pond Estates.

I catch up with Nikki by the sign. "Look at that. It's disgusting," I say.

"It's a sign, Norm," she says, taking my hand.

"That's exactly what it is. It's disgusting."

"Fucking lighten up, Norm." She smiles at me and kisses me quick on the cheek, leaving the ground momentarily. Her body seems too serious for this playfulness, her legs too strong to be so light. Her breasts too determined.

"I love you," I say.

She doesn't take her eyes from the road ahead, but pulls me with her.

People are peering from doorways, afraid to step on their wet steps with bare feet. Some children are racing ahead of us, taking the corner, disappearing for a few seconds before they come screaming back, yelling for their parents and pointing over their shoulders, ecstatic with the adventure they've just discovered.

"Let's go." Nikki releases my hand and begins running against the oncoming children, who are now stopped, trying to decide whether they should run back, or let their parents know what's going on. They can't rip themselves from the excitement and turn on heels to follow Nikki. I join them, all of us running.

The water washes over my feet as I round the curve to the street's concluding circle. Dirty and brown, full of detritus, it runs down the street, flowing fast from behind Steve and Sherry's house. The neatly tended circle of grass filling the center of the cul-de-sac is gone. Under water. It's decorative granite spike pokes through, straight as a lighthouse. The fire trucks' tires are sunk deep enough to appear flat, their shined hubcaps reflect shimmering watery sunlight.

When Nikki stops, turning to gape at me, the water slaps at her calves, curving and flowing around her without stop. Firefighters slop through, their big boots raising splashes as they run from truck to truck around the house, through the yard, where the water reaches their knees.

I run sloshing to Nikki, and we stare. Policemen close their car doors and yell into radios. The city sand truck pulls around in a ten point turn, backs down to the pond, dumping sand as it goes. A brown trail breaks the water's surface and disappears, leaving no mark.

Officials cant their heads into shoulder microphones and wave their free hands in frustration. The front door swings out and there's Steve, screaming at the crowd grouped in threes on the lawn, helpless against the rising tide. Steve's sweatshirt is soaked through, clinging to his gut, his legs bare and white against the dark water. There are eddies around his bottom step. Through the open door I see furniture and the kitchen, still dry, and it looks strange. It looks doomed. Steve looks down at the water swirling toward his door and slams it shut behind him, as if abandoning ship. He takes a few clumsy steps through what had been his front yard.

Policemen approach Steve from all sides, hands out to calm him. Some rest a hand on their guns, reassuring themselves of what power they have when they don't know what is happening or about to happen or what to do about it. Steve clutches his head, turning to take in his house and the crowd, and he sees me. It seems natural to wave, so I do, but then that seems much too friendly and calm, so I stop, which leaves me just standing there, more useless than smiling and waving like a fool. Look at all the experts around me. They don't know what to do. Steve's staring at me, taking in my presence. He looks as if this ups the level of his personal tragedy. He takes in Nikki. When I look at her, she's waving.

"Stop," I say.

"What else should I do?" She holds her hand up, but stops waggling it.

"I don't know, I've never been to a flooding before."

Her hand drops. "We should help."

I look around at the chaos circling around Steve and can't think of one helpful thing I could do. Things are clearly worsening. The sun is only getting warmer, and all that snow keeps melting. What had been a stream behind the dam now flows in a torrent over the top, gushing into the pond, encircling Steve's home. I bet that pavement around the pond was Sherry's idea, and I say so to Nikki. Where is Sherry? Steve is still staring at us.

I take my eyes from Steve, assess the situation. The rise where the house usually sits has been leveled out by the water, its dark, frothy surface extending from what was the pond, out into the street. If they had anything in the basement, they don't anymore. There's a lot of running around, a lot of cell phone and radio chatter, but essentially nothing is being done except watching the water have its way.

My feet are soaked. In the backyard, I see the deck steps emerging from the water. Steve is shouting something at us, his hands cupped over his silly beard. Nikki and I look at each other, not understanding.

Then he waves his arms in sweeping get-the-fuck-over-here gestures. We do. The rushing water is becoming hard to walk against. It seems to take us forever to reach him; it won't be long before the water begins filling the house. We finally get to Steve, and he is haggard—white faced and wide eyed.

"Come inside! Help me!" he shouts in our faces, one hand on each of our shoulders.

Nikki shouts, "Okay!" and runs in slow motion through the flood to the front door, leaving me and Steve behind.

"Hi," I say.

"Let's talk later, Norm," Steve says and tries to rush behind Nikki for the door. He looks ridiculous trying to find the best way to run through the oncoming water. He tries slogging through it, but he doesn't make the progress or attain the speed he clearly wants. He lifts each leg ridiculously high, his bare knees almost hitting his chest, but his progress doesn't improve. He keeps his head low, trudges forward. I follow, though he doesn't hold the door for me. It slams as I search around with my foot, under water, for the front step.

I open the door and close it quickly behind me, for fear of being the one to allow the water in. Nikki is just disappearing around a corner, towards the stairs. Steve is looking around in a panic. He lunges left to grab a chair, stops, and heads towards the TV and stereo. He stops, picks up a laptop from the coffee table. It looks so serene in here. I can't even hear any commotion from outside. There is just the living room, resting quietly. That easy chair looks inviting. A coffee mug rests on the kitchen counter. It is a nice house, and I catch myself looking around, realizing that I'm simply glad for Steve, that he has such a nice place.

"Fucking pick something up!" Steve shouts at me, clutching a laptop and a lamp.

"What do you want me to do?" I say, shouting, though there's no real need.

"Bring something upstairs! F'ing Christ!"

Nikki comes running into the room, empty handed. Without speaking or looking at us, she clears a bookshelf of picture frames and leather bound albums, dropping to her knees to gather it all together and running from the room. We watch.

"That! Do that!" Steve says and eyes the brown leather couch. He tosses the laptop and lamp onto it. Grabbing the armrest, he hefts it up, trying to drag it to the stairs. I lift the other end, immediately pushing too hard and knocking Steve to the floor.

"Sorry!" I say.

"Lift, just lift."

I do, and let him take the lead. He struggles with the couch in a backward run, directly into the wall poking out by the staircase.

"Shit!" he says when he crashes.

"Sorry!" I say.

Steve shakes his head at me and feels behind him with his feet as we climb the stairs..

Moving furniture, even with a friend, is never a good time. Neither of you move at the same speed, there are disagreements surrounding angles and hand holds. But in a flood-forced rush, with someone whose family may have good reason to hate you, there is real potential for violence.

Steve and I smash our way up the stairs. It's my opinion that scratched walls and banged up balustrades are the least of our worries. Steve seems to disagree.

"F'ing Christ, Norm! Watch the walls!"

"Sorry!" I say automatically, then add, "Does it matter?"

"Just carry the goddam couch," Steve says.

Nikki careens around the upstairs corner, stopping short when she hits us coming up. I roll my eyes to her. She looks wonderful, wet and glowing. Her eyes are wide. I smile at her, and she smiles back, dropping her head a notch when she looks at me. I'm doing good, I think. Then her face grays, she looks past me. I turn my head to follow her gaze. It's tricky, balancing the couch on the stairs and looking behind me.

Mother fucker. Destiny. Sherry. They mirror each other on the landing, black eyes and all. They're both wearing sagging soaked pajama bottoms, Destiny's decorated with monkeys. Her necklaces hang out through a hot pink sweatshirt. Their hands are on their hips, feet hidden by shopping bags, and they're furious, fucking furious. The sun shines in beams through the high glass windows behind them. The floor is spotless but for our muddy footprints. Sherry's house is about to be destroyed, or sink, close up like an ark and float away, but what's pissing her off right now, right this moment, is me. It's that I'm here in her house, with her husband.

"Steve!" Sherry says. "Steve. What the fuck is he doing here?"

"Sher, the pond and the snow. The sun. We got to get this stuff upstairs before the water comes in. Grab something, help us. I think a beaver got stuck. You don't understand."

"Beaver?" Destiny says.

I'm still holding on to their heavy goddam couch, my head twisted around to watch their side of this little domestic dispute. I'm just going to drop this couch, let it bump down the stairs and crash into Sherry. Then I'll follow it, and continue out the door. This whole salvage effort is useless, anyway, if the water keeps rising so quickly.

"Mom! What the hell is going on?"

"Your father is in deep shit, that's what happening, Des," Sherry says.

"He's not my real father," Destiny says, then louder, "Thank god."

I can see Steve breathing hard and deciding not to say the first three things that occur to him. His end of the couch is shaking.

He says, "Sherry, you and your daughter need to start fucking carrying shit. Now. Norm is helping me carry this goddam couch. Nikki is upstairs."

"Sherry. What can I do? Just tell me," Nikki says over Steve's shoulder.

"I'll tell you what you can do."

There's a banging on the door, and firefighters fill the doorway, barging in without waiting for permission. They want to know where the basement is and how much water is down there. Sherry's demeanor switches immediately to that of the soft-hearted helpless victim, desperate for assistance and willing to do anything to help. She abandons Destiny at the foot of the stairs to lead the firefighters through the kitchen, down to the basement.

"Let's get this thing moving," Steve says to me. He shouts through heaving grunts as we climb the stairs, "Destiny, put down that goddam phone and start carrying something."

"I got her," Nikki says. She flattens herself against the wall and scooches past us, patting my ass on her way down.

"Gross." I hear Destiny say. Then I'm lifting and pushing again. I feel my lungs fighting against last night's smoke, pumping hard.

Nikki speaks softly to Destiny. Steve and I maneuver up the stairs, silent but for grunts. We work out the sharp corner at the top of the stairs.

"Drop it. It doesn't matter," Steve says, climbing over the arm of the couch and past me down the stairs.

In the living room I don't mention the tendrils of water reaching in and spreading under the door; Steve can see them as well as I. He clears another shelf, DVDs and some photographs. I look at them as he tosses them from the floor onto a brown loveseat: Sherry smiling, holding a little Destiny, Steve beaming behind them. Destiny smiling over Steve's burly arm as he holds a fishing rod for her. The three of them posed in matching outfits, kneeling behind Lacey.

"Where's the dog?" I say.

"Shit." Steve looks around, as if Lacey will be sitting right there, panting or trying to be of use, holding a remote control in her mouth. "I can't look for her now. Don't mention her to the girls."

"Want me to grab a side?"

"Do it. We'll just throw this on top of the couch in the hall." Steve bends to lift the loveseat, and I crouch on my end, seeking a good hold. "Norm."

"Yeah?" I say, still looking for something I can hold on to.

"Thank you."

We're both crouched, looking at each other over the arms of the seat. I see nothing but his eyes and wet baseball hat. "I'll just lift. You steer."

I do that, and we reach the stairs moments after Nikki and Destiny. They race up with kitchen paraphernalia. They're silent, rushing to find a spot to drop a coffee maker, a blender. We follow and toss the loveseat on its back, over the couch. We all reach the bottom landing and split, working silently in our separate groups. Steve and I lift a coffee table. Destiny runs past, kitchen chairs in each hand bang against her knees with every step. The water is now beyond a stream, pooling up steadily before the door. I grudgingly offer Sherry's Dad a silent compliment on the perfect levelness of these floors. In our house all the water would be flowing to the farthest, most uneven corner.

A crash downstairs makes the house shudder. I hear a torrent of swearing, followed by a mad rush of firefighters into the kitchen from the basement door. They're soaked, breathing hard and whispering fiercely amongst themselves; all but one leave efficiently, silently, through the front door. The remaining fireman has some authority the others lack, and he approaches Steve, across from me holding the other end of the table.

"Sir, we need you to leave the premises."

"Fuck that. Norm, let's go." Steve begins a backward run with the table, and I stumble to keep up, past the fireman who looks nervous and furious.

"Sir!" the fireman says. "Sir! You need to take your family outside. The basement door gave way. It's filling up fast."

Steve mutters, "No fucking way." We continue up the stairs, tossing the table down the hall, nearly hitting Nikki coming out of a bedroom.

Our eyes meet, and she makes shrugging, confused motions which I return. Steve trudges downstairs, ready for whatever argument awaits him.

"She's giving up, Norm. Destiny gave up on me," Nikki says.

"Where is she?"

"We were carrying stuff into her room, just to put it somewhere, and she gave up. She's still in there, crying. She just wouldn't listen." Nikki brings both hands up to rub her temples, then that perfume spot behind her ear. Her eyes close.

"You okay?" I say.

"I think." She looks up, her eyes clear, bright against her pale face. "I'm fine. It's just so strange."

"The fire chief just told Steve everyone needs to leave."

"Should we go?" she says, already shaking her head no.

"I'm not leaving if Steve is still here carrying shit."

"I love you, too," she says.

"Thank you," I say, taking a moment to enjoy how this feels. "Should I talk to Destiny?"

"Go for it, if you think it will help. At least get her outside. I'm afraid she's going to get forgotten about in this mess."

"See if Steve needs help. I'm going in," I say, and make a show of pushing up my sleeves.

Nikki makes a leaping descent of the stairs, landing with a splash.

Destiny's door is cracked open, I give a light knock. "Destiny? You okay? Can I come in?"

I hear her sobs and wait another minute before entering, swinging the door wide and leaving it open to the hall. Destiny is curled up in her

319

bed, clutching a pink stuffed bear, her phone clenched tight. The walls are covered with posters: cute animals and shirtless men in equal distribution, a few innocuous bands with perfect hair. She looks like shit. Her forehead and cheeks are red from crying, and both eyes are blackened. There's a nasty cut crossing the bridge of her nose.

"You okay?" I say.

"Do I fucking look okay?" she says to the bear more than me.

"No," I say. "You look like shit."

"So do you, too."

"I know." Silence. "Are you going to help carry stuff?"

"It's stupid."

"We have to save it. Everything is going to get ruined."

"Fuck it." Destiny sits up at the edge of her bed, her bear sitting in her lap like a child. She plays with its ears. "There's nothing I can do about it."

"You can try."

A window breaks downstairs, and we hear Sherry shouting, but can't make out the exact words. They aren't nice. Destiny looks at me, like, see, I told you.

"Well, we can still try," I say. She sits on the bed, says nothing. "Destiny? It's time to go."

"I'm sick of trying."

I look out over the hall railing, down into the kitchen. Things are worsening by the moment. I lean against her doorframe. "I don't think we've really started yet."

She looks at me, her face solid, holding together for a moment. Then she breaks, opens up. Her eyes closed and mouth grimaced, she squeaks out, "I'm sorry, Mr. Mean. I'm sorry."

"For what?" I say, taking a step toward her bed.

She can barely choke out words past the catches in her throat. She wipes away tears with the back of both hands, bracelets jangling. "For the other night. I'm sorry. For all of it. I didn't know."

I have to fight the urge to sit beside her, rub her back. Hug her until she stops. We could sit here until the water reaches the top of the stairs. Until it soaks into her rug, floating the tears away. I stay in the door, letting my tears run, listening to the shouting downstairs. The firemen are back in, trying to force Steve and Sherry out. I wipe hard at my nose, forgetting how much it hurts where it's broken.

"Me too," I say. "It sucks to be sorry."

"How would you know?" Destiny says, and it's a genuine question, without anger. She looks like a child. She looks like what she is. "How would you know?"

I laugh. "How would you know?"

She looks down, fidgets with her bear. I search for something to say. "You can be sorry. Of course. Maybe you should be. Maybe we should all be sorry."

"Yeah," she says. I have no idea what that means she agrees with, but I'm with her. "Can I go now?"

"Let's get out of here, Des."

She rises from the bed, her hair tangled and pajamas twisted, necklaces caught and dragged across her chest. Destiny takes a few steps toward me, and I lean out of her way. She drops the bear at my feet, and walks out the door.

The hall is piled with stuff, nobody up here but us. I have to step over a pile of albums and magazines to get to the balcony railing. Looking down, I can see into the kitchen and living room. There is a foot of dirty water swirling into every corner, filling every crack and crevice. It flows and eddies. Sticks, leaves, and garbage float unimpeded. A beer bottle spins across the water's surface from the basement door, now swinging on hinges in the force of the flow.

Destiny stands open-mouthed with me at the top of the stairs. Everything is moving so fast. As I watch, another step on the staircase submerges, disappears. I can't see the front door, but the shouting carries. Sherry's continuous scream is muffled by water, and bordering desperate. Over and around her wails, firemen repeat their orders to leave. It's time to go. Is there anyone else in here? Is there anything dangerous in here? Is there anyone else inside?

"MOM!" Destiny shouts from the top of the stairs. "MOM! I'm up here! Help me!"

"Destiny! Destiny!" Sherry shouts. She has broken free of the firemen and manifested where the bottom of the stairs should be, but is now all part of the pond. The pond is taking it all back.

Sherry forces her way through the water, taking high slogging steps, barely able to fight the strong current. It surges through the basement door and meets the flow from the front. She's having a hard time with the thigh-deep water, her legs keep getting swept away so she needs to almost swim, flail, until she can get her footing again. Three firemen, their thick jackets and boots weighing on them, are moments behind her. They're shouting, ordering Sherry to stop, and grabbing for her, getting pulled under themselves.

"Stop it!" Destiny screams at them. "Mom! Help me! She's trying to help me!"

Two of the firemen grab Sherry and take a beating from her as they drag her back to the front door. The third looks up at Destiny and heads right to the stairs, his arms out, urging her to jump. He has to brace himself against the wall, knees bent underwater. His unbuttoned jacket floats up under his arms.

Destiny is screaming, hands flapping. I'm frozen in my spot, only feet from her, watching. She's crying and shaking, losing control. I don't think she even hears the fireman urging her to jump. He turns to me. "Sir! We need to get you out of here! Now. Both of you get down these stairs. We'll get you out!"

"I'll get her!" I shout back, and he keeps talking to me, telling me to just get myself down. He'll get the girl.

Destiny chooses this moment to leap. She still has many steps to clear before reaching the fireman. I watch it happen, her hair behind her, a hot pink and blonde blur crashing into the fireman, knocking him back into the water until his boots shoot from the foaming surface and he is forced away, out of sight, into the living room.

Destiny manages to get a hold of the submerged stair railing. Her body stretching behind her, she's tossed over the roiling surface. One hand slips free and she's flipped over, looking at the ceiling with eyes squeezed shut and sounding a wavering moan. At the top of the stairs now, I take in a breath and make the same leap as Destiny, landing on her legs and going under.

It's quiet for a second, dark, and I feel her kicks on the side of my head. I grab a foot and surface into the light. My feet can't find the floor. Destiny is kicking like mad. I don't know what I'm doing. I get both her legs in my arms and work my way up to her waist; my weight pulls her arm free of the railing, and we smash back into the wall pinned by the strength of the water.

My arms are around Destiny, her face next to mine, she doesn't see me though. She flails and screams, taking in water. I see a hand beside me, a flash of yellow arm, and there's the fireman, his helmet gone, face pale.

"Give me the girl!" he shouts.

I can't move. The fireman works his arms between me and Destiny, I feel more than see this happening.

"I've got her, sir! Grab my shoulders! I'm going to turn, you grab my shoulders!"

"I have her!" I shout. I'm afraid to let go.

"Grab my shoulders!"

From my position against the wall I look directly into the kitchen, out through the sliding doors. The water is over the deck, splashing against the glass. I feel the fireman between me and Destiny, tugging at her, shouting. A red kayak floats by the window, bobbing, its tip hits the doors. The deck picnic table is lifted and pushed toward the glass. From the far side of the deck, a huge stainless steel grill shoots across the water and shatters the glass.

In the rush of water through the broken door, Destiny and the fireman are pulled away. Gone. Pieces of glass clinging to wood brush me. I'm knocked free from the wall; now the water inside rushes out the broken door. I'm pulled along with it, hit something solid under the water. I think it's the kitchen island. I reach down for a handhold, but find only drawers that move at my grasps. The refrigerator doors swing behind me. Jars of ketchup, pickles, and a banana bob past. There're kitchen tools in the water all around me. Knives and ladles. A whisk hits my face.

The surface of the island is slippery. My lower back jams into its corner, and I'm lifted up, over, into the spot behind the grill. It's still jammed in the doorway, water pouring around, over it. The picnic table has been overturned and forced against the grill from the outside. It creates a small eddy, the water calmer here. I use the grill and edges of the broken door to pull myself onto the upturned picnic table, poking out of the water. Mustering strength, I emerge, standing on the edge of the table, looking out over the tumult.

I'm outside. The palms of my hands stream blood, cut by the broken doorframe. My precarious balance on the table's edge gives me a view over what had been a yard with a quiet stream and serene pond. Now it's a roiling sea. Trees rise strangely through the surface, waves washing against their trunks. I'm in a boat in a sinking forest. I look at the sun. It's so out of place, the heat and the light. I imagine people all over Garrison looking up, thankful for the warmth, unaware of its purpose today. Today, it's just for me, just for this; it raises the pond to take me down into new found depths. I'm going to allow it. I'm going to offer myself.

From around the corner of the house two fireman come, furiously paddling a canoe. They're down to T-shirts and suspenders. They shout to me, I hold my arms outstretched, straight from my sides, as if I can't hear them. The fireman in front drops his paddle and stands, almost tipping their small boat. His hands are cupped around his mouth, telling me to wait right there, don't move.

The water is over my ankles, covering the picnic table, which is starting to move under me. Something hits my foot, grabs it, wrenching. I reach down to take what feels like, what I assume to be, a hand, and lose my balance. I go headfirst into the water. This is not like swimming. The deck railing rakes my legs as I'm pushed past it, back against it, out over the yard. There is debris everywhere. Everything I grab sinks at my touch.

A large branch hits my chest, and I try to pull myself onto it, but it goes under, taking me with it. My legs feel heavy and twisted. I take in mouthfuls of silt and spit them out, but there is only more. Everything is slower down here, dark things hang suspended in the slants of sunlight. I break the surface and hear voices yelling, screaming for me to come to them. I'm sorry. I'm sorry. I feel pressure, a gripping, working its way up from my feet. I go under again. Deeper, any moment I expect to feel grass beneath me, but I keep sinking.

My elbow is being squeezed. I reach out; I got you, Fitzy. This time it's okay. I got you. Then he's beneath me, clutching my thighs, my knees, grabbing and talking, telling me I'm okay now, I'm okay. I think I've sunk past where the sunlight can reach. Underwater currents tug and push, pulling me into something solid, unmoving. I force my hand to move toward it, above me somewhere. The water is so thick. I feel something at my shoulder, patting, and I paddle, try to turn to it. Opening my mouth to speak, I take in a breath without air, and lights appear, stars, growing closer and brighter. Larger. I wave to push them away, to see who is there. I can just make out his face beyond the lights. My lungs won't work, unable to pump all this through. I hear a voice saying it has me now. It has me, and there is a huge pulling on my chest, forcing my head back against the water, hard as ground; I feel hands all over me, lifting. Something solid, then everything is dark.

The sun is a strange shape. It has lost its circle, cut out by other darker circles, and they're talking.

"He's with us. He's back. He's back."

I blink away the brightness, turn my head until there is only blue sky, then trees, then blades of grass. I'm cold and reach around my shoulders, find a blanket. I'm shaking. I pull the blanket tight, my arms crossed over me. Everything clears around me. It gets dark again, and there is a moment's adjustment until I can make out Nikki's face. She's kneeling over me, her hair dripping onto my face. I watch the drops fall. She's touching my face, her fingers freezing and wonderful.

"You're okay," she says, falling onto me, arms around my back. She pushes hair from my face, mine or hers, I don't know. "You fucking idiot."

"I know," I say and let myself be held.

There are more hands on me, and I hear Dad, then feel him. I push myself to sitting, clutching my blanket. We're surrounded by people, uniformed and soaking. Others wear dripping clothes, holding shovels or TVs or a box of books, photo albums. Someone puts down a small dog, and holding the leash in one hand, starts clapping. Others follow, and it grows loud in my ears before dying out.

On the far side of the crowd, Destiny stands behind Steve and Sherry. They're all talking, waving their arms, pointing up the road. She moves between everyone to lean against Sherry, who, without breaking conversation, reaches out and brings Destiny to her shoulder, smoothing down her wet hair and rubbing her back. Steve puts his arm around both of them. He shakes his head along with his neighbors, all of them beneath the sun, out to join in the disaster. Dad turns me around, and says, "Welcome home."